UNSPOKEN

VOICES

SELECTED SHORT STORIES
BY KOREAN WOMEN WRITERS

Modern Fiction from Korea
published by Homa & Sekey Books

UNSPOKEN VOICES

SELECTED SHORT STORIES
BY KOREAN WOMEN WRITERS

Compiled and Translated from the Korean by

Jin-Young Choi, Ph.D.

Homa & Sekey Books
Dumont, New Jersey

First American Edition

Copyright © by Authors
English Translation Copyright © 2002 by Jin-Young Choi

The publication of this book was supported by a grant from Korea Literature Translation Institute.

ISBN: 1-931907-06-4
Library of Congress Control Number: 2002103287

Publishers Cataloging-in-Publication Data

Unspoken Voices: Selected Short Stories by Korean Women Writers by Park Kyong-ni et al.
Compiled and Translated from the Korean by Jin-Young Choi
1. Korean fiction--20th century--Translation into English
2. Korean fiction--Women authors--Translations into English
3. English fiction--Translations from the Korean
I. Title. PL992.62 895.734-dc21

Published by Homa & Sekey Books
138 Veterans Plaza
P. O. Box 103
Dumont, NJ 07628

Tel: (201)384-6692
Fax: (201)384-6055
Email: info@homabooks.com
Website: www.homabooks.com

Editor-in-chief: Shawn X. Ye
Executive Editor: Judy Campbell

Printed in the United States of America
1 3 5 7 9 10 8 6 4 2

Contents

Translator's Note

Modern Korean literature began during the last decades of the 19th century. Before then, literature was a mere pastime among the aristocrats. With the opening of the country to foreign cultures, however, the situation changed. Instead of the Chinese ideograms, Korean alphabet was widely used to express a newly awakened nationalistic fervor in the form of enlightenment novels.

After Korea was forcibly annexed to Japan in the 1910s, especially during the 1920s, a new literary trend emerged in Korean novels. It was the class-conscious proletarian literature which was soon followed by modernistic works. During the 1950s, the decade of the Korean War and its aftermath, existentialism prevailed.

The 1960s were an age of the young whose dissident ideology called for reform of the corrupt Establishment. The 1970s and the 1980s saw a general resistance, culminating in the 1980 Gwangju Revolt. The democratization of the 1990s seemed to put the writers into a reflective mood. They tend to create either retrospective works or novels probing into the inner workings of individual mind.

Of the twelve authors in this collection, Choi Junghee, Han Musook, Kang Shinjae, Park Kyongni, Lee Sukbong, Lee Jungho, Song Wonhee, and Park Wansuh were born during the Japanese occupation (1910-1945). In childhood, they experienced World War II and as adults the Korean War. They saw death, pain, and hardship but they also observed courage, resilience, and humor in Korean women even in the direst times. Among the older generation, Choi Junghee, Han Musook and Kang Shinjae are no longer living. Park Wansuh, however, is still one of the most prolific and commanding writers.

7

The younger writers, Yoon Jungsun, Un Heekyong, Kong Jeeyoung and Han Kang are the most active creators of works, winning top literary awards. Their fresh look at life in contemporary Korea, their bold experimental style, and their refreshing, often decidedly feministic, voices are representative of their generation.

Choi Junghee (1906-1990), who began her writing career in the 1930s, was one of the early modern women. She became a journalist, and later was involved in a leftist literary movement. Her story, "The Rooster" is a comical folktale of a story showing the parallelism between the main character and his rooster. Han Musook (1918-1993), a keen observer of the life in early 20th century, portrayed Korean women in many of her novels. "The Fragment" is a searing but sympathetic picture of the refugees who fled to Pusan during the Korean War. Kang Shinjae (1924-2001) is an expert in delicately depicting a special beauty that exists in contrast to mundane daily life. "The Young Elm Tree" tells of love between a high-school girl and a college student son of her mother's new husband. Park Kyongni (1927-) is renowned for her masterpiece *The Land* considered a treasure chest of the Korean language. "Youngju and the Cat" is a fine example of Park's delicate but sharp insight into the mind of a woman who lost her husband in the Korean War and her son to a fatal illness. "The Jade Ring" by Lee Sukbong (1928-) is a chilling story of a mother's revenge against her own daughter. Lee is known for her superb description of human psychology.

"The Woman in Search of an Illusion" by Lee Jungho (1930-) is a symbolic tale of the fate of women who had to persevere in quiet desperation. Song Wonhee (1930-) focuses on the Korean War and the life of women after losing their husbands and sons. "Division" tells of two women suffering from their losses.

"The Dreaming Incubator" is a savage criticism by Park Wansuh (1931-) of Korea's prejudice against girls that used to force women to abort female fetuses. Park's fluent and poignant stories about women have an enormous appeal. Yoon Jungsun (1948-), a playwright as well as a novelist, writes about human relationships in a rueful and wistful way.

One of the most critically acclaimed young writers, Un Heekyong (1959-) has won many awards. Un is known for her light and lively style and air-tight form. "My Wife's Boxes" is a study of the pathological psychology of a barren woman told symbolically.

Kong Jeeyoung (1963-) is another young writer recognized for her militant feminism and revelation of private emotions hidden behind the 1980's reform movement. "The Unbearable Sadness of Being" is a story of a recently fired, divorced young designer, with a mother and a daughter to support. Her lover's death in Peru and her hopelessness are exquisitely handled. Han Kang (1970-) is a young and upcoming writer of great promise. "Nostalgic Journey" is about a train ride of a woman to her hometown where her father and sister drowned in suicide after her mother's death.

Jin-Young Choi, Ph.D.
Seoul
March, 2002

Acknowledgement

My most heartfelt thanks go to Veronica Chambers, a novelist and editor, for her helpful suggestions, and to my faithful graduate students, Jin-Buhm Shin, Yong-Jun Park, Eun-Sook Jeong, Young-Shin Park, and Jun-Soo Kang, who did typing and proofreading. I am grateful to Director Hwan-Duk Park and Dr. Jung-Hee Kim of the Korea Literature Translation Institute.

In Korean culture, you are not supposed to mention your family in any complimentary way, but I would like to thank my husband J. J., my daughters Caroline and Sharon and my son Eric for their loving support.

Jin-Young Choi

The Rooster

by Choi Junghee

" "Cock-a-doodle-doo."
Yoon Hansung was startled out of his dream by the
rooster and groggily felt around the space next to him.
"Oh, good. She is here."
He was relieved to find his young wife, Yonsun, beside him.
The room looked as if it were sunk in clear water as the full
moon filled it with blue light. Snuggling close to her, he drew
her hand and placed it on his chest.

Yonsun opened her eyes and squinted at him.

"It's nothing. Go back to sleep."

Yoon eased her back to sleep, squeezed her hand once and
put his other hand on top of hers.

"What a bad dream it was. A strange dream, indeed."

The ominous dream nagged at him. It wasn't about his neighbor Lee Bong himself but Lee's rooster. The cock brazenly
dug his way into Yoon's yard. Yoon took up a long stick from
the corner of the outhouse and tried to shoo the bird away.

"Whoring again, you damned bird. Why don't you chase
your own hen, huh?"

Yoon's stick merely frailed around the dodging rooster, which
in the end succeeded in seducing and conquering Yoon's hen.
On the other hand, Yoon's own rooster fidgeted uneasily, eyeing the couple, but dared not fight the invading cock.

Furious, Yoon raised his stick and smashed it on Lee's rooster
while it was copulating his hen. The rooster dodged again, but
suddenly turned itself into his master Lee Bong who belliger-
ently glared at Yoon. Lee's shoulders were squinched up, his

11

fists raised, his huge oxen eyes full of fire. Lee looked exactly like his rooster when it pounced upon Yoon's hen.

Cold sweat ran down Yoon's spine.

All right, Yoon thought, and raised his shoulders, fists ready, eyes wide open, to fight Lee. Immediately Yoon felt his legs buckling down and his whole body shaking. If Lee made one step forward, he certainly would have toppled down. Lee just stood there glaring menacingly at Yoon. Now, sweat was pouring out of every pore. His hands shook.

"Why won't he fight? Why is he just standing there?"

Yoon mumbled to himself. At last Lee stepped forward, but his head ballooned up so huge that it looked like the head of an elephant Yoon had seen at a zoo. Yoon dropped his stick and tried to run away, but his legs wouldn't budge.

The road in front of him was long and straight with willow trees on both sides. Yet Yoon couldn't run. Afraid, he looked back only to see Lee just rounding the corner of the millet field. "When he rounds the corner, he'll get me." He decided to climb up a willow tree to hide.

It was eerie how easily he could climb. "Whew, I am safe now. He can't see me through the dense leaves."

Underneath the willow branches ran a river. The blue sky and white clouds were mirrored in the river. At the smallest breeze, the willow branches swayed. Between swaying branches, he could spy on Lee. But Lee didn't come. Yoon felt so good that his spirit danced with the boughs.

He even felt like belting out a song he used to sing with the whorehouse women.

"Why not play around, my pal,
This is the time for fun
This is the green green season,
Why not go and enjoy
the mountains and the fields?"

At the instant Yoon reached this part of the song, he saw Lee and a woman emerging from the millet field. Yoon stopped and peered at the woman. The woman was his wife Yonsun. Not only did Lee and Yonsun walk side by side but they flirted openly. She would say something smiling coquettishly, and Lee would laugh and hug her passionately.

"Oh, my God, oh my God. Oh, the whoring pair!"

Yoon couldn't care less if Lee would find and abuse him. With all his enraged heart, he bellowed. But, alas, what came out from him was a weak crow.

"Cock-a-doodle, cock-a-doodle."

Lee and Yonsun didn't come to him, but rounded the millet field and walked into a narrow path toward the mountain. They seemed to have forgotten Yoon.

"So, they've forgotten me."

The two of them walking shoulder to shoulder was the very image of Lee's rooster sweeping his hen to its own yard.

"Yonsun, you dirty whore, you...."

Yoon tried to climb down the tree, yelling and roaring. The result was still a weak crow.

His body felt like a ton. While struggling on a branch, he happened to look down the river. He was astounded. The creature reflected in the river was not a man but a rooster. He had become a rooster, silly and cowardly, fidgeting in a corner, as Lee's rooster made away with his hen.

As the wind picked up, the willow branches swayed more wildly. The clouds flew east with the wind, and rice paddies and fields, being stationary, seemed to flow to the west. The east-bound winds were white while the west-bound fields were green, but Yoon's heart was black. Hugging a sturdy branch, he tried to yell again toward the couple. The sound that came out of his mouth was again a cock's faint crow. He tried again and the result was the same.

He pounded his chest with both hands and woke himself wide awake.

His wife was still sleeping in the blue moon light. In a moment, his rooster began to crow. "What a bad dream. Maybe I was unsettled by the cocks and the hen," Yoon said to himself, fondling Yonsun's hand on his chest.

What started the whole thing was that they began to raise chickens in spite of themselves. They had never wanted to do it. But lately, Yoon began to feel his age and thought about getting some sort of tonic supplement, a stewed chicken, at the least. "As soon as my hands lost strength, money dried up. I cannot even afford a chicken," Yoon used to complain. Yonsun heard it and one day bought a rooster for 500 *won*, out of her own seamstress's earning, because she really cared for her husband and was worried about his waning energy.

However, things began to go wrong. First, the day Yonsun decided to buy a chicken and stepped out of the door, a chicken peddler passed by on his way to Seoul. He rode a bicycle with a basketful of chickens on the back seat. She stopped the peddler and bought the meatiest chicken.

At first Yoon was so happy that he looked at her with adoring eyes. Then he looked over the chicken and exclaimed, "Damn, this is a rooster. It's always been 'a hen for man and a cock for woman.' Don't you know that? Take it right back and trade it for a hen."

Yonsun was dumbstruck. She saw the peddler ride away as soon as he sold the bird. But she ran out to catch up with him. The peddler was gone. She ran all the way to the railroad crossing, but he was nowhere to be seen. Crestfallen she came back with the rooster.

"Why, that's the same rooster," Yoon said. When Yonsun replied, red-faced, "Yes, it is," Yoon's voice had a sharp tone of disappointment.

"Why in hell did you bring it back? They wouldn't change it for you? Don't you know from the olden times that men get tonic power from a hen and women from a cock? Why do you think they use chickens for tonic power?" His voice became more accusatory.

"Ay, ay, ay, I have never seen such an idiot in my life. Where did you buy the rooster anyway?"

Though they had met haphazardly and never loved each other, Yonsun was satisfied with the considerate way he took care of her. Now she was flabbergasted by his unusual outburst.

"Are you just going to stand there, huh? Did you buy it at Suk Nam's store? Go and get a hen."

Yonsun managed to say that she bought the rooster from a peddler on his way to Seoul, and the man was long gone. The old man got furious. Yonsun had to go out again holding the bird in her arms.

But Yonsun didn't come back soon. Yoon became nervous and expectant every time there was a slight noise near the roadside. He sat on the doorsill and watched the clouds change their forms far above the acacia bushes. Suddenly he groaned as if he were hit by something.

He felt enveloped by something he didn't know.

That something seemed to have come from the trees where cicadas made raucous noise. Or it might have come from a breeze floating by. With an involuntary groan, he began to 'see' the house in his hometown where he had lived till he was fifteen and had never gone back in forty years since. He 'saw' his parents and the huge woman, seven years his senior, whom his parents brought for him to marry. He left her ten days later. Now, he even missed her. He missed the garden where flowers glistened with dews early in the morning and the persimmon tree heavy with fruit. He could have as many persimmons as he wanted for himself and his friends. By the way, whatever happened to Na Mi? Why didn't I insist I wanted to marry Na Mi? If I had married her, I would have lived happily with many kids.

Where are Kumran and Oksun? Are they still in Pyongyang? And Sanghong? There are more. If I count all the women I have lived with, they could fill a good-sized oxcart. But, why didn't any of them bear a child? Because they were all whores? Then, why can't Yonsun have a child? Yonsun lost her husband three days after her wedding day, so she was almost a virgin when I met her ten years ago. Why hasn't she had a baby yet? Because I am too old? There are men in their sixties who have produced many sons and daughters. Is it because Yonsun and I are too far apart in age? I am sixty and she is twenty eight. Thirty two years apart. Oh, damn. She could be a granddaughter to someone who married early. Poor thing. She is pretty, she is good and docile, and she is very good at sewing. Why has her fate been so miserable? Why did she have to meet me, an old penniless man whom she has to support by sewing for the town whores? I was wrong to send her out like that. I could have said kinder words. Time flies fast. I have lived sixty years, very unsatisfactory years. Should I live thirty more years, what difference will they make? Time flies by. It's like flipping the pages of a book one by one without stopping. Yoon sighed deeply and rubbed his eyes because he felt tears welling up. For some reason, he cried often lately. He took it as a sign of aging.

Yonsun could not get a hen. Nobody wanted to give a hen for a cock. She decided she had to wait for the peddler to come back. She left a message with several chicken dealers that if anybody wanted a rooster, send him to her. As soon as Yoon saw her cringing at the door, with the rooster in her arms, he said, "I knew nobody would want to give you a hen for a rooster. That's all right. Maybe someone will want a rooster. Or we will sell him and buy a hen." His attitude was completely different from before. However, no one came by looking for a rooster, nor the chicken peddler from Seoul.

One day Yonsun suggested that they cook the rooster. "No. A rooster is no good for a man," Yoon said. "I don't mean for a medicinal effect. Why don't we stew it and share it?" Yonsun pleaded. Yoon merely shook his head. He knew a rooster wouldn't do him any good, but would make Yonsun more plumply attractive, which would make him look older and weaker. In his eyes, Yonsun already looked taut like an air-pumped rubber ball. "Why don't you let it be? Maybe somebody will show up tomorrow," Yoon said. "Then, let's untie it. Otherwise we'll have to feed it three times a day. Let it roam around and find its own food," Yonsun suggested. Yoon concurred.

The first day the rooster was let free, it seemed content to go around under the shades of acacia and cherry trees. The next day, after Yonsun had gone to the market with her sewn garments, Yoon sat alone hoping for a visit by someone looking for a rooster to buy. Suddenly, he saw the rooster desperately escaping from an opening in the fence between Yoon's and Lee's yards, followed by another one. The two birds went several times around Yoon's yard, one fleeing and another in hot pursuit. At first he didn't know that one of the birds was his because his own rooster was white except for a red spot on its breast and shoulders.

The fleeing rooster ran around several more times by the outhouse, the acacia and cherry trees, and, out of desperation and fatigue, jumped into the kitchen. Yoon realized that it was his rooster covered with blood.

"Damn. What happened to it?"

Yoon felt as if a large piece of flesh had broken off his heart. The chasing rooster stood threateningly in front of the kitchen and looked ready to pursue and pounce if there hadn't been a person there.

"You damned son of a cock!"

Thrashing a poker, Yoon chased away the attacker. Then, he picked up his bloody rooster and washed him at the sinkhole in the yard.

"You poor stupid bird. Letting the other guy attack you like this." Yoon sighed and suddenly felt tears gathering in his eyes. No matter how many times he washed, the blood didn't come off completely.

"Now we can't even sell you, you coward. Unless we sell you, we can't get a hen. Do you know that?" The rooster, of course, had no idea and kept going back to Lee's yard, only to be chased back mercilessly.

Another day Yoon's rooster was again desperately fleeing out of the fence opening. Lee's rooster stopped at the hole and went back. For some strange reason, Yoon's rooster meekly followed Lee's back. Curious, Yoon looked over the fence and saw his own rooster getting ready to confront its opponent. Its feathers stood straight up with its neck stretched taut. However, Lee's cock watched it sneeringly, then attacked it, seeming ready to kill it off.

"Oh, Damn. Why did it go there to be beaten up?" Yoon wondered if he should call his rooster or go over to the other side. He ended up just standing there helplessly, because he knew Lee, with his healthy young body, would sit and watch gleefully as his bird defeated Yoon's, and Yoon couldn't take that chance of being humiliated again. Yoon didn't have any particular grudge against Lee, but Lee's youth, his robust health and muscular body oppressed him.

Yoon's rooster came home thoroughly demoralized. Yoon tied it to an acacia tree. Later in the afternoon, an old cackling neighbor woman came by and said, "Do you know why your cock keeps going over to Lee's yard? Because there is a hen there. Why don't you buy a hen, too? Then, you will have eggs to eat, every other day if not every day. Now, wouldn't that be better than just eating your rooster?"

Yoon and Yonsun thought it was a good suggestion. With the money she had been secretly saving to buy a hen, plus two hundred *won* more, Yonsun bought a hen. As was hoped for, the rooster and the hen got along beautifully. They seemed content to stay together in the yard. The rooster began to crow proudly once in a while. Two days later, the hen laid an egg.

Yoon and Yonsun were elated. Yoon punctured the warm egg, sucked its content cleanly, and smacked his lips wistfully. He felt as if he were suddenly regaining his vitality.

"Please lay another one, tomorrow," he silently pleaded, "If I have an egg every day for a month, I will become as virile as before."

The next day, however, a big hullabaloo happened. Yoon had been waiting for the hen to lay another egg when Lee's despicable cock dashed into Yoon's yard. Yoon watched it in fear. The minute Yoon's rooster saw its rival, it screeched and ran into the shade of the cherry tree. Lee's bird ignored the coward and went straight to Yoon's new hen. He conquered her in no time. In a minute Lee's cock herded the hen with the proud mien of a proprietor. In the meantime, Yoon's rooster cringed and watched, not daring to come near them.

"Alas. What a shame," Yoon lamented. His lamentation sounded exactly like the screeching of his silly rooster. Yonsun came out, temporarily pinning her needle on her jacket front. Yoon began to rant as if the whole thing were her fault.

"Go right now to Lee's! That damned cock of his stole our hen away. How did the fucking cock know we had a hen?"

Yoon's face and neck flushed furiously. Yonsun sidled away from him toward Lee's yard.

She made some noise trying to shoo Lee's cock, but there was no more noise nor did she come back. Curious and agitated, Yoon looked over the fence on his tiptoe, but, alas, he could not see anything: the pumpkin and pea vines, which had been young only days before, were now so thick and entwined that they made a green screen. Besides, they were swaying wildly in the sudden gust of wind.

"Only a couple of days ago, they weren't like this. They are so dense you can raise a tiger in them," Yoon said to himself. He had the feeling that those pushy growing plants were choking him. Their waving leaves seemed to be mocking him. "Why isn't she coming back? What's she doing there anyway?"

A hot anger flamed up in his belly, but in a calm voice, Yoon said. "Dear, where are you?" Yonsun must not have heard him. Instead he heard the old neighbor's voice.

"Your rooster is a coward. If he's strong, other cocks won't dare come near your hen. You know a cock takes after its master. That husband of yours has no energy, that's why."

"That damned old hag!" Yoon almost felt dizzy but managed to find a hole among the green leaves and stems and peeped.

Through the prospering corn stalks, cucumber vines, and pumpkin leaves, he could barely see the old woman, Lee and Lee's wife. Yonsun stood there in a daze with the stick hanging loosely in her hand. He wanted to yell to his wife to bring the hen home right away, but no sound came out of his mouth.

"Even if you take your hen back, it will be no use. Your cock's the problem. He can't keep his hen. Ha ha hee hee," the old woman said. The woman's sunken cheeks joggled as she laughed. At this, Lee's hippo-like face expanded in laughter while Lee leered at Yonsun.

"Damn! Damn! I could kill him. That old witch talking dirty like that to those young ones! Why don't thunder bolts hit her!"

Yoon was seething inside, but couldn't utter a sound. His vision slowly blurred into a green curtain in which the faces of Lee, the old woman, Lee's wife and children, and his own wife Yonsun, all mingled. Everything seemed a slowly spreading green ink blot. When the wind picked up, the corn stalks, pumpkins, cucumbers, and peas shook in wild waves, growing by inches in front of his very eyes.

Yoon calmed down enough to think that not his ominous dream, nor Lee's rooster, not the old woman, nor Yonsun was responsible for his lot, but those green things, the earth, the universal truth, were. He knew.

The Fragment

by Han Musook

When Taehyon opened the soggy flap of a door and stepped in the warehouse, a foul odor assailed his nose. He slowly wove through a narrow passageway to his partition and flopped down on his unwashed covers without removing his shoes. On the rough straw mat, his wife had fallen asleep, her face the very image of exhaustion. Beside her, his three unwashed and emaciated children were sleeping as well.

On the other side of the boundary, consisting of battered soot-encrusted pots and bowls, and small bundles of kindlings, lay the young couple, fast asleep, their heads touching at a 90-degree angle. The rain water dripping through the roof only made it into the buckets scattered around the room, half the time. The drops that missed drenched the sleeping lovers' incongruously pink cover.

Because of the cold wet air Taehyon had let in, Old Man Bae began to cough and sat up in his allotted space nearest the door.

Rain kept dripping down from the ceiling, and a dim candle-light cast ghostly light upon pale, gaunt faces, some with their mouths agape. Everyone, young and old, looked like huge worms.

In one corner, an infant began to whimper. The baby's mother instinctively groped to put her nipple in her baby's mouth, while the baby rubbed vigorously its tiny face here and there on its mother's bosom, till it found the mother's nipple and sucked on it loudly. The father mumbled something and rolled over, pulling the cover away with him. Suddenly exposed, several children cringed into shrimp-like crouches with their hands between their legs.

The rain water dripped down more insistently till it began to pour down. Everyone, who had been sleeping in their allotted partition, began to sit up one by one. Children whimpered as adults tugged at the slowly soaking covers. Even in the bone-chilling weather, the warehouse reeked of a terrible odor.

"Aah," sighed the man who had rolled over with the cover off his children.

"Winter rain, what a curse!" the man's wife sat up and covered her children.

Old Man Bae's coughing became so bad that he could hardly breathe as his wife watched him helplessly. A gust of wind rattled around the flimsy tin roof. Water drops flew off the flap of the door.

"Brr.... It's so cold," mumbled the children still in sleep.

Taehyon came to himself and covered the children with the urine-smelling damp cover. As he sat alone, a self-scorning leer lingered around his mouth. In this soggy warehouse, his children slept on a thin piece of straw mat on the bare cement floor. Yet, he didn't think of covering them until they said how cold it was.

"All I had was an excuse, a mere excuse," he thought to himself. He had done everything, he said, to save the young lives. But deep in his heart, he had a searing remorse and pain. His old parents appeared in his mind's eye.

"Don't worry about us. Take good care of yourselves," they said standing in the falling snow, with tears brimming in their eyes.

"I want to take you with us, but I'm not sure what might happen to you on the road in this cold weather. But how can we leave you here?" he said to his parents.

What a lie it was! By then, he had already packed and was ready to leave with his wife and children. He had already decided to abandon them when he made such a lame excuse to his parents.

"You young ones must save yourselves. Don't let us old folks get in your way. Stop worrying about us and leave at once," his mother said.

"Oh, Mother!" he burst into tears and she patted his back.

Taehyon covered his face in shame. His unfilial lies and schemes and guilt! The sin of leaving his old parents behind, his hypocritical mask, and his coercion of them to extract their blessing. His crocodile tears when he knew how afraid and sad they were behind their loving encouragement.

"Ah, it's so cold," his child said. To him, it sounded like "You're a hypocrite." He was a cold-blooded hypocrite not only to his parents but also to his family.

The wind continued to roar. Someone was nosily urinating into an empty can. Under a palm-size window in the ceiling, ten families were living in that warehouse, each in its allotted space.

The night was deepening. Taehyon's infant daughter began to cough. She'd had whooping cough for sometime. Coughing led to vomiting. His wife held the tiny baby and watched her pale face, but he refused to look at them.

"Oh, the poor little thing threw up, didn't she?" Mrs. Song commiserated and sighed. She put more covers on the baby and rocked it needlessly and sighed again. Eventually her sighing led to a sobbing lamentation over her own dead child.

"Sungil-ah, Oh, my Sungil-ah! Only five years old and dead, oh, oh."

Everyone had heard about the five-year-old boy who died on the road when they were fleeing for refuge, but no one seemed to have actually seen him. So, people felt a little doubtful and showed only casual sympathy. On a gloomy miserable night like tonight, nobody did even that. There was only silence. "Oh, my poor child, oh, oh, my dear child. If only that damned car didn't explode, we could have hung onto a train and made it here. But this cruel mother dragged the little one in the snow for miles and miles. This cursed mother forced the little one...oh, dear God." Her lamentation went on. Her husband merely cleared his throat and filled his pipe.

"You see, this ogre of a mother threatened to leave him behind if he didn't keep on walking. I even beat him. I dragged him. Oh, this monster of a mother. I deserve to die," she wailed. Her husband merely coughed.

"Oh, my poor, poor Sungil. Why did it have to snow so much! They said there was a village over the hill, and we wanted to get there before sundown. So, I forced him. He just dropped on the snow and didn't move. Ever again. Oh, my child."

"Now stop it. That's enough," her husband said, tapping his pipe. But his hands shook visibly. There was no way in the world to express his pain and sorrow over the death of his son whom he buried on some unknown spot in the snow-covered field.

The wind hissed and roared through the leaking roof. Old Man Bae's dim eyes filled with tears. Trying to hide his tears, he coughed and bent his head. His wife sniveled, covered him, and crouched beside him, needlessly smoothing with one hand the coarse wet straw mat.

"Oh, my cursed life, oh, oh," Mrs. Song moaned and fell silent.

Old Man Bae looked over at Mrs. Song, and with trembling hands, calmed himself. Huge pouches hung beneath his eyes while bushy white brows framed them. His nose tilted upward and deep lines creased his forehead and cheeks. His lips were pale and slightly open. His eyes were filled with fear. His was an unforgettably tragic face.

One day a friend of Taehyon's came and declared after he met the old man, "The very symbol of our tragic age! I take my hat off to him as a sign of my respect."

Today Old Man Bae's face was sadder than ever. Nothing was known about this old couple except that their son was on the front line. They rarely spoke. They ate so alarmingly little that it seemed a miracle that they were alive. Wrapped in silent sadness, they made no noise except the man's coughing.

Outside, the storm raged on. The eyes of the people took on more and more uneasiness. Jee-Sang, a longshoreman, also woke up from a deep sleep, scratching his armpits. Flakes of dead skin showered down from his long unwashed body. Then, he hunted up a louse and crushed it. Perhaps excited by the popping sound, he took off all his clothes and began lice-hunting. It seemed he derived a sick thrill from noisily popping the fat lice.

"This city of Pusan is a nasty place. Even its weather is weird. Why on earth does it rain in the middle of winter, will somebody tell me?" Mr. Chung grumbled.

Mr. Chung, another worker on the dock, put a couple of empty cans to catch the rain water, which, as if to gall them all, evaded each and every can.

"It has rained so much this winter that soldiers on the front are battling with the mud rather than the Chinese marauders, I heard," said Lee Sangho, the husband of the young couple, who worked at a printing office. His voice was as soft as a woman's.

"Oh, oh," Old Man Bae moaned.

"Sir, not every soldier dies. Please, try not to worry," consoled Lee.

Old Man Bae again put his shaking hands on his chest and nodded his chin up and down. His sorrow was his own and no word came out of his mouth. From time to time, he burst out moaning. The old couple was the parents of not only a Republic of Korea soldier but also of a die-hard Red guerrilla. September 25, 1950, right before the UN forces recaptured Seoul, their older son, the guerrilla, disappeared without a good-bye into a storm of cannon fire.

They remembered his piercing eyes and tense face. They didn't know whether he was alive or dead. Then, their darling younger son, who might be battling with mud and the Chinese invaders, went to fight as well. Brothers on an eternal ideological parallel, but they were both their beloved sons.

"Oh, oh," Old Man Bae moaned again.

"God, I can't sleep," blurted the young man who lived alone across the aisle from the Songs. He had been sleeping under a blanket, completely covering himself from head to toe. He had a straight high nose and brilliant eyes. His name was Kim Byongmin, but, for some reason, people called him "Young Man." Nobody knew what he did for a living. He often came home late and he seemed better off than anyone else in the warehouse. He wore an old American Army shirt and had an American Army blanket.

Next to him was a woman named Shin Miryong. Rain didn't drip into her space, but she had been up for sometime listening to the rain.

"On a night like this, anyone under a roof is a happy person. Anyone who has a warm corner is also a happy person," Shin remembered reading in one of Turgenev's books. "Am I happy because I am under this so-called roof?" she asked herself. No. Do I have a warm corner? No. This is no more than a warehouse where human fragments were blown into by the mad storm of a war. This is some storage for worn-down, wretched, miserable human fragments. She knew she herself was not a whole being but a fragment with no human emotions but an instinctive tenacity to survive.

She felt the intent gaze of the Young Man. Overwhelmed by a shivering excitement, she turned pale. A 25-year-old war widow, she knew what suffering was. She hid herself under her cover and groped for her nonexistent mother as if reaching for a savior.

Someone moaned. Rain kept pouring down into the deepening darkness.

"Oh, no, sir. You shouldn't do this," Mrs. Song chirped.

"It's all right. My wife is not well," Taehyon said.

Taehyon blushed in spite of himself. Why was he blushing? What was he anyway? Like everyone else, he was a mere refugee. All refugee men carried water, made fire and did other sundry chores. Why did he alone look so awkward? With downcast eyes, he put his empty bucket in a long line of empty receptacles around a hydrant from which a thin trickle of water was dripping down. No one knew how long it would take to fill all the empty buckets of all sizes and shapes.

Among those waiting in line, there were a man with graying hair, a little girl barely taller than her bucket, and occasionally a prettily made-up young woman in a silk dress. While waiting interminably, Taehyon felt that his hands and feet had gone numb. "So, this is how my wife brought home water for me to wash myself." He thought of his wife's sallow face, swollen from malnutrition.

Young girls used their waiting hours for knitting. While wives gathered in small groups to chat, their eyes were alert for anyone who might try to cut in. A rice-candy peddler leaned against a wall listlessly jangling his huge scissors once in a while. A truck sped by throwing up a cloud of dust. The waiting people and the buckets were soon covered in a thin layer of dust.

"What a curse this is! I can't stand these refugees. Can't get water, prices go up, our houses are in a shambles. Oh, God! When on earth is this going to end?" A middle-aged woman with protruding cheekbones complained in her thick Pusan dialect.

"Now, what did you say? You think we wanted to come here? You don't know what hardship is," Mrs. Song immediately retorted.

"You all ought to be ashamed of yourselves," the woman persisted.

"Ashamed? You people in Pusan won't share even water with us refugees. Shouldn't you be ashamed? Somebody ought to dump you in the sea to make you see straight."

"Good heavens! You are loud."

"Pusan is disgusting. I don't even want to hear its name," Mrs. Song gesticulated with her arm to show her disgust.

"Who told you to come here? We never invited you."

"You think we wanted to come?"

"What strange people you are. I've never seen such brazen bunch," the woman decried and shoved Mrs. Song.

"Who do you think you are, huh? You struck me! Okay, now let's have it out!"

Mrs. Song's face turned red and curses streamed out of her mouth.

The Songs had been a comfortable farming family before the war. Mrs. Song used to be a respected lady in her town. The war took away her dignity, her sense of shame and rationality, and left her only with rapacious energy for survival. She quarreled with strangers because it made her feel alive.

For a long while Mrs. Song cried and carried on before she got to the hydrant and filled her bucket. She put it on her head, gave the woman a mean look, and stalked away to the warehouse. Taehyon followed her with his full bucket, resting at every few steps. He felt overwhelmed by Mrs. Song's vitality. What was he then? Nothing but a hypocrite, a heartless man, a deceitful son, and above all an incompetent.

On his way to the warehouse, he saw the refugees sitting on rusted rails and hunting lice in their clothes. They were the ones who lived in permanently stalled rail cars.

There were more and more peddlers selling candy, gum, matches, and cheap cigarettes to longshoremen. The peddlers were mostly women in discarded Army pants, their heads covered with old towels. A group of rugged dock workers sat on their heels in front of a woman cooking bean pancakes. They drank rice ale, belched loudly, and wolfed down big chunks of hot bean-cakes. Taehyon felt his mouth water, having had little food in the past few days. The smell of bean cakes pierced through his empty stomach. By the time he arrived at the warehouse, he felt faint.

Mrs. Song, also a seller of bean pancakes, had already begun to grind mung beans on a stone handmill.

"How are you?" she said, smiling, her bluish gums exposed. In her smile, Taehyon could sense a shade of pity and slight reserve.

Taehyon's heart sank. It had been months since the families began living together under the same roof, but he had not been able to open up to anyone. He felt like a sole outsider. Now that there was little possibility of escaping the crowded warehouse, he knew he had to discard his old pride. But at the same time, the distance he maintained was the only way left to him to hold up his pride, without which he would be nothing. In this squalid refugee life, his incompetence seemed ironically a vestige of his superiority.

He put the pail beside the two stones that served as a fuel hole. From the clean air outside, his nose suddenly inhaled the unspeakable stench inside. His eyes took a few minutes to adjust to the darkness.

His wife's swollen sallow face was not on a pillow but on a bundle of old clothes, her disheveled hair loose. Her breathing was short and labored. At her head, his 4-year-old son, his dirty hair matted on the head, his unwashed face smeared with nose drivel, sat spooning into his mouth some gruel from a pan between his legs.

His wife opened her eyes and tried to smile at him, but her attempt resulted in a grimace. As if to hide her unclean appearance, she pulled up her cover. Her hands were coarse and knobby. She had fallen to this bottomless pit with her incompetent husband, Taehyon thought, because she was a woman who was sensitive to her husband's defeats and blamed herself.

In the few years before the war, he had often felt bored by her. But, now, as he looked down on her gaunt unwashed face, his heart went out to her. Into the back of his mind loomed the image of his wife in her bridal pink skirt and yellow gold-embroidered jacket, standing like a spring flower. He was a handsome young husband, the only son of a wealthy land owner, as well as a graduate of the Kyungsung Imperial University.

However, what had he become after graduation? Was he one of those honor students who became failures once they were outside of the school walls? Was he a fish on land? His downfall came from his pride and refusal to accept his incompetence in the real world. He often changed jobs as he began on his slow downward spiral. As long as he stayed in Seoul, he managed well enough. But once in Pusan, filled to the brim with job-seeking refugees, he had spent all of what little he had had. Eventually, he ended up in the warehouse.

While looking down on his wife under the smelly covers, he thought he saw the angry faces of his old parents, perhaps gone mad by now from hunger or already dead. Their accusing eyes were glaring at him.

He had to get out. In the street, Mrs. Song was still grinding the beans while the young wife, the next-door neighbor of the Songs chatted loudly. The young woman, with Taehyon's daughter on her back, was washing soiled diapers. Taehyon's eyes burned. In shame, he turned his eyes to the messy dump in the station yard, piled high with broken rails, disintegrating freight cars, and other debris.

There stood on the dump his older son, Hongin, in patched army-blanket pants. Beside him was the Songs' son, Dushik. The two boys were making obscene gestures to a UN soldier and his heavily painted girlfriend.

A line of freight cars, loaded down with people hanging on the doors and the roofs, roared by. A tall young man strolled down the road and was gladly greeted by the two boys. It was the Young Man. He came down and held the boys' hands on each side.

Taehyon had much to thank the young man for, especially since his wife became ill. Nobody knew what he did for a living, but he had a Zenith radio, an incongruous item to the warehouse life. He smoked American cigarettes and ate with the dock laborers. While Taehyon received vague, totally inappropriate respect, the Young Man was an object of his neighbors' curious wonder and envy.

Mrs. Song went so far as to call him insane.

"You are home early today," Taehyon greeted him.

"Yes," the Young Man said.

To each of the two boys, he gave a stick of American gum and waved them away. He watched them scamper off and sat on the rail beside Taehyon.

"Would you like one?" he offered a Lucky-Strike cigarette. Shamefacedly and awkwardly, Taehyon accepted the cigarette which the Young Man lit for him with a lighter.

Such sweet aroma he hadn't had in a long while.

"Won't you sit down? You must be really worried," the young man said.

Taehyon's face burned, but he said, "I don't know how to thank you for all the care and help you gave us."

The Young Man seemed to disregard the remark and sat silently for a while. Then, he grinned suddenly and asked, "Mr. Park, have you ever felt the pleasure of blasphemy?"

The Young Man looked away from Taehyon as if he didn't expect an answer.

"Yes, the pleasure of blasphemy, the opposition to common sense. Ha. Ha." The Young Man laughed, exposing an endearingly irregular front tooth.

"Do you know, Mr. Park, what I do these days?" the Young Man asked Taehyon, his two brilliant eyes focusing on his face. There was only silence between them.

"I have a lot of money in my pockets. Where do you think I got it? How do you think I got it?" Taehyon found himself getting a little afraid of him.

"Mr. Park, I don't mind throwing it all away. I don't care because I don't need it. But," he paused. "I threatened my father. He wasn't to blame except for pinning all his hopes on me, his only son, and belonging to the rich class. He didn't do anything wrong, but I threatened him anyway."

"I did an unforgivable thing. I don't think he gave me the money because he was afraid. Maybe he felt threatened, I don't know. If he did, he could have used any means of.... Aah, I don't know what's what. I can't see any meaning in anything. Nothing means anything. Isn't that abominable? I don't know what I wanted to ask you," the Young Man said.

"You know, Mr. Park, I wish my father had punished me, then I would have been able to see things more clearly. Now, I'm utterly confused." He kept his hand on his forehead as if trying to put his thoughts in order.

"When I see other people who go back on track after a time of confusion, I marvel at them. I used the word blasphemy, but actually I don't know its meaning or where to apply it." The Young Man shook his head.

"Was there ever an age when the word justice was used so carelessly, or principles were so convoluted and transgressed? I no longer know the meaning of guilt. People who judge other people are no longer human beings, are they? It may sound funny to you, Mr. Park, that I am thinking of all these things now. Things that are considered sinful on one side are hailed as sacred on the other. The most inexcusable things are rationalized without a moment of hesitation. I don't have to go on, do I? But, to my great misfortune, I saw too much. Yes, I saw too much with my own eyes."

"So, I have become unable to distinguish between good and bad," the Young Man said.

"It's the tragedy of our century. Don't think too much about it," Taehyon said.

"But, please hear me out. I had two very close friends. Being an only child, I loved them both passionately. They were young, healthy, bright, and beautiful young men. We went to the same university where we energetically pursued truth and beauty and enjoyed our life. Then, the war came. The war was a storm that turned people insane."

"And, here I am, left alone. One of them was killed by the Reds in the summer and the other was dragged north by them. To me, they both might as well be dead."

"They were not alone," Taehyon mumbled, helpless to comfort the Young Man, who continued.

"It was during our exodus from North Korea. My family rode a truck down to Inchon and stayed there until the last moment. Then we had to get on a boat. The scene on the dock was pure bedlam, thousands of people milling desperately to get on board. The boat was a small private one and it was already full, far over its capacity. But hordes of people, screaming, mad with fear and desperation, kept climbing onto the boat. No one held out a hand or offered a word of encouragement, but they kept coming aboard until the boat seemed about to capsize. At that moment, I saw something no human eyes should see. A few big rugged sailors appeared and began kicking the climbing people off the boat into the sea. Many of them drowned. Ever since then, I have suffered this utter confusion. What I couldn't bear was that the sailors' action was rationalized as justifiable self-defense, because the boat would have capsized otherwise. From that moment on, my life has become rudderless, my personality dehumanized."

Taehyon remained silent.

"I came to view everything differently. The war...and...but without some sort of conviction, I fell further into confusion. I didn't want to live because my life became a burden of shame. To escape from it, I resorted to roiling other people's lives but I was the one who got hurt most." The Young Man put his hand on his forehead again as if he were dizzy. Choosing his words carefully, Taehyon began to talk.

"You seem to have propensity for suffering."

"What?"

"You may not like what I've just said, but you do. Shall I go on?"

"Yes, please."

"If you came to doubt all the exigencies and restrictions of life...."

"Yes. I did."

"Then, I will tell you what Roman Roland said, 'I believe in God only as a being who is conscious of his own inner self.' Try to rely on a morality that begins and ends with you." The Young Man gazed hard at him without a word and stood up. He quietly repeated to himself, "I believe in God only as a being 'who is conscious of his own inner self.'"

Taehyon suddenly felt ashamed and rose from the rail. He blushed at such words as morality and God. Who was he? Ever since the War began, his family had survived by selling whatever he owned, but he had never ventured to the market himself. He had no courage to do that, and he was now lecturing to another man. What gall!

His wife had earned a little by peddling cigarettes in the street until she became ill. Since then, they had been selling every little thing they had in possession except an old suit of his. The suit was made of expensive material but in old outdated style. His wife treasured it as if it were a family heirloom. She knew it was the only suit he could wear when he went for job interviews or after he got a job. In the past few days, Taehyon's eyes kept turning to that suit.

"What, what in the world happened? Oh my God! It couldn't!" Taehyon could hear the loud tear-filled voice coming from inside of the warehouse. It belonged to Mrs. Song who had said happily, earlier on the day, that soon we would all be going back to Seoul.

"Oh, my God, how could such a thing happen?" Mrs. Song burst into a keening wail.

Mr. Song came in with his head hanging low and threw himself down in his partition. Mrs. Song continued to cry and wail.

"What in the world happened?" everyone asked.

Mr. Song turned away as Mrs. Song began a long lamentation.

"Oh, the heinous robbers! Why didn't they give us poison instead? They killed us anyway!"

"What is she talking about?"

"Oh, my God, they took away everything. How could this happen? What I had to sell, I got with my own money and some borrowed money. We had to eat. And those damned rascals took everything, everything!"

"What does she mean?"

"The American MPs and Korean police blocked every entrance to the Pusan International Market and carried off everything in it in Army trucks!"

"You mean only illegal American goods, right? I have been hearing about a raid for sometime," Lee Sangho broke in.

"Then, why didn't you tell me, huh? How could a neighbor be so heartless?" Mrs. Song screamed.

Lee Sangho blushed with embarrassment. Mr. Song bellowed, "Stop it!"

Mrs. Bae who had recently lost her old husband looked at them blankly. There was no light of life in her eyes. Deep in her heart were buried her two sons, and her husband whom she had buried unceremoniously like a piece of garbage.

"What a pity," Taehyon's wife whispered, feelings of sympathy written on her swollen yellow face.

Taehyon glanced at his sick wife and at his one remaining suit, a symbol of his old world, to which he was desperately hanging on. He sighed and frowned as if from pain, and walked slowly out of the warehouse.

Outside, on the old broken rail, the young wife was playing with his infant daughter. She cooed and whispered baby-talk and buried her face in the baby's tiny bosom. The baby giggled. Early spring sunshine was warm on their heads. The 20-year-old wife had irrepressible joie de vivre despite the unspeakable squalor of refugee life.

It was indeed spring. Through the smoke, soot, and dust that covered the rail yard, green things were sprouting up. Early mornings, spring mist hung midair. Even in the dark refugee quarters, a new air of hopefulness stirred because of the news that Seoul would soon be recaptured by the UN Army.

The young woman was baby-sitting his daughter. For some reason, though no one was watching, she blushed deeply. Her heart-beat quickened as she felt a new life stirring inside her. She held the baby close to her heart and rubbed her cheeks against the baby's.

The Young Man walked slowly by the woman in measured steps. He was thinking of Shin Miryong, the young widow, whom he had just seen on the street. The widow had stirred him. She had permed curly hair, archy penciled brows, blue eye-shadow on her eye lids and dark-red full lips. By her make-up and clothing, Miryong showed unhesitatingly what she was. One day she spoke to the Young Man who had never even accosted her.

"Sir, have you ever experienced something like this? It was in Seoul that one day I went out, all dressed up in my best clothes, when it began to rain. Fortunately I had an umbrella with me, but all I cared about was how to keep my white socks and long skirt from rain and mud till I got back home. I hiked my skirt and walked carefully, avoiding puddles. So I succeeded and got to Chongro though that took me almost half an hour. Then, suddenly, a car came from behind me and splashed water all over me from head to toe. I was so angry. I glared at the back of the car, but what good was it? Then, something entirely unexpected happened. Once splattered with muddy water, I could walk freely. I didn't have to avoid wet places. I didn't wait for a street-car but walked merrily all the way home. I even stepped into the puddles. How I enjoyed the freedom! It was great. It could be called the pleasure of ignominy, couldn't it? Once I didn't care about keeping my clothes clean, I could walk with such freedom, such abandon!" the young widow said and laughed.

The Young Man could still hear her ringing laugh. He was suddenly reminded of what Taehyon had said, "the morality that begins and ends with you," but he couldn't be convinced of that; and that is why he was trudging back to the messy, smelly warehouse. He went in and flopped on his straw mat without taking off his jacket and shoes. After a while, he woke up from his reverie and sat up in surprise because the girl-like face of Lee Sangho had a strange expression. The Young Man stared at Lee, who fidgeted a while before confessing.

"I have been drafted to the Second National Army," Lee grinned awkwardly. Upon hearing the news for the first time, his wife winced and turned pale. Taehyon walked in and stood beside him with a somber face. The Young Man joined him, but neither of them spoke, merely watching each other's face. They themselves were targets of the drafting agency and didn't know what to say.

> "On the hills of Nak Yang
> Lie graves, high and low,
> How many heroes were
> Ho, ho, ho...."

Jeesang, obviously pleasantly inebriated, was singing loudly this old song as he entered the warehouse. He held in his right hand a fish on a string and a bunch of spinach in the other.

"Come, come Mr. Park, er.... These here are for your lady...heh, heh," Jeesang awkwardly offered the presents to Taehyon, and dropped himself heavily in his corner. This rough longshoreman, Jeesang, would feel insulted if Taehyon refused.

Especially because Jeesang respected Taehyon, the intellectual.

"Thank you so much. I don't know what to say," Taehyon said.

The good-hearted Jeesang was pleased and a smile appeared on his thick leathery face. Taehyon, also relieved from tension, nodded at Lee Sangho, and went to look at his suit to take to the market the next day.

The Young Man lay quietly in his corner. Apparently Lee Sangho's draft summons shook him up. Taehyon couldn't tell whether he was re-organizing his thoughts to leave the warehouse or he was more confused than before.

From outside, the smell of rice being cooked floated in. Taehyon's baby daughter woke up and began to cough on the young woman's back. Other cooking odors seeped in and mixed with the typical putrid air inside.

Taehyon sat beside his wife near the portable cooker and opened the pot with some unidentifiable thing boiling in it. He stirred it with a thick iron spoon.

Jeesang lay on his back humming a tune, which sounded strangely comforting to Taehyon.

After the long enervating crying spell, Mrs. Song sighed deeply, blew her nose on the inside of her long skirt, and slowly walked out with a cooking pot.

No one stirred to light a candle. Darkness gradually descended on all.

The Young Elm Tree

by Kang Shinjae

Whenever he comes to my room, he has that clean smell of soap that sends a momentary tingling sensation down my back. The first thing he does when he comes home from school is take a shower and ask me for some snack. I often wonder why he asks me, a clumsy girl who is a menace in the kitchen. He certainly knows he can just go down to the kitchen and open the refrigerator or simply order the servants. Nonetheless, I like to do little chores for him because I love to be alone with him.

I don't know what I should call him. Legally we are brother and sister. But both of us know, often very self-consciously, that we have no blood kinship.

When I come back with a tray of cold cider, glasses, and some crackers, I find him looking out of the window. I love him more than ever at such moments when he shows his most pensive and serious profile, seldom seen by other family members.

"What have you been doing?" he asks me, returning to his usual cheerfulness.

"English composition. You broke my stream of thought," I answer teasingly.

"All right, let me see if you are a writer material," he jokes.

It was only last spring that I was brought to this house in Seoul after spending most of my childhood and high school years with my grandparents in a small country town. My mother had lived with me there until she married Mr. Lee, an economics professor and a middle-aged widower who owns this house. I didn't particularly want to join my mother in her new life, but one day Mr. Lee came and insisted, though very politely, to my grandparents that I be with my mother and him.

In the living room on that spring day, my mother introduced me to Mr. Lee's son.

"This is Sooni, my daughter, and your new sister." Then she turned to me and said, "This is Hyun, your new brother. I hope you will get along well." My mother was very cautious, and I could read her anxiety which was well hidden under her composure.

She continued, "He is a junior in the Physics Department at Seoul National University, and a top honor student. Sooni was regarded quite bright in the town, but I am afraid competition with Seoul students will be tough for her."

I looked at Hyun, taking in his pair of light gray pants and the brown open-neck sweater worn on top of a light brown sports shirt. He had heavy eyebrows that made his face rather somber, but he had a firm jaw and a high forehead suggesting broadmindedness and a gentleness that came from self-confidence. He was of medium build and height. So, I thought mischievously that he was the only son of my new stepfather, and we, an eighteen-year-old girl and a twenty-two-year-old man, were suddenly cast into a brother-sister relationship.

I thought to myself, "Yes, he looks like a genius type. Let's see how I can get along with him. I think I will like him all right."

I never called him "brother" as anyone would in other families, because I did not want to use the word and also because I was not accustomed to calling someone brother. For that matter, I could not quite bring myself to address Mr. Lee as "father" either. The word does not come easily to me as I have never met my own father.

My grandparents and my mother simply told me that my father had died before I was born. But the day my mother married Mr. Lee I happened to overhear my grandparents.

"We should have allowed her to marry Mr. Lee a long time ago. The poor girl has had a sad life because we insisted on marrying her off to that now-gone fellow. How stupid and blind we were when we thought we were doing the right thing for her."

"No use talking about the past. But didn't we get Sooni? I hope they will be happy now that they are at last married to each other."

So I know Mr. Lee and my mother were not newly met, arbitrarily arranged mates. But I haven't said a word about my discovery to anyone.

As the peaceful and serene days went on, Hyun and I became closer. I was happy because Hyun turned out to be gentle, friendly, and infinitely generous to me. Sometimes his generosity irritated me because I coveted a more serious attention from him rather than a mere brotherly permissiveness. His gentlemanliness made a striking contrast with my "bratiness" bred on my grandparents' doting. We both were fond of the big, rambling ivy-covered brick house with built-in modern appliances, and a spacious lawn. We also had a tennis court just off the garden, where we spent a great deal of time together.

After Hyun munched crackers, he suggested, "Let's go play tennis."

"All right. You will never let me become the top student in my class."

I put down my pen pretending that I was really interested in my work.

We went down to the tennis court and exchanged a few strokes. I was unusually poor because I could not concentrate on the game.

"What's become of you? Your game seems to be getting worse."

"Oh, never mind. It happens from time to time."

I was restless and uneasy in our outwardly calm family life. I was not satisfied for I felt there was something ambiguous in my relationship with him. When I was alone with him, I felt a joy mingled with sorrow, even though I tried to be the picture of casualness itself. As it began to darken, we started home. In the garden I took off my shoes and walked barefooted.

"Why don't you go to the shoe mender and have some tacks nailed to your feet? Then, you won't have to wear shoes," he always teased me.

"Because I like to walk barefooted. I feel as if I were back in my carefree old days."

He did not seem to catch the implication of my remark or pretended not to, because, after a brief silence, he brightened up.

"Hey, let's stop at the fountain and have some medicine water. It will help you regain your tennis skills."

We walked to the little fountain which was merely a little hollow place amid huge rocks. The fountain was in the absurdly large garden beyond our fences in the estate of an old court official who subsisted on a generous pension. He was a very old man in his eighties and came leaning on his cane to see us play tennis. He never showed any special interest or made remarks, but stood there for long hours, watching us. To speak the truth, the lot which we were using as our tennis court belonged to him.

Later we found a little gourd dipper beside the fountain. I guessed that it was the old man's gift; perhaps he saw us scooping water with our cupped hands and provided the dipper. Hyun handed over a dipperful of water to me. I drank from a corner of it and handed it back to him. He drank from another corner.

I glanced at him while he held it to his lips a brief second with the same brooding expression flickering on his face and disappearing the next second. It was only a split-second facial movement which I caught without letting on that I was observing him.

"When you drink, you'd better pray that you will play tennis better next time. It is supposed to be tonic water," he said playfully.

"All right. But it is not that important," I sighed at his seemingly calculated indifference to my strange moodiness.

"Let's go home, it is getting dark," he said, brushing off any further conversation between us.

When we came home, dinner was ready. Mr. Lee and my mother were waiting for us. "I am not hungry, mother," I said and went up to my room to look out of the window. Dusk was softly descending upon the garden.

I know Hyun always goes to the dinner table and carries on a polite conversation because he is extremely well-mannered. His father, Mr. Lee, is a taciturn type who is happy when everything is quiet and peaceful, and everybody is well-fed and well-cared for. He has been very busy these days preparing to go to America as a Korean representative to an international conference and is rarely seen at his beloved study. It is a big honor and he must attend many official meetings and farewell parties.

At last I was alone in my dark room, curled up in my bed and began to wonder. What will happen to me if I keep on loving him as I do? Is it absolutely impossible for me to form a different relationship with Hyun? And what does he think about it? Is he really my brother? The word itself stifles me. It is so absurd. What does his occasional gloominess mean? Is he thinking of the same things as I am?

The next afternoon my mother called me to the living room and showed me a bulky letter.

"Sooni, I don't see you at all these days unless I call on you. And I want you to know that I am most interested in everything that happens to you and you are expected to tell me and discuss any problems with me."

She gave me an already opened letter. It was a love letter from a friend of Hyun's, a medical student, who is the eldest son of a government minister who lives next door. He plays tennis with Hyun and me frequently. I was not annoyed at all with my mother for opening the letter.

I read the very romantic letter, which was unbecomingly delicate in contrast to the boy's robust physique and outgoing disposition.

He carried all of his six younger brothers and sisters in a jeep every morning to their respective schools. One day when I was coming home I met him who was bringing two of his sisters in the jeep.

"Jump in, we are on our way home," he said good-naturedly.

"Thank you. Why, you have only two today?" I said.

"When we come home, it is up to everybody to catch this jeep. If they miss it, they have to ride a bus."

"That sounds like fun."

This kind of casual friendship was all I maintained with him. Therefore, I was astonished to receive such a long, earnest love letter from him.

"Sooni, you are no longer a little girl. I wonder how you are going to answer that. If you need my help, tell me so any time," my mother said.

I wanted to answer, but how could I tell her the truth? I wanted to say, "Mother, what would you do if told you that I am in love with your 'son'? Will you be on my side as you always say? I took the letter up to my room and decided to take a walk in the garden. I went as far as the fence and climbed on it dangling my bare feet. Soon I heard little girls' giggling and dogs barking. Then I saw my admirer running with two German shepherds followed by his two sisters.

"Oh, hi, taking a walk?" He blushed in spite of himself.

"Yes, it is so cool out here. Oh, Hyun says he would like to have a tennis match with you one of these days," I tried my best to be casual.

He told his two sisters to run ahead with the dogs and stayed behind.

"May I presume that you have read my letter?" he said, suddenly serious. "I hope you will give a serious thought to it and understand how I feel."

"Yes, I have read it, but I don't know how to answer it yet," I said almost inaudibly.

"You don't have to answer me right away, but please think it over."

I could not stand the awkwardness any more, so I began to walk toward home. "I hope to see you soon," he said noticing that I didn't want to prolong our conversation.

My heart stood still when I found Hyun in my room. His face was full of anger as he glared at me with his intense black eyes before he opened his mouth.

"How kind of you to leave the letter open, for me I presume?"

I said nothing.

"Where have you been? Why don't you answer me?"

I just looked at him defiantly.

I was determined not to respond to him no matter what. In the tense silence, I felt a stinging slap on my face. Then the door slammed. I stood there stunned. Then my heart began to pound, not out of anger but out of a bursting joy. So, he is in love with me, too! I wanted to shout this news to everybody. Instead, I went back to my bed, tears streaming down my cheeks. My whole self was brimmed with happiness, oblivious to our artificial family tie.

That night Hyun and I took a walk in the little wood beyond the court official's estate, and I fell into his arms ecstatically, fearfully, and crying.

Happiness, however, was brief because living with him in the same house as his sister became unbearable. A few days later when I was still half in a dream, forgetting my school work, meals and my beloved tennis, my mother called me and said, "You don't look good. Are you all right?"

When I said yes, my mother who is used to my swinging moods said, "Your stepfather has been invited by an American university to do research for a year. The government has given permission for me to go with him. Hyun told me that he had no problem with my accompanying his father and I want to know how you feel about it."

My mother was cautious as she had always been but she sounded as if she felt guilty about leaving me again. Her announcement was a thunderbolt to me. Me to live with Hyun alone in the big house though there were two servants!

"It is okay with me, mother. I know you will enjoy the trip," I said, playing it cool. My hands began to sweat, though.

"I am glad to hear that. Thank you. Maybe I will ask one of your grand aunts to come and live with you here," she said. But I knew which aunt she meant, one of her maternal aunts who was old and deaf, and wouldn't make any difference as far as my situation was concerned.

On a fine August day, my mother and Mr. Lee left for America. The day after, I packed up my clothes, shoes, books, souvenirs, tennis racket and went down to my old home where my grandparents were still tending their peach orchard. I made a firm resolution not to ever return to that big house. I was afraid to be with Hyun alone because I loved him too much to make him suffer. I would suffer alone.

I quit school, without letting either my parents or the school know why I was leaving. I felt spiteful at the turn of the events, but at nobody in particular. I said a brief goodbye to the old aunt, the two servants, telling them that I would be back soon. When I was at last back in my room in the little cottage of my grandparents, I suddenly felt unbearably lonely and apprehensive about my future.

Everyday I climbed the little hill behind the orchard and leaned against a young elm tree. The sky was blue and clear as ever; the bushes and shrubs were green and fresh. My grandparents didn't have the slightest suspicion about my return from Seoul and rarely inquired about my plans. They were affectionate and gentle as they had always been and seemed quite satisfied with my mother's remarriage to such a distinguished scholar.

It was the last Saturday in August when the edge of breeze suggested the coming of the fall and the skies began to assume the transparent autumnal look that I stood against the elm tree thinking of Hyun, mother, Mr. Lee, and my uncertain future.

From far down the hill I noticed a man climbing toward me. My heart literally stopped—it was Hyun. I leaned against the sturdy tree to steady myself when he came within a few hundred feet from me. He didn't come nearer.

"Now listen to me, Sooni. What happened between us cannot be undone, and neither of us can forget our love for each other. But don't despair; there is a way out for us. For instance, we can go abroad and be together. Do you understand me?" He was calm and almost stern. I nodded in a mist of tears.

"Only promise me that you come back to Seoul and finish school. I have found a room for myself, and one of your mother's friends promised me to give you room and board. I will rent the house. If you agree to this, come down and pack your things."

I was too overwhelmed to make any answer. I nodded like an embarrassed child and looked up into the deepest autumn sky, which seemed to promise me infinite happiness.

"Now come down to the cottage and get ready to leave," he said, smiling at me and offering his hand. It was more than I could have imagined. But before I went with Hyun, I paused to take in the view from under the elm tree. I knew that I would always cherish it as the spot where, in my hiding, love had found me.

Youngju and the Cat

by Park Kyongni

Youngju lost her father during the Korean War and her younger brother last summer. She had thus become an only daughter to her mother, Minhei, as Minhei herself had been to her mother. It was something like a fate. It was Sunday and Youngju was reading a picture book she had read so many times that she could remember every word in it. After a while, she closed the book and skipped over to the window and gazed at her own reflections. She smiled and then frowned. In a little while, she began to whisper to her own image.

Outside, the sun was setting but the boys were still engrossed in sledding on a patch of ice on the street. Youngju blew steam on the window pane, and with a fingertip drew faces and wrote a line of poem she knew. Then, she erased them all. She looked at the golden sunset descending slowly behind the roof of a house across the street. She put her fingertip between her lips and kept looking at the reddening sky.

Round and square, round and square
Ice patterns frozen so beautifully on the window
Pretty like the pictures ducks draw in the pond

Last winter, Youngju used to sing the song with her brother. They fought, too, over who should get the first chance to draw on the frozen pane. A cat that had been dozing beside the brazier stretched itself and rose. "Adele, Adele," Youngju called the cat and picked it up in her arms. The cat licked her hands.

Youngju was ten. She was so small and delicate that her classmates called her "Baby." She was like a newborn chick, soft and small-boned, with eyelids almost transparent. But her eyes were sad. The lonely sad-eyed daughter playing by herself tugged at her mother's heartstring. That is why Minhei got a cat for Youngju, who had always wanted one. The cat had light brown and yellow stripes on white fur.

After thinking long and hard about the best name they could give the cat, Minhei recalled the name of the beautiful servant girl in the story of Count Montesquieu, Adele. To their delight, Adele grew in good health except once when it ate some meat and had a stomach trouble.

Adele kept licking Youngju's hands. Suddenly Youngju put down the cat and stacked two cushions, one on top of the other. On each side of the cushions she placed a pillow and spread some towels and a wide skirt that belonged to her grandmother. Holding a feathery duster, she sat herself on the make-shift throne and gravely intoned, "I am the queen. Adele, you are a lady-in-waiting. Do you understand?"

The cat was indifferent to Youngju's shenanigans, instead, it stared at her toe protruding from a hole in her sock. Then it pounced on the toe and bit it. "Ouch. You cheeky witch!" Youngju scolded and hit the cat with her duster. The cat skulked into a corner under the desk.

The light came on rather dimly. Youngju coaxed the cat out of the corner and draped toy pearl necklace around its neck and some silk cloth over its back. "What a nuisance," Adele seemed to say, while rolling away from Youngju.

"Adele, you pest, your mom is trying to dress you. Be still, will you?" Youngju began to spank the cat with her duster.

Minhei came in from outside and quietly observed her daughter playing with the cat. Youngju seemed to have forgotten her brother. Minhei grieved for her son more as she watched her daughter who looked oblivious to the absence of her brother. "All right, forget your brother and live a happy life," Minhei thought, feeling more desolate than ever. Youngju was falling asleep with Adele in her arms.

One day Minhei's old classmate, Junghee, moved to live nearby. Junghee said there were rats in her house and borrowed Adele. When Youngju found about her cat, she didn't complain because she liked Junghee's children as much as she liked Adele. Junghee had several children who called Youngju "big sister," which made Youngju very proud. Sensing Youngju's loneliness and attachment to the cat, Junghee did everything to please her friend's delicate daughter.

Finishing her homework after school, Youngju went over to Junghee's house. She missed Adele and wanted to play the "queen game" with it. She came home as darkness fell on the neighborhood. A few days later, Minhei paid a visit to Junghee's house, and Youngju wordlessly tagged along. The children were absorbed in their play, paying no attention to the whereabouts of the cat.

Minhei had a long talkative visit with her friend and stood up in embarrassment when dinner was about to be served. Junghee wanted her to stay for dinner, but Minhei couldn't do that. Youngju followed her mother into the yard and said cheerfully to Junghee, "Ajumoni, Good-by."

As soon as they got home, Youngju covered her face with her hands and began to sob. "What in the world happened? Didn't you have a good time with your friends?" Minhei was at a loss.

"Oh, Mommy, Kwangsu kept hitting Adele. My poor, poor Adele. But I couldn't scold him because he is a baby."

Minhei was surprised. Youngju seemed to play so well with her friends, but she was crying inside. Was she also hiding her sorrow about her brother's death? Was she putting on a serene facade for my sake? Oh, God, what a child! To hide sorrow and darkness deep inside, that was hard even for adults. And a small delicate little girl who has learned by herself the nuances of human emotions.

It was too sad, too dark. Looking at Youngju, Minhei felt as if Youngju were a miniature of herself. Junghee once said, "Your daughter Youngju has a much more generous mind than you. She is not so particular as you. You know, you think too much about every little thing, but she seems much more accepting than you. Besides, she is so cheerful. You ought to watch her when she plays the queen game. She is really something."

"I know, but she doesn't show how she really feels."

"She always plays that queen game of hers. Well, I wish she would someday be a real queen."

"You are crazy."

Minhei smiled sadly. She also wished for some sort of a miracle to happen to her daughter, but she knew it was unlikely.

"Maybe we need nursery tales because our life is so bleak and unpredictable," said Minhei as she watched Junghee nursing her baby.

Sunday came and so did Adele. Youngju was reading a French story and asked, "Mommy, what is the Bastille Prison?"

Minhei explained it while looking into the eyes of her daughter. Youngju's pupils wavered a little and suddenly Minhei was dizzy with an oncoming headache. She laid herself on her stomach as she knew it was a symptom of her anemia.

My present life is no better than life in prison. True, I have freedom, but I have no freedom to survive because I have no means of making a living. I live in a constant fear of abject poverty. Minhei closed her eyes as tears gathered in them.

"If I died, what would happen to Youngju? She would be an orphan wandering the streets. I understand why people kill their children first before they commit suicide. But, if you have the courage to die, you can do anything, even selling your own body."

Dinner time. Minhei and Youngju sat with the small low table between them. If you think about what may ensue after you die, the very thought of suicide is nothing more than sentimentalism, Minhei thought. She began to chew a spoonful of rice. The things in her head felt like they were grating against one another, like rusty machines. Dizziness crept up again and she had to lie down.

Youngju came around the table and sat in her mother's place. "I am your mother now. And you are Youngju, understand?" Youngju said to the cat and patted its head lightly. The cat meowed in response.

"Now don't spill food. Eat like a lady," Youngju glared at Adele.

The cat was too busy eating the anchovy she had fished out of her soup.

"Tut, tut, you eat like you have been starving for days. What horrible manners," Youngju said mimicking her mother's voice. Forgetting her headache, Minhei laughed. Youngju laughed, too.

After dinner, Adele was comfortably ensconced in a carton with only her head above the box top. The cat looked adorable.

"Mommy, Adele is so cute, isn't she?"

Youngju picked up the box and put it on her head.

"Sweet rice cake, sweet rice cake," Youngju yodeled like a peddler selling rice cakes at night in back alleys.

Minhei jumped up, as if stung by a hot iron, and began to slap Youngju.

"Why on earth did you do that? Is that what you want to become? A night peddler?"

Youngju quickly put the box down and stared at her mother.

"All right! Be a peddler after I die. What a sight you will make!"

Minhei regretted immediately, especially her second remark. But Youngju's eyes remained as calm and clear as ever. Minhei buried herself under a coverlet. What an unbelievable curse she blurted. After a long time, she came out of the cover and sheepishly grinned at her daughter.

"Youngju, will you hand over that book to me?" Minhei asked gently. She smiled at Youngju who smiled back at her.

Adele, playfully rolling a walnut on the floor, slowed down and came meekly to Youngju's side. Youngju seemed to have put aside the incident with her mother. She was gently rubbing the floor with her fingers while the cat licked them. She pushed away the cat, giggling.

"Stop giggling. Aren't you mad at Mommy?"

Youngju made a serious face, but soon began to giggle again as the cat tickled her toes. Surprised by the sound of Youngju's laughter, Adele went back to chasing the walnut around the room.

Minhei watched the cat and the walnut.

"Time, fly as quickly as you can. When my face is full of wrinkles and my hair is gray, I will not think about the mournful cries of a night peddler anymore," Minhei prayed.

A cold gust of wind was blowing outside.

The Jade Ring

by Lee Sukbong

In a corner of the tearoom, Yonju sat alone as her face gradually darkened despite the cheerful Italian music from the stereo set. She was preoccupied with her mother's vindictive remark: "I shall see how you end up. It will be sooner than you think!" The day she moved to a small apartment Yonju found for her, she spat out the near-curse. It was three days ago. For Yonju, her mother's move gave her the first freedom she had had in eight long years, during which her mother nagged her over every little trifle in her life.

To her surprise after her mother's move, Yonju didn't feel like "Good riddance" as she had thought. She felt rather remorseful that she might have taken away from her mother her sole pleasure in life—nagging and criticizing her daughter's every action and every decision. At the moment she was thinking of this.

"A penny for your thought," said her cousin, who ran a notary public office nearby. He flopped himself in a seat across from Yonju. Yonju respected him because he always gave her good counsel on matters of life, especially family matters.

"Are you on your way to office?" Yonju smiled at Dongjin.

"I am coming from my office. I have something to talk to you about."

Dongjin took out a pack of cigarettes and put it on the table, a sign that the talk was going to be serious.

"May I ask what it is about?" Yonju felt herself becoming tense.

"You made your mother move to live alone, I understand. She came to my house this morning."

"I did."

"Why this sudden move?"

"It wasn't sudden at all, Dongjin. I have endured as long as I could. I couldn't take it anymore."

"Between family members, there shouldn't be anything you can't endure."

Yonju faltered as Dongjin's gentle argument began to close in on her. But Yonju couldn't capitulate so easily. She had to convince Dongjin, the most important relative; otherwise, she knew she would be branded as "an ungrateful child" by the entire clan. Yonju hated being called an ingrate.

"You know how she is. She nags and whines over everything and nothing. Since my divorce, she has become worse. It's been eight long years!"

"You must understand she was a young widow with two daughters. If she hadn't had that kind of difficult disposition, she would not have remained single all these years."

"I know. That's why I have endured this long."

"Then, what was the cause for your change of mind, may I ask?"

Yonju hesitated. Mother must have told him about it. She looked down and waited for Dongjin to start reasoning with her. But did he or anyone else have a right to intrude into her privacy? No! She looked up.

"Didn't Mother tell you?"

Dongjin lit a cigarette and puffed a long minute.

"That you're involved with a married man with children."

He smoked in silence.

"Yes, I am."

"She told me that you kicked her out because she said a few words about it."

Yonju smiled a crooked smile. That much was true.

"Yes, I admit that was the direct cause. Every time he came to visit me, she swore and cursed in the most vile language. She called us every name in the world, dirty whore and whoremonger and many others. Then she would spit at the door of my room. So I asked him not to come anymore. Then I thought about which one, Mother or the man, I need more for my life."

"But he is a married man."

"You know one's feelings are not regulated by some formula."

"That is why you should try, I mean, try to live by family rules."

Yonju lost her desire to continue to talk with him, because she thought his counsel seemed limited to practical matters. She felt suddenly lonely and bitter, but could not stop the conversation.

"My conclusion was that Mother was somebody I needed in the past, but the man was the one I need now and will need in the future. That was why I asked Mother to move out."

Dongjin rubbed out his cigarette, obviously displeased, and looked at her straight in the eye.

"I will tell you what I think. If you must see him, do it somewhere else, and bring your mother back."

Yonju smiled, not as a sign of consent, but of silent refusal. Hyungsok was hers, only when he lay in her room in a robe, away from all the restrictions. She could no longer tolerate their secret trysts filled with anxiety and guilt. She didn't even want to think about resuming them.

"You have taken good care of her all these years, why risk being branded ungrateful now?"

Dongjin rose heavily and walked out.

Yonju rose, too, and walked over to the counter. "Was it really because of Hyungsok that I wanted my mother out of my house? No doubt that was the most immediate cause, but the real reason was that I wanted to be free. My frayed nerves could no longer hold up. I wanted to live in peace, free from anyone's interference." And yet, Dongjin's parting words sank like a stone in her heart.

The tearoom began to fill up with nearby salary men thirsting for a cup of morning coffee. Waitresses were busily moving between tables while Yonju watched them in brooding silence. She was reaffirming her determination not to let her mother move back in. To her dismay, she saw her younger sister Yonsuk enter the tearoom. Yonsuk, content in a happy marriage, rarely left home, and her sudden appearance forebode some unpleasant news. Yonju did not move.

"Big Sister, can I have a minute with you?" Yonsuk asked coldly.

Yonju took her to an empty table and sat across from Yonsuk.

"What is the matter?"

"How could you do this to me? Is it true your jade ring is missing?"

"What?"

"Your jade ring. Is it really missing?"

"And if it is?"

"Did you say I stole it?"

"What?" Yonju could not believe what she had heard.

"I heard it from Mother last night. I was so angry and hurt that I cried all night. If my husband weren't there for me, I would have killed myself."

"Do you really believe Mother?" Yonju was icily composed after grasping what had happened.

"Why on earth would Mother say such a thing if it wasn't true? Why would she make us enemies for no reason?"

"It is true the ring is missing. I found it gone on the morning when Mother moved out. I used to keep it in my dresser drawer and for a couple of days I didn't look in. But never, ever did I suspect you. You were there the night before Mother moved out, that's all."

"Then, for no reason at all, Mother is trying to estrange us, is that it?"

"If you believe what she said, there is nothing I can say. But I must tell you this. As long as you believe Mother, you and I had better not see each other."

"Pshaw! Now I know. You kicked Mother out, and now you are cutting your only sister out. Mother is right. You are so infatuated with that guy that you've become blind."

Yonju closed her eyes and breathed deeply in order not to explode.

Yonsuk's pointed chin thrust aggressively upward. With an icy sneer, Yonju glared at her sister's chin, the same pointed chin as her mother's. The night before her mother moved out, Yonsuk came and supported wholeheartedly Yonju's decision. Yonsuk had said that in this modern age, it was desirable for grown-up children to live apart from their parents.

And now, she was criticizing the same decision with such vehemence.

"I'll tell you one more thing. Mother said it was that man who stole it," Yonsuk almost hissed those words. Yonju turned pale and her lips trembled.

"You'd better leave now."

Yonsuk stood up with a triumphant sneer and left.

Yonju made her way into the kitchen and drank a glassful of orange juice meant for a customer. Holding the empty glass, she moved slowly to the window. Outside, it had just begun to snow and the snow flakes looked tentative and timid. Hyungsok's face emerged among the snowflakes. He couldn't have heard what Mother had told Yonsuk, but Yonju felt deeply sorry. "He had endured all kinds of invectives from Mother, but he wouldn't tolerate her accusation of stealing the ring." Yonju went to the counter to call Hyungsok. She wanted to hear his warm and friendly voice, but he was out with a visitor.

Yonju sat on a spare chair behind the counter. Into her agitated and infuriated state came the image of the jade ring. It was assessed by a jeweler to be worth more than two hundred thousand *won*. It was a gift from her former husband who had brought it from Hong Kong. But the very ring caused the beginning of their estrangement when exactly the same ring had been given to another woman. Yet, Yonju had an unusual attachment to it. It had the color of an old mossy pond and its deep green seemed to hold an unfathomable mystery in it. It also had a magically calming effect on her.

Losing the ring was a blow to Yonju, but she never suspected anyone close to her because all of them were dear to her and they in turn held her in love and esteem. She didn't even doubt the maid, a middle-aged widow who had lived with her for more than five years without one incidence of dishonesty. Maybe I put it somewhere else and forgot or I might have taken it out and lost it. More than anything else, she wanted to prove Hyungsok's innocence.

She felt thirsty again. Instead of calling a waitress, she went into the kitchen again. She was too agitated to stay in one place. In a corner of the kitchen, Sanghun, the errand boy, was standing with an angry face. The groceries he had brought were left on the cooking stand.

"It's cold out, isn't it? Did you get everything?" Yonju asked cheerfully, purposely ignoring his expression.

"I want to quit here today and go back to my hometown," Sanghun said. He was almost rude.

"Why do you want to do that so suddenly?"

"Why should I stay here when I am accused of being a thief?"

"What? Who in the world accused you?"

"Oh, don't give me that surprised look. You did. You said I stole your jade ring."

"What?"

Yonju slapped him.

"Why do you hit me? What have I done to you?"

"You fool. If I ever had any doubt about you, would I have left you in charge of the kitchen? Think about it, you fool."

"Then your mother lied to me? Why? Why did she make up a lie like that? I cannot stand being called a thief."

"Do you really believe what my mother said? Do you?"

Sanghun began to cry. Perhaps he was sad that he could not believe Yonju.

"If you do, there's nothing I can do for you."

Yonju sank on a chair. She had brought Sanghun, a distant relative, from the country to help her run the tearoom. During the three years he had been with her, he had been scrupulously honest, and there had been no shady business to worry her. In other words, Sanghun was indispensable to Yonju.

"If you do, there's nothing I can do."

She poured a big spoonful of sugar in a glass of cold water and drank it. She left the kitchen and saw the tearoom packed with people as it was lunch time. The counter chair had been taken away to make an extra seat for a customer. Yonju leaned on the counter and watched the people coming and going. Hatred of her mother began to fill her like a cloud of black smoke. She could see through her mother's purpose in lying to Yonsuk and Sanghun. By estranging everyone dear to her and alienating her completely, her mother wanted to make her realize how much she needed her.

Yonju ran out into the snow. A glistening white blanket covered everything. For some reason, the scene reminded her of the long well-pressed white apron her mother used to wear long ago. As a child, Yonju would press her face in it which always smelled sweet. Her mother called the smell "the scent of fire." At times when she put her head in it and stretched out on the warm ondol floor, her mother told her, "I am giving up my best years for you girls." As Yonju grew older, however, her mother's words chilled her. Her mother was expecting to be repaid for her lost youth, a very high reward for the lonely years of her young widowhood. Yonju kicked at the snow. No, no, I will not. If mother's reward demanded sacrifice of my own youth, I cannot and will not give it to her.

Yonju stopped at the red light. Too impatient to wait for the green light, she took a few steps and stopped in the middle of the street. Suddenly she remembered the day nearly eight years ago. Her mother had found out that Yonju's husband had given the same jade ring to another woman and told the news to Yonju. How animated, how gleeful her eyes were when she was tattling on her son-in-law! She was vengefully taking her daughter back from her husband. She was going to keep her daughter and squeeze every last morsel of reward from her. Hatred mixed with pity filled Yonju's heart. She walked and walked aimlessly until cold and fatigue stopped her.

She entered a coffee shop and called Hyungsok. He was the only one who could calm and comfort her. He was in office and said he was going to call her. He suggested that they meet at a place, not at her apartment and hung up before she could protest. His voice was forbiddingly gloomy. Yonju's hands shook at an ominous feeling that something terrible was going to happen. She was too shaken and tired to walk around while waiting for him. Drinking warm coffee, she sat and brooded.

The one hour was unbearably long. Why did Hyungsok insist meeting her outside when he knew how much she disliked it? Why was his voice so dark and gloomy? Oh, my God, did Mother go to him and accuse him? As Yonju left the coffee shop, she shook her head trying to erase the doubt. Even if her mother had met and accused him, Hyungsok was not the kind of man to be swayed by her mother like Yonsuk and Sanghun.

It was getting dark. She stepped into the cafe where Hyungsok was waiting for her. He had a martini glass in front of him.

"You look so haggard," he said in his usual warm, intimate voice.

"Maybe because I am so cold," Yonju smiled, relieved and comforted by his voice.

"Why don't you have something that will warm you up?"

Hyungsok called a waiter and ordered a martini without asking her.

"That will be too strong for me."

"On a day like this, one needs something strong."

"On a day like what, may I ask?"

"Oh, just a cold snowy day," Hyungsok said with a smile.

Yonju sipped her martini slowly having nothing more to say. She sensed that there was something meaningful in his remark. When she finished her drink, he suggested moving to another place because he said the bar was too oppressively small. They went to a spacious nightclub where he again ordered martini for himself and for her. As they got pleasantly inebriated, he came around the table to sit beside her and held her hand.

"Shall we dance?" he asked in that intimate voice of his.

Yonju withdrew her hand and looked at him straight in the eye to see if he was making fun of her.

"Why, you don't like me anymore?" he asked.

Yonju turned to look at the stage where a male singer was singing a tango under the dizzyingly psychedelic illumination.

"If you have something to say, say it, please," Yonju said calmly. Hyungsok lit a cigarette and slowly blew smoke rings.

"Your mother came to see me today."

"She did?" Yonju's heart sank, but she kept her composure.

"She told me that you suspected me of stealing your jade ring."

"So, you called me out to interrogate me?" Hyungsok denied it loudly.

"Then what?" asked Yonju.

"She scared me. She was like an avenging witch in old stories. I am sorry to say this."

"So?"

He called to a waiter and ordered another martini. Until the drink came, he closed his eyes and kept smoking. Then he opened his eyes as if he made up his mind.

"Er, I'm truly sorry to say this but I want to get out of the ring of people in her grasp. She even made up a lie to take you away from me," he said quietly after taking a sip of his martini.

"I understand." Yonju gave him an icy smile. Everything was over. Her love and her trust, for which she would have given her life, were over.

She tried to stand up but couldn't. It wasn't the martini but a big hole in her heart that crumpled her legs, she thought. To fill the void, she picked up his glass and drank it up. Otherwise, she felt she would never be able to get on her feet.

"Look, Yonju, I will take you home."

Yonju's penetrating look at him was like an icicle.

"Never mind. I can go home alone."

She stood up. As she walked carefully out of the club, tears began welling up.

It was about midnight that she arrived at her mother's apartment. After wandering around several hours, she managed to catch a taxi going near the apartment. As soon as she rang the bell, her mother answered.

"Come in," she said in her usual even voice.

Yonju was surprised and relieved that her mother didn't complain about her coming back so late or ask where she had been. But tonight her mother's even voice grated on her nerves. She found it even repulsive. In the living room, there were pieces of clothes scattered on the floor. Her mother hurriedly pushed them to one side. They were her mother's new or just washed clothes all torn apart at the seam.

"I was so lonely and bored that I decided to resew them. I have nothing to do, nowhere to go, so I thought sewing would give me...."

Her tone didn't have a trace of whining, though. Yonju found herself getting nervous. She had come to her mother to have it out with her, to have a battle, fierce and brutal. But she couldn't bring herself to say anything because what her mother just told her was a heartrending confession of loneliness. Yonju gritted her teeth and recited to herself every word she had meant to say.

"You must be completely satisfied now that you have alienated from me everyone dear to me. As you schemed, I lost everyone and here I stand. Are you happy? But forcing your child to sacrifice her happiness cannot be the right way to earn your reward for your lost youth. I am going to fight for my happiness even if it means disobedience and estrangement."

Yonju's mother stopped fidgeting with her cloth pieces and brought out her iron. She began to iron them one by one like a child playing with a toy. Suddenly Yonju's eyes widened. On the middle finger of her mother's left hand was the jade ring, too big for her bony finger.

UNSPOKEN VOICES

Yonju quietly stood up averting her eyes from her mother. She was too afraid to meet her mother's eyes. If she did, she knew she would lash out words too horrible to hear.

"Going?" her mother looked up. Her voice was still even and calm, but her pointed chin was trembling, ever so slightly.

The Woman in Search of an Illusion

by Lee Jungho

This is a story neither real nor unreal. It may very well be a story my mother told me when I was small. For some reason, it has held me for years and will not leave me. That is why I sit here on this rock watching, through the tree branches, the young boy-monk at the temple.

I do not know when I began this habit of loitering around this Buddhist temple. Nor do I know how long ago the enigmatic story set its roots in my mind. I only know that I linger around this temple and spy on the boy, because the story tenaciously holds me in its grip.

The young monk looked heartbreakingly sad with his shaven blue head and shining eyes. The gray pants, tied tightly under the knees, seemed too stern and cruel for such a young boy. His pink fuzzy cheeks were eons away from the Great Awakening he might be striving for.

The boy-monk came out of a side door of the main hall and hurriedly went into the kitchen. He brought out two soot-encrusted iron bowls and stopped in midstep as if caught in a dizzy spell. A thick carpet of leaves covered the yard after last night's rainstorm. The boy-monk hasn't had time to sweep them away.

There was a deep yearning in his eyes as he stood on the leaves and looked up at the clouds. The parted pink lips were chanting a verse of the scriptures. A falling leaf slid down his chest, and he jumped and ran to the side door.

The wide Han River came into my view. The river ran around the mountains, its golden waves wrapped by the green hills. A red mud road stretched under the purple clouds. The clouds hanging limply and the waves, moving quietly, converged in the distant horizon.

The green trees, as protective as walls, darkened the temple and its yard. The crescent moon, a silvery sliver, hung in the sky. More than a thousand years old, the temple was famous for its glorious surroundings, but for some unknown reason, few visitors came by and the temple was visibly declining. If someday in the distant future, when the boy-monk grew hoary and died, the temple would surely collapse, if not in loneliness, then of neglect.

I snooped around the side door the boy-monk entered. A pair of white rubber shoes lay on the step, but there was only silence behind the closed windows.

I circled around the main hall and the meditation hall. There was no boy-monk anywhere. I went back to the gingko tree under which I had been sitting. I lay on the yellow leaves, waiting and praying, but the boy-monk never came out.

Whoosh! Leaves rained down on my shoulders and skirt. Noises exploded in my head. The noises were not from the waves or the winds. They were the sounds of the earth shaking, rocks splitting, and the world exploding.

The Han River ran in the middle of the two army camps, North Korean and American. The American bombardment continued all day long.

"Mom, I cannot make one more step," the girl whined and flopped on the ground.

"Get up, or we will die."

"We'll die anyway."

"Get up, please."

The mother pulled her daughter's arm.

"Mom, I'd rather die here." Blood seeped out from the girl's leg.

Boom, bang, crack....

The mother and the girl held each other and buried their heads in the grass. They didn't know how they had strayed from the other people. There was no one around, but cannons continued to boom. Boom! boom! Trees and rocks soared up and crashed upon the two. The mother covered her daughter. The mother wasn't afraid to die, but she couldn't lose her daughter. In her forty years of life, the mother's only wish was for her daughter to grow up a fine young woman, marry, and raise a happy family. Her philandering husband who despised her had tried to take the girl away, but no, she wouldn't let him. She wouldn't allow even a little scratch to be inflicted on her daughter. She wanted revenge, by her daughter's success to flaunt to him.

Suddenly, the cannons stopped. The two women climbed on a hill. The day was waning into a gray evening. The mother scanned the shores of the river and spotted something. It was a small hut at the end of a hill.

"Child, there is a house."

They climbed down the hill. There were two cottages, one empty, with its walls crumbling. They crawled around the house and found a door made of cement bags strung together.

"Hello," the mother's voice trembled. There was no answer.

"Hello," the mother raised her voice a little.

A face emerged from the cave-like darkness of the room. A little boy about four or five peeked out and drew back in.

"Hi, little one," the mother stepped nearer when a gaunt bearded old man in rags peeked out.

"Grandfather, we are lost. May we stay here one night?"

The old man just stared at her.

Gathering her courage, she asked again.

"Please, let us stay here tonight."

The old man waved them in.

The room reeked of a foul odor, but was fairly large with a straw mat on the floor. The mother and the daughter sat down in relief and told the old man that, come dawn, they would rejoin the refugees.

The mother untied her bundle to take out a rice cake and rice candy when the old man brought in a bowl of cooked barley. The barley was so old that it was rotten hard. The mother put the cake and candy in front of the old man, but he ignored them and lit a long bamboo pipe.

The little boy's eyes were shining at the food. A moon beam seeped through the warped window and lay across the mother's lap.

"May I ask why you didn't join the refugees?"

The old man just kept smoking.

The mother thought the old man was resentful of their intruding into his hiding place.

"Grandpa cannot talk," the little boy piped up.

The boy's voice was clear and innocent.

"...."

The woman looked at the old man again and turned away.

"Little one, where is your mommy?"

"Mommy ran away."

"And your daddy?"

"Daddy died."

"Grandma?"

"Grandma died, too."

The woman sighed. She felt the old man was glaring at her. She looked down at the sleeping face of her daughter and then turned to the boy.

"Little one, why didn't you and your grandpa leave here? How do you live?"

"Boat, boat, Grandpa's boat...."

"Oh, I see. Grandpa is a boatman."

The boy nodded.

The old man lay down on the mat and turned to the wall. The woman gave the cake and candy to the boy. The boy ate them, noisily, and in a little while, he was sound asleep.

Hours slipped by before the woman sat bolt up listening for the booming noises coming from far away as in a dream, like a huge mountain moving or a herd of beasts rushing. The noises came nearer. They were definitely metallic noises.

Boom, boom, crack.... Boom, boom, crack....

Iron wheels turning, engines bursting, things exploding, and the earth shaking.

The woman shook the old man awake, and pointed her fingers outside and to her ears. The old man went outside and hurried back in. He tapped the woman's shoulders, put his fist on his nose, and made a wide circle with both arms.

The woman didn't know what to make of his wild gestures. He repeated them two or three times before it suddenly dawned on her that American soldiers had arrived.

"Oh, my God!"

The woman woke up her daughter and just circled the room in shock.

"Grandfather, please, please hide my daughter! Oh, my God!"

The old man stood there blankly.

"Please hide my girl, for heaven's sake. Please."

The mother cried and clung to the old man.

"Mom, please," said the daughter.

"Oh, my God, we are dead. How could this happen?"

The mother sobbed over her daughter and pleaded to the old man.

"Please hide my girl, please, Grandfather, Oh, my God, Oh, Oh...."

The old man's face brightened up an instant and made some quick gestures.

"...er...er...." He swept his hair back, put his hands together as if in prayer, and looked far into the distance.

The woman couldn't tell whether he was urging her to pray or telling her they would go to heaven.

"...er...er...."

Suddenly the old man grabbed the girl's arm and dashed out, the woman in hot pursuit.

Outside, it was bright as noon. The Americans must have crossed the river. The three of them lay flat on the ground under the neon-like lights. The Americans were shouting to one another, while the three crept through the wood, around a hill, and into another wood where a huge tile-roofed house loomed before them. It was definitely a temple. A monk's chanting floated out of a dimly-lit prayer hall. The chanting sounded hauntingly eerie.

The old man opened the door and went in. The mother and the daughter followed. The chanting monk slowly turned around. The flickering candles cast deep shadows on his face.

"What is the matter?" the monk asked.

The old man and the monk seemed to know each other. The old man made some gestures and the monk approached the two women.

"Reverend sir, please save us. We got lost somehow, and now I might lose my daughter." The mother bowed deeply to him.

"Follow me." The monk went into the side door of the hall. There was his room.

"Stay here and you will be all right."

The mother and the daughter sat down, but still felt uneasy.

In the room, there were a chest, a low table with a thick book on it, brushes and an Indian ink-stone, still wet, a stack of white rice-paper, and a red prayer robe hanging on the wall. All these things looked ghastly mysterious.

All of a sudden, the mother trembled violently. Heavy foot-steps were drawing near as if a crowd of people were rushing in, helter-skelter, while shouting loudly to one another.

The mother took hold of her daughter and stepped into the hall.

"Reverend sir, I am afraid. Please let us borrow one of your robes for my daughter."

The monk nodded and turned his meditative eyes to the golden Buddha. The woman put a robe on her daughter and sat her beside the monk. The mother sat behind them.

Three days have passed since the day some Americans came and peered into the girl's face. The monk's fluent English worked like magic in sending the Americans back. Now, night was deepening. The head of the mother, sitting beside the medi-tating daughter, drooped as she was overcome with sleep. The American army was stationed in the wood and nobody knew when they would move on. That was why the mother sat up-right with her eyes closed, but in fact, she was sleeping. She didn't realize that the monk and her daughter had slipped out of the side door.

The boy-monk came out, wearing the long outer robe. He seemed in a hurry. There were tears on his face. Where was he going? From the cottage on the hill, a young boatman about twenty or so came out and ferried the boy-monk across the river. The boy-monk ran along the red mud road that wound around the hills. He ran and ran.

A bright yellow gingko leaf fell on my skirt because a bird flapped its wings and flew off. I cannot see in this hovering haze.

I pick up the leaf. My eyes see only the yellow color. I close my eyes. I hear the waves crash on the rocks. I open the window and feel the cool wind against my breast. My house is a lowly cottage but the windows open to the breeze and beautiful flowers in the yard. The walls around the yard are tall but they cannot block out the sound of the waves.

A pale young girl leaned on her mother's lap and watched the sky darken and began to count the stars. She counted the stars every night. Suddenly she trembled and burrowed into her mother's bosom. She saw something move.

"Are you frightened of something, dear?"

"A ghost, Mommy."

"No, it's Yongnyo."

"Yongnyo? Oh."

The girl calmed down and looked up at the stars. She was silently talking with one of the stars.

Yongnyo was a very pretty woman, but she had a tattered rag around her waist in summer and winter. If she didn't have a rag, she wore a straw cord around her waist, and she always hummed a song. They said it was a lullaby. She went into any house she happened to fancy, looking for something, because she was said to have lost a very important thing.

"Mommy, why did Yongnyo go mad?"

The mother gently rubbed her cheeks on the soft hair of her daughter.

"She did something terrible."

"Something terrible? What? Did she steal money?"

"Something worse than stealing."

"What can it be?"

"Well... Yongnyo was the only daughter of a very rich family. Her father and mother doted on her."

But as time went on, her father wanted a male heir, and had relations with other women. Consequently, the father and the mother had endless feuds and made the daughter always unhappy and nervous. Because of her emptiness and outrage, the mother pathologically clung to her daughter. She wanted to raise her daughter to be a happy and successful woman and avenge her husband's infidelity and neglect. She wanted to flaunt her daughter's success and triumph over her husband. And she treated her daughter like a drop of dew.

Then, suddenly, Yongnyo fell ill. She began to lose weight and her complexion turned sallow. Her mother felt like a thunderbolt had struck her. Desperate, she had many doctors examine her girl.

Yongnyo, however, was not sick. She was with child. Now, the mother got sick. She beat her daughter till blood oozed out from her wounds, but what good did it do? She couldn't kill her. Death was preferable to being shamed in public. Public pillory would ruin both of them.

Yongnyo's mother built a small shed where she imprisoned her once beloved daughter Yongnyo, who, banned from contact with anyone, ate and slept in the shed.

"Mother, please kill me," Yongnyo pleaded.

"You shameless ingrate. Be quiet, if you have an iota of concern for me."

Yongnyo couldn't kill herself, but couldn't live there, either. She whiled away her days in tears.

"Mommy, is having a baby such a terrible thing?"

"Yes, it is, if an unmarried girl has a baby. It brings ruin to the whole family. People kick them out of the village and pull their house down."

In late fall when trees began to shed their leaves, the baby's birth was imminent. One day the mother disappeared and returned in the dark of the night. She pulled Yongnyo out of the shed and dragged her into the mountain. Yongnyo, ten months pregnant, could hardly walk. Besides, she had been shut in for months.

"Mother, I can't move anymore," Yongnyo pleaded, but her mother dragged her more urgently. Yongnyo flopped on the ground.

"You shameless ingrate, you want to see your parents die in public shame? Get up and walk." Yongnyo held her big stomach in her arms and pushed herself forward with clenched teeth. Thinking her mother was going to kill her deep in the mountain, she felt her legs crumble. She feared her mother, who, at the moment, looked as cruel as a butcher.

They stumbled on for what seemed like hours, but the mother urged Yongnyo on even more. On the other side of the mountain, there was a farm house Yongnyo's family owned. A tenant farmer, who had served the family for three generations, was loyal and trustworthy. The mother had arranged for the man to be there.

Fallen leaves stuck on their legs. Yongnyo had to hang onto a tree as she felt a searing pain in her stomach.

"Mother, oh, please," she moaned. She slid down and writhed in pain under the tree. Unable to carry Yongnyo on her back, the mother spread armfuls of leaves and laid the girl on them. Yongnyo clutched the leaves in her arms in pain. She struggled to suppress herself from screaming.

"Waaa...."

The baby's first cry echoed through the mountain.

"Mommy, what happened to the baby?"

"It was given to somebody."

"Who?"

"Who? I don't know, dear."

"Who is the baby's daddy?"

"I don't know that, either."

"Oh, poor Yongnyo. So, that's why she keeps looking for something. Her baby. But, Mommy, how did she become mad?"

"Yoo-hoo. Yoo-hoo!"

Someone was calling. I stood up. I saw two people standing on the other side of the river. One was the boy-monk, but the other one, I didn't know. The boat crossed over and brought them back.

The boy-monk ran, followed by a man in a dark suit, holding a black leather bag. They went into the side door of the temple. A long time passed before they emerged from the door, the man first and then the boy. The boy folded his hands together and bowed deeply to the man. The boy's shoulders shook piti-fully all the while.

After the man left, the boy-monk brought out a big broom and began to sweep the spacious yard all the way to the bottom of the mountain. The boy was crying.

The boy stood still in the middle of the yard and looked up at the sky. His face, with the clean-shaven blue head and the dark clear eyes, was inexpressibly sad. The gray pants, tightly knot under the knees, seemed too stern for the pink-cheeked novice monk. Too young to know the eventual nirvana, he long held the white clouds in his eyes in absolute stillness.

Then, with bowed head, he began to walk slowly to the side door of the main hall. I stepped toward him.

"Little boy," I called. The boy stopped and glanced back briefly and went quickly in the door.

This is a story neither real nor unreal. An old story that I might have heard long ago, it would not let go of me. That is why I watched the young boy today, and perhaps I will come back tomorrow and tomorrow.

Division

by Song Wonhee

An ear-splitting explosion shook the house to its foun
dation. I hurried down into the cellar where my hus
band was.

"We can't stay here. Let's get out." My husband put Jinee
on his back, but Youngee was gone. A strange woman stood
beside my husband.

"Who are you?" I asked.

The woman turned around. "Oh, you are Mira, aren't you?"

"No, I'm not."

"Then, who are you?"

"I'm his wife," the woman said as she held my husband's
hand.

The woman smiled serenely.

"How did you come here?" I asked.

"By walking. There's no one at the DMZ or at Panmunjom."

"Mother, mother, what am I going to do? His wife has come
from the North."

My mother glowered at me. "Oh, great! I warned you, didn't
I? Now, I wash my hands off you."

"Mother, mother," I tried to call but no sound came out of
me.

I sobbed. "Why are you crying?"

I turned around to face Mira's mother.

"You are Mira's mother, but you died. How did you come
here?"

"No one stopped me at the DMZ."

"I thought you were my husband's wife," I said.

"Oh, there is Mr. Lee coming toward us."

"Dear, honey," I called, but my husband passed by me as if he didn't know me.

I opened my eyes to find myself tangled in my covers. Thank heavens, it was just a dream. I sighed with relief. My forehead and breasts were soaked in perspiration. Lately I often dream such dreams at night. Even on broad daylight, I am seized by paralyzing hallucinations.

The night before last, I had another dream in which I was frantically shutting my windows to avoid seeing the marching North Korean troops.

Why do I keep having such dreams? Freud would say dreams are made of what exists in outer reality mixed with what lurks in the subconscious. On the other hand, dreams can be the very reverse images of what is real. Dreams can be omens, too. Mira's mother died a few days after I had seen her in that first horrible dream. She glared at me a moment and faded away. Then, last night I saw her again in my dream. I am thinking about her because of the letter I received yesterday.

The death of Mira's mother was totally unexpected. Dying of a heart-attack at forty five! She must have been exhausted, raising three children alone in these dire times. Even men find it hard to survive. And yet, instead of trying to understand her, I had only felt hostility toward her. Maybe she hated me more than I did her. We were like two enemies on the opposite ends of a taut rope. Perhaps I should not have read the letter I received yesterday. No, no, I should have read it before she died. Alas, it's too late.

I looked down at my husband's sleeping face. His eyes were sunk deep above his prominent cheekbones. He'd had to take care of Mira's mother's funeral single-handedly and was bone-tired. Lately he has been more depressed than ever. I can only guess at his inner turmoil. As Turgenev said, other people's inner world is a dark forest. Is my husband "other people"? Strictly speaking, yes. There is always a fissure between a wife and a husband.

Is it wrong of me then not to forgive my husband for holding another woman deep in his heart? In our case, things are more complicated. He left a wife and three children in the North. If I dwell on the fact, will people think of me as selfish? On the other hand, is there a woman who can be generously accepting a husband forever hanging onto his past? Isn't it natural for a wife to want to possess her husband from head to toe? However, no one can possess another person in entirety. Is it just wishful thinking?

I didn't think of all this when I married him. In fact, I didn't want to. People said I was big-hearted, but I might have been merely too lazy. I had been a school teacher until twenty eight; people branded me as an old maid. Having no courage to live in spinsterhood all my life, I became afraid. When I decided to marry a man who had a wife and three children in the North, I had reasons. Above all, he was a good man and unification of the country seemed all but impossible. So I decided to push aside everything else and trust myself to the hands of Fate. It seemed that I was a mutant to my parental heritage. My father had been imprisoned for his participation in the 1919 anti-Japanese uprising and my mother suffered for hers; both of them were endowed with a strong resistant spirit. But I was a daughter who decided to live docilely by the dictates of Fate.

"What time is it?" my husband asked. I looked at the clock. It was 6:30.

"Is Jinee still sleeping?" he asked. I listened for our son.

"Jinee, Jinee, let's go for our morning walk," my husband called.

"Um, um, yes," Jinee answered sleepily. Jinee and my husband are unusually close, though Jinee is nine and my husband forty nine, a late but proud father.

They always take a 30-minute walk before my husband leaves for work. I don't know what they talk about during their walks, but one day Jinee said, "Mom, is it true I have an older sister and two older brothers?"

"Who told you that?"

"Dad said they are in North Korea. Is it true, Mom?"

I didn't know what to say. That night, my husband and I had an argument.

"Did you have to tell that to a child?"

"He will come to know it sooner or later."

I was surprised because I didn't understand what he meant by the remark.

"You didn't have to tell him in advance."

"I had to tell him, so he will know that we are not enemies."

"I feel like I'm living with only half of you."

"Nonsense. Jinee is learning Korean geography at school and I wanted him to know where my hometown was."

I wasn't appeased. Our marriage had been happier than I had expected, and my husband had been so loving and trustworthy that I became blind and smug.

The window began to lighten up by the rising sun. My husband opened it to let in the fresh dewy air.

"It's a fine day. Why don't you go out? It will do you good and ease your nervousness."

But I was too depressed to accede to his advice. I didn't mention the letter I received yesterday from Mira. It will remain a secret forever.

"I had a strange dream last night."

"What kind of a dream?" he asked. But how could I tell him that I saw his wife again in my dream?

"It was a very unpleasant one. I don't know why I have such a dream so often."

"When you are not well physically, you tend to have bad dreams."

No, it was the other way around. The kind of dreams I have oppresses me and there must be something that causes them.

"In my dream I saw your wife and Mira's mother. You said you were taking refuge only with Mira's mother."

No sooner had I said it than I felt a jabbing pain in my heart. It was self-inflicted. Jinee called and my husband left the room without a word. What did I expect him to say? Staring at his retreating back, I felt my eyes burn. Lately I have often felt this way even before I read Mira's letter. I have felt empty and lonely, especially since my husband began to work at the Unification Research Center and Mira's presence loomed unbearably in my consciousness.

"Why in the world do you have to work at the Center?" The fact that he worked for unification sent a shock wave through every part of me.

It was like a stone thrown onto the quiet surface of a lake. My husband sensed my apprehension and tried to put me to ease.

"My work there is purely academic. It has nothing to do with what you are worried about."

The center was a political research institute composed of college professors doing academic studies on Korea's unification. My husband kept saying that what they did there would not bring about actual policy changes. Nevertheless, I couldn't let the matter go.

"If our country is unified, what are you going to do?" I asked. It might have been a foolish question, but I felt as if unification were imminent.

"If my working there bothers you so much, I'll reconsider the matter," my husband said when he found how serious I was.

"It's not a matter of whether or not you work there. I wish unification would never come," I blurted out.

"How childish you are," he said and drew me into his arms.

"I don't want it, I don't want it!" I cried.

"A silly child," he said quietly, but the heartbeat I felt on his chest was faster and stronger as if he were in pain.

This morning I mentioned again the painful dream I had had, causing yet another sort of pain. It was a torture for both of us. Why did I do it? What was I looking for? Was I begging for a confirmation of his love? Am I not sure of his love? Am I wishing that he would not go back to the North even after the country is reunited? But I know he will have to. Will he come back then? All I can do is wait and see. If I were a fatalist as I always claim, why am I so agitated? I don't understand myself. Ever since he began to work at the Center, I have been having frequent headaches, restlessness, sleeplessness, and nightmares. My legs would buckle at the mere suggestion of his ties to the North.

Several years ago, my mother decided to enter the Sungga Buddhist Temple, because she said, she had come to a profound disillusionment with human life. This and the letter from Mira's mother contributed to the worsening of my anxiety. I felt threatened on all sides.

At Mira's mother's funeral, I found myself shaking so uncontrollably that I had to leave abruptly. Her death drew a deep sense of guilt from me. She had died of a heart-attack, but I couldn't shake off the feeling that I might have been part of the cause of her death. Alarmed by my condition, my husband took me to Dr. Koo, a friend of his.

"You are suffering from neurosis," Dr. Koo said to me.

"I think you, too. Is there some problem?" Dr. Koo said to my husband with a wink and a meaningful grin. My husband laughed it off, but I was ashamed of myself for being so obtuse about his problems. I had been completely wrapped up with my own misery.

"Dr. Koo said you have neurosis, too. Why didn't you say anything to me?"

"Don't you know he was joking? He knows how much younger you are than I."

I am twelve years younger to be exact, but I have never felt dissatisfaction with my husband. Dr. Koo apparently took it in the usual male way.

My husband and Jinee must have returned from their walk. There was much movement and noise. There was also an unfamiliar voice.

"Mom, somebody is here."

"The Reverend Abbess from the Temple. Your mother has had a stroke," my husband said.

"Oh, my God."

My dream was an omen indeed.

Before I went out to meet her, the nun stepped onto our hall. She had visited us a couple of times before. In fact, she had befriended my mother, who had lost her husband and son during the war, while we were living in Pusan as refugees. She eventually succeeded in converting my mother to Buddhism.

"How is my mother, Reverend Abbess?"

"She collapsed during our evening prayer last night. I'm sorry."

"Why didn't you call us last night?"

"It was too late. Besides, she recovered her consciousness for a while."

"Then, how is she now?"

"She has been unconscious since about 4 o'clock this morning."

"How far up the mountain can a car go?" my husband asked, referring to the high perch upon which the temple sat.

"About half-way."

The question was whether to take a doctor with us or to bring her to the hospital.

"I think we should take her to the hospital," my husband decided.

"Will she agree to come down?"

"Dear, she is unconscious!"

At times like this, I tend to get irrational while my husband makes calm decisions. My legs were about to buckle down.

"Why don't you stay home? I'll take her directly to the hospital."

But I couldn't stay behind alone.

"No. I will come with you."

It's been five years since my mother went to the temple in spite of my repeated plea not to. The last time I saw her was this past summer when I noticed how weak she looked and asked her to come home with me. But she refused adamantly. She was 66. She had borne six children, only two of whom had survived, my brother and me. However, during the Korean War, my brother was conscripted as a "volunteer" and never came home.

War always takes away what is most precious in one's life. The apple of my mother's eye, my brother grew up to be a fine young man and a college freshman when he was taken away. It seemed only yesterday that my young mother laughed happily at my brother's acceptance by a college of his choice. Now, her hair has turned white. If he were alive, my brother would be 36, but my memory of him is not that of a grown man but of a fun-loving teenager. My mother's sudden decision to rid of all her earthly connections was also her way of resisting to my marriage.

Ten years ago when I decided to marry, my mother objected strenuously.

"Of all men in the world, why do you have to marry a man who has a family in the North?"

"Mother, having someone in the North is like having no one."

"Isn't the North a part of this country?"

"We hear news by the hour about what is happening in space, but we haven't had any news about people who disappeared during the war. It's been nearly twenty years."

"Are you saying that we will never be reunified?"

"How do I know that? But as things are now, reunification may not come within our lifetime."

"You sound like you don't want it. Well, that's to be expected, since you married a man with a wife and children in the North," my mother said angrily.

"Mother, what I am thinking or saying doesn't matter. I'm merely stating the fact. Your anger won't help either."

"If I don't want unification, who will? Why can't I say that I want to see my son again? The country was divided more than twenty years ago, but nobody dares demand that we do something about it. What kind of spineless people are we anyway? Are we going to live and die like this, dumb and numb? Even an earthworm wriggles when stepped on. Ah...what a miserable world this is!"

"Mother, don't be so outspoken. You may get into trouble."

"Why on earth not? Am I committing a crime? They can arrest me if they want to. I'll scream alone, if I must, that I want to see my son again!"

"They'll say you're crazy, besides, you are not the only one. Other people with equal pain are bearing it quietly."

"Why don't those smart people speak up, huh? What do they want? I'm so sorry that I didn't go mad. I'm an old woman now, but long ago I proudly joined the anti-Japanese movement. I cried 'Long Live Korean Independence,' I did!"

"That was another age, Mother."

"No, it was the same. Even then, there were people like you. Your kind."

She was right. It was the same. In every age, there was a wall, and some people courageously resisted it while others accepted it meekly. I married my husband despite her unwavering objections, because I didn't really understand her desperate yearning for her son. My mother and I have kept a relationship of pure resistance to each other. Even after I married, she refused to live with us and chose to enter the secluded temple, away from me.

Soon after the April 19, 1960 Student Revolt, she signed a petition that called for an exchange between the South and the North, for which she was jailed for a month by the military who seized the power in a coup d'etat the following year. When the prosecutor asked her who had instigated her, she replied, "No one did. I signed it because I want to have my son back. Is that wrong? Can you possibly imagine what it's like having a son in the North? Do we just sit and wait? Is that all we're going to do?" Her answer embarrassed the prosecutor who released her within a month. For a year or so afterward, she slowly regained her health. One day she declared, "I'm disgusted with everything," and moved to the temple.

At that time I resented her and felt rebellious. What was I rebelling against? It was perhaps her sharp insight that saw through my hypocrisy, my selfishness, and my negligence. I was afraid of her.

"You, my only daughter, have become a concubine. Our family never had such a shameless woman. I'm ashamed before my ancestors," she said. How I hated her at that moment.

"Mother, please don't be so hard on me. His family is up in the North. It's no problem."

"Why isn't it a problem? My own flesh and blood is there."

I couldn't say anymore for I was filled with hatred for her callousness toward me as if she wouldn't mind bad luck descending on me, as long as she had a chance to see her son again. Our mother-daughter relationship was like that of two precipices facing without a bridge between them.

Once I told her about my husband's good deed of sponsoring Mira's education, but her response was, "I told you. He's doing it because he's trying to ease his conscience. He's so sorry that he can't do it for his own daughter in the North." I was taken aback by her answer and felt furious about her stubborn, skewed view, but later she was proved right by the letter Mira sent me.

When my husband first told me he was going to pay for the education of Mira, the daughter of his closest but missing friend, I was moved by his generosity and didn't see any extraneous motive behind it. As time went on, however, I became increasingly vexed by it. I was often jealous. It seems that a person who fails to see reality tends to fall into his own fantasy world. My uneasiness turned to serious vexation by the time Mira went to college.

First of all, Mira's tuition was a sizable chunk out of my husband's rather meager professor's salary. Last fall, I happened to find a receipt for a new coat he had bought Mira, which alarmed me. I didn't mind his buying a new coat for her, but I minded his not telling me about it either before or after the fact. He obviously wanted to hide it from me. To make matters worse, I've heard rumors that he and Mira were often sighted by my friends. Anxiety and anger left me in throes. The fact that Mira was no longer a young girl continued to bother me till I was overcome with jealousy.

One day at a college reunion lunch, a friend said to me, "Your husband and a college girl are often seen together. Is she the girl he has been sponsoring?"

"When did you see them?" I asked.

"A few days ago at a concert and again in Myong-dong. Don't be too trusting, dear. These new college girls are not as we used to be."

"He has a daughter about Mira's age in the North," I said lamely, but I was shaken inside.

"Does he now?"

"Yes. When he left, she was eight, so she may be married by now," I said.

"So, he has done all that because he misses his own daughter. I see. But don't be too naive, dear. Men are not so trustworthy in that area. You know, only the other day there was an article about a man and his friend's daughter,..." my friend said.

"Well, since he doesn't have a daughter here and now, his feelings for the girl may not be entirely fatherly," another friend chimed in. I was getting more nervous.

"By the way, what are you going to do when unification comes? I think I will open up a consulting office for people with such problems and wait for you," another joked and everyone laughed, but me. I must have looked too serious, for the joker said, "Don't worry. Unification won't come in our lifetime."

"Frankly speaking, I don't want our country to be reunited with the North. Unification will bring only confusion. I like the status quo."

"I agree. I don't want it either. My hometown is Wonsan, but I'm sure my parents have passed away by now, and I don't particularly want to go back there. I like the security and comfort we have now."

"Right. I feel the same way. After twenty years of separation, even the memory of your parents fades away. I think it would be the same for husband and wife."

People say that forgetting is the result of passing time. Do all people forget as time passes? I know there are people who miss their loved ones more as time goes by, such as my mother, Mira's mother and perhaps even my husband. None of my friends wanted unification for different reasons from mine. I feared losing my husband but they didn't want their comfort and peace to be disturbed. Ultimately though, their reason and mine are the same, because we all want to keep the present status.

On my way home after lunch, I was feeling extremely agitated when, as luck would have it, I ran into Mira. A most disastrous encounter. Mira's shy smile looked to me like a diabolic smirk, my emotional state being what it was. Her smile seemed to tell me: "I'm closer to your husband than you are. We have something special between us that you can't even guess at." Was it my morbid reaction? Was I being paranoid?

She was a tall slender woman with a well-developed bosom. I was beside myself with jealousy.

"Mira, you are no longer a girl. People talk about you and my husband. So, please don't go around with him too often. It bothers me," I said. Was I out of my mind? No, I was completely sane.

Mira blushed deeply and through her slightly open mouth, I remember seeing her even white teeth. Yes, I was sane and calm.

That night I exploded.

"Aren't you aware of what people are saying?" I screamed at my husband.

"What in the world are you talking about?"

"Mira! People are suspecting your motive behind your fatherly facade."

My husband was silent.

"Why are you so quiet," I raged. "Does my honesty cut you to the quick?"

The next moment I felt a sharp sting on my left cheek and my eyes blurred. My husband's furious face danced vaguely before my eyes.

"So, Mira is so important to you that you use violence against your wife," I thought, but couldn't say. My eyes remained blurred.

"I'm sorry. I'm so sorry, but I didn't think you would stoop so low," my husband said.

"Did you think I was a saint?"

"I'm sorry if Mira's presence bothered you so much, but it is a part of our fate. Besides, she'll soon graduate."

Mira is my fate? I didn't understand. The letter I received only yesterday provided the answer.

"Dear Mrs. Lee: How are you? I want to go to see you, but I don't feel like going out yet. I'll be all right soon. I'd like to thank Uncle Lee for doing so much for my mother's funeral.

"A few days ago, while cleaning out my mother's drawers, I found a letter addressed to you. She seemed to have written it last winter but didn't mail it. I don't know why she didn't. My guess is that she thought her frank letter might be misinterpreted by you, instead of helping you understand her. After I read it and thought long over it, I decided to mail it to you. My mother must have felt a premonition of her impending death. That is why she wrote the letter, I think. Even though you may find parts in it that displease you, please read it to the end. I hope it will be of help to you to understand my mother who had fought all her life against the wall of reality. With my warmest regards to you. Mira."

Dear Jinee's mother:

I am not sure if I should write this letter to you, but I feel I must. I am not writing it out of anger but to tell you my thoughts and wishes.

A few days ago I saw Mira crying in her room. I asked her what was the matter, but she refused to answer. Pressed further, she finally told me that she had been reprimanded by you that afternoon. I knew immediately that there was a misunderstanding, and such a misunderstanding was the most fearful thing. Back in my room, alone, I couldn't help crying myself. I was not rehashing the pain of the Korean War experiences and bemoaning of my hard life. I thought what you said to Mira was actually meant for me. As much as you disliked me, I kept my distance from you. I am sure you know it. It seems we are hating each other for no reason. No, there is a reason. We stand on either end, with Prof. Lee in the middle. As you know very well, Prof. Lee was my husband's closest friend and our two families were so close. I am not saying this to upset you, but rather to tell you my story in a clear and orderly way.

When Prof. Lee left his family back in Kaesung, he couldn't help it because his wife had just given birth to their third child and his elderly mother refused to leave home. Besides, everybody believed the ROK Army and UN troops were temporarily retreating for a strategic purpose and Kaesung would be reclaimed very soon. In the January 1951 retreat, unlike at the sudden outbreak of the war in 1950, tens of thousands of people took refuge every day by car, truck, or train.

My husband was a reporter when the war broke out in 1950 and pushed north to Munsan to gather news and came back to Seoul to check up on his family, thus losing his chance to escape Seoul. For two months he had hidden in the ceiling of our house until one day our neighborhood was bombed, forcing him to get down. He was immediately spotted by a North Korean internal security man and was taken away at gunpoint. It was just before the September 28 recapture of Seoul by the UN Forces. Our family was utterly devastated after he was kidnapped like that.

All around us people were leaving every day and Mira, then eight, kept asking why we weren't leaving, too. I had Mira and two more children, six and three. I didn't know what to do. After our neighborhood became empty and silent, I collected myself and frantically ran around seeking help, but no one cared to help a family with three small children. No relatives, no neighbors.

At such a moment, Mr. Lee dropped by out of concern, because he lingered on in Seoul thinking of his own family back in Kaesung. He said he expected an empty house. Immediately, he packed and led us out of Seoul on foot. On the road, Mira once lost a shoe and Mr. Lee carried her on his back. At night when we were jammed in some strange room with other refugees, he would take off his coat and cover my children. Finally we got to Pusan where I managed to find a job. But on important matters, I relied on him for advice and guidance.

To all of us who prayed for the northward push of the UN troops, the sudden news of the armistice treaty was a thunderbolt. Especially the new truce line placing Kaesung in the North shocked Mr. Lee so much that he fell ill. It was unbearable for us to see him suffer so terribly. It also reminded me that my husband, perhaps incarcerated somewhere in the North, might be suffering worse than we were. One day Mira asked innocently what people were eating in the North, Mr. Lee quietly left the table.

Mr. Lee remained in Pusan even after we moved back to Seoul. He continued to study biology, his life-time passion, and write articles. Occasionally he would come to Seoul; I noticed how shabby and haggard he looked and advised him to re-marry. There were other people who urged him to do so, but he wouldn't hear of it. In my advice to him, there was a tinge of unease, because, if he remarried, my own husband might have done the same in the North. Yet, seeing Mr. Lee the way he was was painful. On one hand, I commiserated with his suffer-ing and wanted him to settle down; on the other hand, I wished he would wait for his family as I was doing for my husband. But, as you know, for a man to live alone isn't an easy thing.

Mr. Lee once asked me, "How would you feel if your hus-band were living with someone else?" I fell in stunned silence for a few minutes.

"Well, it doesn't look like we will meet again anytime soon. I would hope that he would meet some woman to share his life. I only hope he is alive somewhere. I am sure your wife in Kaesung feels the same as I do," I answered slowly.

The next year, he came up to Seoul and told me happily that he was going to marry a colleague of his at his school. Frankly, I was a little disappointed. To all the people who had been suffering the same fate, his decision seemed an act of betrayal. Even if his life was a continuing misery, as long as he took it courageously, I felt encouraged by it and held some sort of hope for my husband. But I thought it over and decided to be happy for him because I knew how much he loved his wife and his decision was made in pain. Time and years of separation seemed to dim even the deepest love held in human heart. His remarriage, I knew, would have made his wife utterly bereft if she had known, but times were such that we couldn't think of love alone. My one fervent wish was that my husband be alive until we would meet again. After his marriage, Mr. Lee's health improved noticeably, I am sure, because of your loving care. I was thankful for the good turn in his life.

I wonder if you remember the day we met near the Duksu Palace. Jinee was a small child in his father's arms. Mr. Lee had a camera slung over his left shoulder. He was happier than he had ever been since the war. You told me you three were on your way to the palace. You looked the very picture of a happy family.

Only two years ago, Mr. Lee was so worried about his family in the North and now I admit the green monster of my jealousy raised its head. I went so far as to hate you. And it was I who had urged him to remarry. I guess a woman's heart can never be gauged objectively. There was no reason why I should hate you, but while looking at you and Mr. Lee, I was assailed by a cold premonition that my husband would never come back to me.

Could it be my misapprehension that you were distant and cold to me when we ran into each other on the street or when we visited? The first thing to come to my mind was Mira's education expenses. When you married, I asked Mr. Lee to stop the payment, but he always said, "Who knows? Your husband may be doing the same for my family in the North. I'll pay for her education till she graduates from college." I have always felt guilty about this. I knew neither of us had much money and footing the tuition for years wasn't easy.

Last fall Mr. Lee offered to buy a new overcoat for Mira. He seemed proud that Mira was soon to graduate after ten years of his sponsorship. The daughter he had left in the North was Mira's age and he seemed to consider Mira his own daughter. My guess was that he had helped us all these years not because my husband might be doing the same for his family but because he wanted to pay for his error of judgment and appease his conscience somewhat.

That day he told us he had begun working at the newly established Unification Research Center as a faculty member. I was surprised that such an organization came into being. I was thankful and as excited as a young girl, though Mr. Lee told me the Center had yet to make realistically effective policies. He also said that you were extremely anxious and nervous.

Whereupon Mira asked him, "Uncle, what would you do if our country were unified? Will you divorce one of your wives?" Then she added, "Mom, do you think Dad has remarried there? I don't think my dad has." I suppose a daughter tends to idealize her father. At that moment I watched Mr. Lee, who had a quiet, bitter smile on his face, but I could see the intense anguish beneath it. Then, they went out to shop for a coat for Mira, looking very much like father and daughter. Watching their backs, I knew how deeply I missed my husband. My heart ached unbearably.

Should I meet my husband someday in the future, I would not resent his new attachment, but rather try to understand it. I think we can come to real understanding and forgiveness only after experiencing profound suffering and pain.

Sixteen years. It has been a long time. I have lived only by the dint of my will to survive. Breathlessly trying to live one day at a time while yearning, at times hopefully and at other times hopelessly, for my husband, I have survived so far. Whenever I was exhausted or dejected, I wished I had someone I could lean back on. Several years ago I heard your mother was sent to jail for signing the petition for a North-South detente, which moved me deeply. I hear she's gone to live in a temple. There seem to be many ways to do a patriotic service. It doesn't necessarily require swords or guns.

Our country was cut in half nearly twenty years ago and we have been cut off from our husbands and fathers, but we don't seem to lament and bemoan, as some foreigners pointed out. But we know we all live day by day with a throbbing pain deep inside us. I lost my husband when I was only twenty-nine and people urged me to remarry, but I couldn't give up. Perhaps this year or next year, or the next, I've waited for his return along with my children who barely remember their father. Even if I die now, I have a hope that my children will continue to wait for him. Forgetting is the most horrible thing for us.

On the surface we seemed to have forgotten the War and try to avoid any mention of it, but have we been really healed? The internal scars and the ruined landscapes have slowly been replaced by the booming economy and mushrooming skyscrapers, so foreign visitors praise that we look like a nation without a worry, only bent on ever-spiraling development. A country under the bluest sky, they say.

Your admonition to my daughter not to bother you anymore indicated that our family's fervent wish for the return of my husband must have threatened the peace of your family. But I will continue to wait for him even if he might be inaccessible to me by now. I shall wait for him even if I should die in a mud pile, bloodied and wounded. I shall wait for the day. Please forgive me this long wordy confession.

Mira's mother

Did I ever feel the kind of wound and pain that Mira's mother did? Yes, I did. I lost my brother and my father who never got over his son's disappearance. And, Mira who had been a source of my anxiety for years. Now I realize that it was pure jealousy. I felt threatened by her. Her mother's pain was on a different level, compared to which mine was almost meaningless. Now that I look back on my life, was I ever deeply wounded or did I ever think seriously about anything? Did I ever have anything that could be called solely mine? I have lived easily, compromising myself to reality, lying to myself in order to hold onto comfort and ease, because I valued security and comfort above everything else. Mira and my mother were threatening figures. I wasn't different at all from my complacent friends.

In my college days, I, too, had skepticism about life and the courage to rise against unjust reality, but I was no more than a youthful idealist. Those days are long gone. Then, what am I left with? The realization that the wall of reality cannot be overcome by me alone or a few people; life is no big deal; nothing has much meaning anyway; life isn't filled with only suffering and sorrow. I have lived like the flow of a river. Inertia. Even an earthworm wriggles when stepped on, my mother said, criticizing my lack of energy or gumption. She didn't go to the temple out of resignation or desire to find solace. She had waited for her son till her hair turned white and she will continue to wait till she dies.

I didn't know how long we had been driving. The car stopped midway on the mountain slope. The driver and the nun told us to get off and walk up. My husband and I followed the nun.

"Are you all right?" my husband asked me.

My legs didn't shake anymore. The brilliant morning sun shone directly upon my face. The sun that had shone millions of years was lighting up every dark corner of my soul, my hypocrisy, my egoism, and my otiosity. I looked up at my husband with renewed respect. And I prayed for my mother's recovery more sincerely and fervently than ever.

The Dreaming Incubator

by Park Wansuh

My sister's sweet voice coming out of the phone was breathless and urgent, with a heavy dose of spoiled child's irresistible appeal.

"Big Sister, it's okay with you? Right? Oh, my God. I'm going to be late again for the faculty meeting. The principal will glare at me. Big Sister, you regret it from the bottom of your heart, don't you? Making me move near you? Well, it's too late. For me, it's just perfect. I'm going to cling to you like a leech. Heh, heh."

In one breath, she said everything she wanted to say, plus a joke, and hung up without waiting for my answer. What she had asked me to do was attend her son Sulgie's kindergarten talent show in the afternoon, because she couldn't possibly leave her school at that hour. She said she had to finish her semester-end report cards.

My sister was a home economics teacher in a high school. It is absurd that she is a home economics teacher. Her main talent lay in doing the least possible household work, as she had neither the ability nor the inclination of doing it.

She had insisted that she would have only one child to be the best mother in the world, but when she had Sulgie, she didn't quit her job.

During her prenatal and postnatal maternity leave, she said she seriously considered quitting, but finally decided she couldn't do it. From then on, I have become her private tutor in interviewing part-time maid applicants and training the maid. I bought groceries not only for my family but also for hers to teach the maid how to cook basic dishes. I even made sure that her baby's diapers and coverlets didn't have detergent residues on them.

We had lived on the south of the Han River. South of the River is a kind of new upper-middle class area, but not too near to each other. Thanks to my car, I could go and help her out. However, on the days when the maid took a day off without advance notice, she would bundle up her baby and unload it at my doorstep and run off to school. She and her husband each had a car, so mobility was no problem. Occasionally, when her husband brought the baby, I felt guilty about my sister's working and pretended to be overjoyed to take care of it.

Furthermore, what annoyed me was that she always forgot a thing or two necessary for babycare. I would get mad at her but I felt so sorry about the baby being carted around like a package that I would calm myself. I had three children of my own and a husband to take care of. I was lucky that my husband thought my extra babycare was due to my excessive love of babies.

My sister, however, never seemed to be grateful to me, thus earning from my family a nickname "Shameless fox." After a whole day of backbreaking work, I'd never get a word of thanks; instead, she'd barge in and inspect the baby, holding it up, and even smelling it, and say, "why does the baby look smaller?" or "why does the baby look so shabby?" I couldn't say a word but wonder how could a person be such an ingrate.

Considering it a sign of generation gap, I couldn't bring myself to hate her for doing what I'd never dream of doing. In fact, it was I who suggested to her to move to our apartment complex. I knew she would depend on me more, but I never thought she'd move so quickly. But, as soon as I made the suggestion, she sold her house in no time but didn't concern herself to find a new apartment. Now it was my turn to worry because real estate was going up rapidly, and she was indifferent. I worked myself to a frenzy and finally signed a contract the minute an apartment in the building next to me was put up for sale. My sister hated small things to bother her, but big things like selling and buying a house, she did with no hesitation. Since she moved, I would be called upon to do more and more for her, but I couldn't even complain. It was all my doing.

It's been nearly five years since my sister moved. The baby has grown to a kindergartener, ready to go to school next year. For all the things big and small I was doing for her, she expressed her gratitude in so frivolous a way as "my life near my Big Sister has been a pure taste of honey." On the other hand, she complained about gaining weight, an inch a year in her waistline, because I made her life so easy and sweet. Meanwhile my family had accepted the fact that I did all the things for my sister because I loved babies. But they were wrong. I loved my sister more than her baby. No, no, that's not true, either. It wasn't love. The truth was that I wanted, quite zealously, my sister to intrude into my life.

Brooding over all this, I didn't realize until I got to the kindergarten that I had forgotten to bring the video camera. My sister had asked me to video tape every interesting scene in which Sulgie had a part. The camera belonged to us. My husband had bought it in Japan, not particularly because he was interested in taking pictures but because he wanted to have the things other people had.

It was therefore mostly used by my sister's family as they had a little boy and went on excursions often. They borrowed the camera, but we never asked them to show us what they had taped. My sister might have thought of me as cold, but I wasn't interested in seeing on video the people I saw every day.

I liked movies and TV dramas because the people in them were far from me like the stars in the sky. What they showed me was not reality. I hurried back home but couldn't find the video camera. My sister had asked several times and Sulgie was the main character in the play; I had to find the camera. It was very important that I take pictures of him. Playing a role in a drama meant becoming someone else than yourself.

When I looked for something with increasing anxiety, there came a moment when I forgot what I was looking for, and all my thinking stopped. It was a kind of momentary dementia. My husband called it my middle-age phenomenon and joked about it. But I was just forty, not a day over. Some of my contemporaries were having late babies, thus giving me a hope for rejuvenation. Me, a demented middle-aged woman? Never.

Thinking of this made my hands shake. It wasn't because the camera was expensive. Once in a while I found I had misplaced my keys when I had to rush out, or my daughter's indoor shoes I'd washed when she had to go to school. At such times I had the same symptom of losing sight of the visible things as if they were fading away or of losing the thread of thought entirely as if I were becoming nullified. It was scary. Fear and despair.

If my husband happened to notice it, he would speak to me gently and calmly.

"Listen, honey, stop and think logically. Now, take a deep breath. Forget about the missing thing. Then, try to recall where you saw or used it last. Now, take it easy. All right?"

Under the kind guidance of my husband, I would trace back to the time my daughter's indoor shoes were washed. Yesterday was a day our part-time maid came, so she was the one who washed them. She had the habit of drying them on veranda on the top of a soy source jar. Then, in late afternoon, while watering the plants, she would find them still not dry enough and move them to the radiator in the bathroom. At last, my lingering suspicion that the shoes might be in the foyer shoe cabinet or on my daughter's desk, dissipated quickly. Sure enough, I found the shoes dry on the bathroom radiator.

Even though I succeeded with my husband's help, I didn't feel pleased. On the contrary, I felt things got worse, because he treated me exactly the same way as he did his mother. His exaggerated and hypocritical kindness and respect, the nauseating tactic, was applied to me, too.

Nevertheless I used his back-tracing strategy at my sister's apartment after remembering that she had never returned the camera. I mobilized the help of her maid, a rather slow-witted woman, and searched every corner of her apartment, finally finding the darned camera.

I must have lost half an hour. The talent show had begun. Sulgie's kindergarten was known for its excellent facilities and teachers not only in our neighborhood but also in many well-to-do areas south of the Han River.

While other kindergartens had to pass out free flyers or resort to door-to-door visits, Sulgie's picked its children on the first-come first-served basis, which resulted in long lines forming before dawn at its gate on its opening day. The early morning long lines in turn helped make the kindergarten more famous and rumors were spreading that next year people would form lines in sleeping bags the night before the registration day. Two years ago, my sister sent her maid in her place around four o'clock in the morning and succeeded in having Sulgie admitted. My sister was elated.

The kindergarten looked as rich as its reputation. The trees, already neatly wrapped in straw mats for the winter, stood proudly like mink-coated aristocratic ladies among the bare evergreen trees. The playground devices were neat, well-made, and I walked proudly as if I were a parent of a Seoul National University student, across the yard and into the tidy one-story building. The curtains with fairy tale figures against clear window panes reminded me of the new-born babies room in a hospital. My heart beat fast but I didn't hesitate.

The auditorium was packed with parents and relatives. On the stage, the children were doing a folk dance with boys and girls paired. There was a big poster pasted beside the stage and I was relieved to see that Sulgie's play was right after the dance. I had thought using a video camera would be too conspicuous, but I was surprised that there was a crowd of adults, everyone with a video camera, milling around the stage. There were more adults under the stage than the children on stage.

All of a sudden, a fight broke out between a pair of dancing children. The two began to wrestle while the music blared on and other dancers were divided into those who went on dancing and those who stopped to watch the fight. It happened in a flash. Teachers leapt onto the stage, followed by some parents, to break up the fight. There were giggles among the audience. The music stopped and the children went off the stage.

"Why did they pair two boys? That's what caused it."

"What could they do? There aren't enough girls."

"Then, why did they decide on a folk dance when they knew there weren't enough girls?"

The teachers calmed the ruffled feathers of the pair, and the dance soon resumed, but without the boy-only pairs, the stage was half-empty, and the audience seemed to lose interest.

The next program, Sulgie's play, was about a wolf and seven baby goats, as my sister had boasted, Sulgie was the wolf. His entire graduating class was in the play, some children playing rabbits, squirrels, ducks and storks, and other spectators watching the goat family's struggle for survival. Sulgie fitted the role, being taller and bigger. He wore fur-like cloth wrapped around his body and huge clawed shoes. He looked menacing and adorable.

Holding the camera, I shoved through the crowd trying to find the best spot. When I looked through the camera, however, I couldn't see a thing. I panicked. The lens was apparently closed, but I didn't know which button to press. Of course, it wasn't the first time I used the camera. When my sister wanted to be included in a scene, she would turn it over to me, but then everything was set and I had only to push the button.

The mother goat looked back on her babies several times before she went off the stage. The wolf who had been hiding behind a big rock was about to emerge. I still could not see anything. Just as I had always felt at such moments, I felt faint and my hands began to shake.

"May I help you?"

It was a low, very pleasant male voice. A tall man was grinning behind me. His grin, however, was not a sneer. He lowered himself to my eye-level, touched a red button, and returned the camera to me.

"Try it. You will see now."

Before trying, I looked up at him. He had a kind and good face. As the wolf came forward from behind the rock, I looked back at the man and asked. "Do I just hold it up like this?" The man bent down and touched something when the English words "stand by" changed to "camera." I saw the words for the first time.

"Have I just been holding the camera without taking any pictures?" I asked the man, a little irritated. But he laughed as if to reassure me, and I laughed with him. He tried to explain to me this and that, finally I sighed resignedly and shrugged my shoulders.

"Shall I take pictures for you?" he asked. I nodded, handing the camera to him. He handed me his brown envelope obviously containing some documents.

"Take good pictures, please. The wolf is my nephew."

I wanted to make sure he didn't take pictures of other children. He moved back behind the crowded mothers for he was tall enough. It occurred to me he might be a camera thief, so I looked back again and again. Whenever the player's performance caused laughter, I looked back to give him a sign that such moments were worth taping. He glanced at me, too. Our eyes met several times and I was excited.

The shared pleasures of watching the children's play gave me such an uplift that being jostled and looking repeatedly back didn't tire me.

After the show was over, the man and I walked out together. It seemed natural, but it wasn't. Most of the parents stayed behind to compliment the teachers. My sister would have wanted me to do the same. The schoolyard was empty when we slowly crossed it in the deepening dusk. The kindergarten faced the back gate of our apartment complex. If he didn't live in the same complex, we had to part there. I looked up at him to see in which direction he would move.

"You look cold. Shall we have a cup of tea somewhere?"

It was an unexpected offer. Because of his rather excited voice, I guessed that my eyes had enticed him. I must have shown him how reluctant I was to part.

I followed him, not too eagerly though, to a rather nice coffee shop. Under a dimmed light, with quiet music floating in the air, I sat across from him and began to feel extremely uncomfortable. It was so unlike me to sit with a strange man. I had never done it before.

I decided to assume an aloof and dignified air as if to tell him that it was entirely his fault to have brought our encounter to this point.

"Did you say it was your nephew? I mean, the wolf?" he asked, quite easily.

"Yes. My younger sister's son. She lives in my neighborhood. She is a teacher, so I substitute for her once in a while."

"Very similar to our situation. My wife and I both work, so when things like today happen, my mother-in-law stands in for us. She is on a senior citizens' tour, though. My wife doesn't know I was there, because I promised my child this morning behind my wife's back, that Daddy would be there and she should try her best. By the way, don't assume that your nephew was the only star. My daughter was a star too. I had boasted to my boss that my daughter was a star in a play and her Dad had to be with her," he said.

"Then, you did better than ordinary working women. I guess men have more leeway at workplaces than women."

"Depends on workplaces. I work for a magazine, so it is easier to make up an excuse to leave my desk. But I can't play hooky for no reason."

I remembered the title of a well-known magazine on the envelope I had briefly held for him. So, this man was not some suspicious vagrant; I was relieved.

"If your daughter was a star, was she the mother goat?"

"No, no. The mother goat can't be the star. The real star was the baby goat who hid in the clock and brought the play to a happy ending."

"Oh, that little baby goat. She was so pretty and smart."

"Not really. Only the role made her so," he said. His modesty enhanced him in my eyes.

"You may be right. My nephew is big for his age but he is a weakling. He has been beaten up by a girl. But he enjoyed being the big bad wolf and a threat to the girls. I don't know what a big deal being a boy is. By the way, how many girls and boys do you have?" I asked.

"No boys. I have two girls. A first grader and that little goat."

"Oh, my goodness. Then, you should have more children," I said.

"No. Two is enough. They are healthy. Our ability is limited. Besides, I don't want to contribute to global ecological problems."

"You may say so, but I don't believe you. Deep inside, you must be envious of other people who have sons. I know you are sad and miserable. An old saying goes, 'a son-less man will want to steal a boy if possible.' But with today's technology, you don't have to steal. All you have to do is make use of every possible method." I was surprised at my chattering in such an abandoned manner and stopped myself.

I was unspeakably ashamed. I felt as if my underwear had accidentally slid down before a crowd. Luckily, he didn't seem to notice my shame. Perhaps he was pretending. In that case, I should be afraid.

"I didn't say I wasn't disappointed. When we were expecting our second child, I did wish for a son. Isn't it human to want to have both sons and daughters?"

"But that's different. Do you know the people who had a son first, say that they want a daughter the second time, but they are lying? They just say that. If they get a son again, they are never sorry, never; instead, they puff up with pride as if they owned some secret son-producing skill."

My voice, I realized, had gotten hot and bitter. The man inclined his head and said, "I don't know that. Besides I don't understand why I have to know that."

"You are not happy, are you? I know you aren't because having no son is a big factor in an unhappy marriage."

"Why are you forcing these opinions on me? I don't feel that way at all."

He seemed acutely embarrassed. I was upset because he was the first man who denied without any qualms that having no son had any relation to happiness. I wasn't going to let him go so easily, a man who so nonchalantly negated my long-held belief. He was definitely a phony and it was my duty to peel off his mask.

"Do you like baseball?" I asked.

I decided to use a different tactic. My scheme began to assume a more definite direction.

"How did you know? I like all sports but I am crazy about baseball," he brightened up at the change of subject.

"Then you must go to the baseball park often," I said without showing my triumphant "gotcha" feeling.

"Of course. Especially when high school tournament is in season. My old high school had a famous team. I wasn't a player, but even now I've got to scream and yell at a high school game a couple of times a year to feel really good. It makes all my stress evaporate."

"You go alone?"

"No, of course not. I meet up with old high school friends. After the game, we get drunk because our team lost, because our team *won*, and because we had missed each other. I come home stone drunk, often bringing home a couple of drunken friends, infuriating my wife every time."

"Don't you ever miss taking a son to the games?" I asked him with narrowed eyes.

"Good grief. You are back at it. To be honest with you, I do get envious when I see a father and son yelling and cheering together. I even tried to interest my elder daughter in baseball, but I let it go when I began to see that she was becoming more and more reluctant as she grew older. Well, there is hope still, my second daughter. There are fewer women at the games, but there is no reason why women can't enjoy baseball."

"Why don't you change your attitude and show your wife that you are so envious of men who have a son to take to the ball park that you want to die."

"But why on earth would I want to do that to my wife? I don't want to hurt her. She is not to blame."

"Hurt? It should be more like humiliation and defilement. But it will make her seek out ways to bear a son," I said.

I became so rapt in my argument that I lost the last shred of self-consciousness. As it slowly dawned on me how empty my argument was, I began to dread what he might say.

"Well. If we had only sons and my wife complained about not having a girl to help her in the kitchen, I'd still not want to have a daughter for that reason. I think it a blessing that we humans cannot decide the sex of the babies. The existence of such a divine resort! I'm thankful for that."

Saying this, he made an exaggeratedly big gestures of raising his arm and looking at his watch. A blatant hint that he didn't want to talk with me any more. I found him incredibly naive to believe in what he called a divine resort because everybody knew we had passed by it long ago. How old is he, by the way? The same as I am or a couple of years younger. I felt lost and listless. He seemed to think I had nothing more to say and took his leave.

"I'd like to excuse myself if you don't mind. To speak the truth, I'd had an interview lined up and stole a short time to see my daughter."

"You know all the tricks, don't you?"

"Tricks? People may think my job is fairly free, but I often have to work when they sleep. Well, good-bye. I'll pay for the coffee."

He hurried off. Unnecessarily fast. Did he think I'd bite him? How naive! But the more naive he looked, the more I wanted him, not for any intimacy but to toy with him just a little longer. I stood up and followed him to the counter, but did not insist that I pay. I hated people fighting over the pleasure of paying. I merely watched him pay and get changes as I cooked up a cunning scheme.

"May I have your namecard?"

"For what? I wonder if I have any on me."

Instead of searching inside his pockets, he merely patted them on the outside, a transparent attempt to buy time to decide whether to give one to me or not. I saw through him and found him irresistibly cute.

"For no other reason than I'd like to send you a copy of the tape. My nephew was the male star, and your female star was in it," I said in a matter-of-fact way. He positively brightened up.

"But of course. Yes. When you see the tape, you may find some scenes focused on my daughter. I hope you'll understand and forgive me."

He was beaming as he held a namecard toward me. I gave it an indifferent glance before putting it in my bag, nodded to him, and walked off.

"Even if the tape doesn't turn out good, please send me a copy. I'll look forward to hearing from you."

I heard his loud words behind my back and couldn't help smile a triumphant smile. While walking slowly, I prolonged my enjoyment of his very pleasing bass voice on every step I took.

After dinner I was watching TV when my sister called. My two daughters had gone to after-school tutoring and my son was doing his homework in his room. My husband was in China on business.

"Big Sister, won't you come over for tea? When did your picture-taking skill improve so phenomenally? The tape is simply great. Really, out of this world! You ought to see it."

I had left the camera at her home on my way from the kindergarten.

"You are not impressed with my great skill?"

"That's not it, Big Sister. I never said this before but do you know how bad your pictures used to be? I'm not that good, but mine were passable, but yours? They were positively unbearable. Even so much as one cut of yours among many pictures could be picked out, you know. And then, suddenly, this masterpiece! It is a master-piece, a work of art! Your camera was almost always at my place. When did ever you learn to take pictures like that?"

My sister was positively buoyant. When I told my son I was going over to his aunt's, he didn't even look up. He merely said, "Okay by me." At the foyer I asked him if he wanted to go with me to see the video tape I made. "I'm not interested," he mumbled. I shouldn't have asked. An eleven-year-old boy! Couldn't he have said, "Mom, I'm too busy," or "I don't like home videotapes." He was all of ten years and seven months. What on earth was he interested in? I was so miffed that I wanted to barge in and grab him by the shoulder and yell at him what an unspeakable torture I had to endure to bear him? I got hold of the edge of the shoe cabinet and took a deep breath. I was shaking from the deep inside of my body and soul.

My sister's family was having the evening family hour, with their thoughtless maid giggling and folding laundry, among the three.

"Ajumma, you are getting prettier everyday," I said, without meaning it.

"Big Brother must be having booming business. Half the time he is abroad, isn't he? I'm afraid I might forget his face," my brother-in-law said. He was having dessert with my sister and Sulgie.

"Going abroad doesn't necessarily mean booming business. He has the same problems and troubles as the rest of small-and-medium sized businesses."

"You always say such things, Big Sister. A very wifely modesty. But he is definitely not a small or medium business-man, is he now?" my sister cut in.

"Then, are we a 'jaebol,' you think?"

"You certainly are. You are a real estate jaebol, definitely several cuts far above those small businessmen who have to plug a big deficit hole with small profit all year long. You know, for other people doing business is a life-or-death struggle, but for my Big Brother, it is a recreation, a leisure activity. That's why he makes so much money," my sister went on. She was referring to the building my father-in-law had built on the site of the old house when the then city government decided to lay a street in front of it. After he died, my mother-in-law has been managing it and my husband is expected to inherit.

"Maybe I should quit my bank job and go work for Big Brother and learn business," my sister's husband said.

"Forget it. How can you be sure he will accept you any-way? I don't dare hope for the bank president's wife, but I will be happy to be the wife of a branch manager," my sister said.

When my sister pushed the rewind button, her husband picked up his cigarette box and retreated to the master bed-room, and the maid to her room.

Sulgie's eyes took on a bright expectant look. The tape be-gan and I was completely sucked in. In contrast to the crude drama I had seen, what I was seeing on tape was an entirely different drama. The childishly cute mistakes and the surpris-ing acting performances, even the awkward little scenes that helped make the play so heart-warming were caught expertly on tape. The 30-minute-long tape was indeed a masterpiece because we all had shared common affection for the children.

But I wasn't just watching the tape. In truth, I was facing the man eye to eye. The last scene showed all the performers dancing around the stage, holding hands and waving goodbye.

Sulgie had fallen asleep on the sofa and my sister yawned loudly. She didn't say a word of compliment, obviously bored to tears after seeing the tape four times. Pretending boredom myself, I asked her to make a copy for me. I came out of the building into a dark night. A crescent moon hung on the edge of the roof. Ah, Nature reveals herself even in this concrete forest.

My son was sleeping, but it was not yet time my daughters returned. A high school junior and a ninth grader, they had to be picked up at their private institute. So, the neighborhood women had organized a car pool system, for which I was forced to learn to drive, despite my extreme fear of mechanical things.

To wait for them, I turned on a video of a film called *War of the Roses* I had borrowed after my husband left for China. Generally I don't enjoy videos or movies. Sometimes I can hardly follow the story line. It is very rare, therefore, that I would want to see a video tape again. Whether it means the movie is a good one or not, I don't know. For some strange reason I feel guilty about wanting to see the movie again and decide to return it before my husband comes home. The movie wasn't really a big deal. It was merely about a feud between a husband and wife; no, it wasn't a feud, it was a fierce battle, a war. Energetically, cunningly, cruelly, and persistently they hurt each other. Even the Nazis and Jews, the South and North Koreans would have fought with more room for human sentiments. What hatred! But what egged me on was my continued search for their motive, the seeming absence of which made me anxious that I must have missed some key element.

The movie was a nightmare and I couldn't understand myself why I felt compelled to watch it repeatedly. A worse horror came from the scene in which the husband sawed in half his wife's shoes. His eyes were bloodshot. Every time I saw the scene, I had a hallucination that the woman's shoes were the body of my son. I woke up perspiring when the movie ended. The doorbell rang and my two daughters came in. They asked me if I was not feeling well. My head felt like a huge drum in which small rocks were rolling around and crashing into one another. "I must have dozed off while waiting for you. I had a horrible dream and I feel kind of headachy," I said.

On the calendar, I saw three days remaining before my husband's return. Only three days. My younger daughter asked me if adults had bad dreams, too. Becoming an adult might mean having no fears, I almost said, but instead I patted her slender back.

I did not see the movie again. My sister brought me a copy of the video and urged me to show it to my husband, as if she expected everyone to dote on her son. However, my husband was always rather indifferent to family pictures even to those he himself had taken. But I decided to show it to my family and they merely endured it without asking who had shot the tape. The anxiety I felt when I asked my sister to make a copy was somewhat eased, and yet there was a residue of guilty discomfort about the attraction I had felt to a strange man.

To a housewife like me, such feelings were not new, perhaps even trite and banal. I knew that in hindsight, I'd feel foolish. But there was something different about the man I had met. Somehow it galled me that there was a man in Korea who was neither unhappy nor desperate about not having a son. In one way or another, I had to confront him and make him confess his true feelings. Otherwise, I would never be able to completely erase the strange uneasiness inside me. I was sure he was hiding behind a mask. I called and told him that I wanted to give him the tape in person. His welcoming warm voice pleased me. I wanted to chatter on like a girl.

"I was amazed at your photo-taking skill. The tape was superb. For a while I thought about sending it to your daughter by Sulgie, but I changed my mind. The tape is good enough to deserve our having another cup of tea together," I said.

"Really? Is it that good? If so, you should buy me tea this time."

"Sure. Why not? I'll buy you tea this time, but you should buy me tea next time for the copying service."

I was so happy that my voice sounded like a young girl's. I was going to squeeze the last drop of pleasure from our encounter. We made an appointment.

My sister, who came to borrow a cup of sesame oil, kept looking at my face.

"Why are you staring at me? Is there something on my face?"

"Uhuh, but somehow you look different, younger and prettier. Anyway you look more alive. You know, you have always been sort of languid and listless. I wonder what happened. Good heavens, are you in love with someone?"

"Shut up, you scandal-monger. Take this sesame oil. I won't expect you to pay back. Why don't you just take yourself out of my house, huh?"

"Have I ever paid you back anything? You are always cooped up in the house anyway. How can you meet anyone?"

After my sister left, I wanted to verify what she had said. Carefully I inspected every part of my face in the mirror. I looked different indeed! Young, pretty, and fresh, how wonderful it was! Since then I have tried in every way possible to look younger, prettier, and fresher. For a moment I even forgot whether I was excited or annoyed about the existence of a Korean man who didn't despair over not having a son.

While watching my son, I thought of the man. I liked measuring my son's height against me. I was five feet five inches and never weighed more than 110 pounds, so I looked tall and slim. My 11-year-old son was approaching my height. When he was small, I marked his growths on a door post, but, since he entered school, I preferred putting my arms around his shoulders. It gave me a secret pleasure to hug him close to me and hear his exclamation that he could hear my heart beat. As he grew taller, he stopped yielding to me so readily, but I still craved bodily contact with my son. He grew up healthy and strong like a tree. Even when he wore pants, I could feel his long and sturdy legs.

I was thrilled just to have him in the house, for he filled not only my arms but the entire house. Even in his absence I felt proud and fulfilled because he was the very height of my achievement as well as the source of my incomparable happiness. I loved my daughters. I loved the eldest because she was the first-born, the second because she was the last of my daughters. I had never discriminated against my two daughters who nevertheless didn't measure up to my one son in giving me the deep, rich sense of fulfillment.

To keep my date with him, I made up my face as carefully as never before and tried on several outfits. My sister's comments were her first remark that had pleased me. I left home well in advance to have my car washed. The place I casually mentioned to him was in fact carefully chosen for its romantic ambience, easy access, and large parking space. My driver's license had been obtained after numerous failures in tests and I was still a very shaky driver. The only driving I did with any confidence was picking up my girls. My driving delimited the range of my social activities. My husband kind of laughed at me but seemed relieved by it, which he called "a mother's dutifulness to her daughters." As he pointed out, I had so far not found any other use for my car.

Today was different. I wanted to shine. My makeup, my attire, and my car, too. I handed my keys to a deeply bowing uniformed doorman with a superior smile and stepped proudly into the hotel. I had watched enviously as other women parade in and wondered if I could ever pull it off. Today, however, I thought my actions were quite smooth.

The man was waiting for me at a table overlooking the Han River. "I am young and lovely," I quietly intoned to myself like a mantra as I walked toward him. "Have you been waiting long?" I asked and slid into my chair. I was immediately disappointed at his tired and worn look. I felt embarrassed at my overwrought preparation. "No, I've just got here," he said and yawned unabashedly. Looking at his chin covered with messy stubbles, I felt insulted.

"I'm sorry. I was on night duty last night," he said, halfheartedly suppressing another yawn. I ordered coffee and looked out of the window. Savoring the warm coffee helped me calm my anxiety, but I was still in the dark as to what I really wanted with this man. I didn't want to have an affair with him, but the unfamiliar emotional confusion he had aroused in my heart bothered me. I merely kept staring out of the window. I saw a waterless pool, a well-paved road stretching to east and north, and the river that had looked exotic in summer with yachts and cruise ships floating on it. Now flocks of winter birds replaced them. What would happen to the birds when the river froze over?

"There was a big pond. In the fall, many ducks came flying to it. One night the pond froze solid. What happened to the ducks? They flew away with the frozen pond. There was no pond any more." This was from a movie I had seen long ago. The futility of life. Perhaps the scene I was seeing now was not real but a fantasy only I could see. I felt an insistent stare at my cheek and turned to him. His quietly alluring eyes were watching me.

"You look so lonely," he said. He looked surprised at my sudden turning and avoided my eyes as if dazzled. I was sure he was attracted to me, otherwise, why would he turn away to avoid a bright light? My expression hadn't changed from the beginning. If he thought I looked lonely, then he saw through me. I was. But that was not important. The fact that he could see my loneliness beneath my elaborate makeup and expensive clothes proved that he was drawn to me. I found myself losing my self-control; at any minute I might fling away etiquette, appearance, or honor.

I felt a premonition of falling into a stupor as a person might before the oncoming of a cerebral hemorrhage or epileptic fit. Unless I brought up the businesses at hand, I was afraid I might lose my composure.

"So, the tape was good," he asked, waking me from my daze. I took the brown envelope out of my bag and gave it to him. In an exaggeratedly animated manner, I told him how Sulgie's family and mine had enjoyed it.

I had the bad habit of carrying on nonstop once I started talking. I was like a person who had to blow a balloon until it burst. I wasn't just a normally garrulous person. It took me time to open up and I was discriminating about whom I was talking to. I chattered on about the kindergarten's successful publicity campaign, problems in preschool education, the questionable quality of the teachers, right down to the difficulties of handling today's children, and more.

My husband called my uncontrollable garrulousness a "sickness." Once he had called me from abroad and asked me about the family. When I merely answered "yes" or "no" he said, "Don't worry about the phone bill and tell me more." He didn't know he opened up a dam. I told him every little tidbit about our first daughter, second daughter, and son. I chattered on and on until the moment I realized he had hung up.

"My wife will like it. Thank you very much," he somehow managed to squeeze in and glanced at his watch.

"Will you still insist that you like daughters better?" I was myself surprised at my question. I had no control over what came out of my mouth any more.

"You want to talk about it again?"

Yes, I hate the idea that a man like you exists in Korea, pretending to be happy about having only girls. I'm not going to let you go free, do you understand? He seemed disgusted with me for a minute, then composed himself coolly.

"I never said I preferred girls, because it means the same as preferring boys. Both ideas are on the same level. I don't like what people are saying: in old age, parents of girls will travel by plane while parents of boys will travel by bus. That is not in any way different from calculating what will bring more profit—what I shall plant for next year's harvest or what business I shall get into to reap more profit. That sort of attitude will only harm male-female relationship. Maybe, the day will come when girls' parents will gain more profit, the way the male-female ratio is rapidly becoming lopsided. Didn't you see the fight at the kindergarten? There weren't enough girls, and little boys resorted to physical strength like primitives. But, wait till they are grown up. What gives strength in adult world? Political power and money. You know how many truck loads of dowry a girl's parents send to the groom's family if he happens to be a doctor or a lawyer. Maybe it will be reversed, and a girl's parents will just sit and reap the profit. Instead of sending her to her husband's family, perhaps, in the near future, the man will have to come to the bride's family if he wants to marry at all. So, what difference will it make? A losing business is changed to a profitable one, and a woman is still rated by commercial values. The more profit, the more commercialization of women. The result will be furthering of women's education toward better commercial values. As for men, material desire and sexual desire will boost each other, and finally, a pretty woman will become a number-one asset and a symbol of power. In other words, women's dehumanization will result in men's dehumanization."

The man became different from an attractive man whose first impression I liked or an unkempt tired man, now sitting in front of me. He has become what we used to call the "dissident demonstrator" type, a street fighter for freedom and democracy. I could detect the passion underneath the messy appearance.

"In that case, you must mean that women will always be contemptible beings judged for commercial values, regardless of their number. And yet, you say you are satisfied with two daughters, isn't that hypocrisy?" It wasn't my intention to persuade but to provoke him.

"You are persistent. I already told you I was disappointed when we had the second daughter. Why are you forcing me into your corner? Because the sex of my children is not their fault nor any human fault, I want to remove as much as possible the kind of prejudice that made me disappointed when they were born and help them become their own masters. I believe that is much more important than raising a son. I was once what you might call a dissident student, a demonstrator, and it took me seven years to graduate from college. I caused my poor mother so much pain. The idealism of that time has been frustrated but I am still proud of myself of that time. I am what I am now, compromising endlessly to provide daily rice for my family. But the past I and the present I are the same person, and this belief is kept up by being a good father for my girls."

"I was right," I thought to myself. "You were a dissident. I saw through you, but I didn't understand everything you said." I shook my head.

"It's all right if you don't understand me. I guess I was born with something called a sense of justice or conscience. I admire people who struggle on though oppressed and alienated more than people who succeed at the cost of others' lives. I am proud to be on the side of underdogs. You know, even among my friends who made lots of money or hold powerful positions, I feel like I am a white crane among dark chickens. Just because my social idealism was frustrated, I cannot give up my effort to realize equality and love in my family, can I? In my old days, I used to agonize over the discrepancy between our thoughts and actions, and argue with my comrades. I was often disillusioned. But now, within my own family at least, I want to live for justice and try to influence them in the right way. Isn't it a small step toward changing our society for the better?"

"Don't you think expecting too much of your daughters would be another way of putting stress on them?"

"I don't mean for my girls to become sons. Man and woman alone are incomplete and that's why they are equal. I think Nature is beautiful, not because each species is complete but because of the harmony among different species. You know, the inequality between sexes in our country has gone far enough to destroy the most profound law of natural harmony, that is male-female balance. Frankly, I am scared. I don't even want to think about how the imbalance comes out in real life situations."

I was conscience stricken. I changed my posture and cleared my throat. The secret I hid away deep inside me seemed to have been uncovered. I had lived dreading that the secret might be bared; on the other hand, I wanted it to be exposed. On this matter, I had always been ambivalent. I sensed that my self-control was again on the verge of collapsing. I managed to whisper, "But unlike animals, human beings have to carry on their heritage. Perhaps that is why the problem emerged. Even though we build a society of complete equality between men and women, the eventual, final inequality will still be there because generations are preserved by the male line. Don't you agree?"

"I know that is why daughters-only families are pitied by others. Even my mother, a very open-minded lady, blurts once in a while that my family would be flawless only if we had a son. My wife and I did not have an easy time of it, as you may easily guess. Then, if you think about it, what is succession of generations? Having children to succeed is enough, isn't it? Why does it have to be connected to family name? My wife and I rationalized and consoled ourselves, too. Paternal succession is a present system in most parts of the world, true, but does it mean that man contributes more to creating a human life or leaving more of his characteristics in the genes of his offspring? No, of course not. Man and woman are absolutely equal in the amount of contribution they make to creating the most fundamental unit of human life. In short, the bloodline is carried on either by sons or by daughters. If man's instinct is to continue his life through posterity, sex is merely a shell, devoid of any meaning. I really believe this."

"Sex may be merely a cultural shell, but the fact that women from the beginning let their children take on their fathers' names proves that women are inferior, don't you think?"

"Not necessarily. You know, people began to have family names fairly recently, and family name is definitely culturally nurtured and connected to women's inferior economic status. I don't think it was because men were superior, but women didn't have the need for it. Women knew who their children were. Men pity women's trouble and pain in having and bearing children, but they are sometimes envious of women. Women are fortunate that they are absolutely sure of their children they bear, but men cannot be sure. There is always a drop of doubt at the bottom of men's consciousness. Women saw through men and decided to emphasize how the children looked like their father and even document their paternity. For these, women dumped on men the duty of providing for their family."

"Sounds probable, but the difference between man and animal lies in culture. How can you ignore that?"

"I didn't mean to ignore culture, but to say we should enhance our culture to a higher degree. What I mean is we should expand the concept of posterity. It's not enough that daughters can carry on the family line. Childless couples and priests also have the same wishes. Knowing that the world will continue to exist after our death helps us curtail our bad instincts and lead a more righteous life. That is the concept of posterity; in other words, that is the love of one's race and the love of mankind. This is how I think of the issue."

I sighed. I pitied him.

"Since you have thought out such a thoroughly reasoned argument about why you don't feel deprived, it seems to me the reverse is true. How deeply disappointed you must have been. I feel sorry for you."

This time I didn't want to provoke him. I would rather stop our conversation.

"You are right to some extent. But it was not an excuse to console myself, but a piece of my mind about the wrong direction our society is heading for. A kind of reaction to an oncoming crisis."

He gazed at me insistently. He was paying me back the pity I had shown him. But how ludicrous. How dare he pity me? Ridiculous. After a minute he began to speak again.

"Last year, I covered a story about childless couples who would go to any length to have a child. So I visited several OB-GY clinics."

Oh, my God. What is this man going to say? I must get out of here. Despite my inner turmoil, his pleasant low voice held me on my seat.

"I was the one who proposed it. You may laugh at me as a sign of my inferiority complex about having no son. Since the male-female ratio was becoming more lopsided every day, I thought it worthwhile to look into the matter. I think there was a bit of curiosity on my side, too, about other people who had sons so easily. As you know, throughout our history, there have been numerous son-producing secrets. Incidentally, such secrets had never seemed to succeed in breaking the man-woman balance, which means those secrets were useless. But, what has brought about this phenomenal imbalance now? Modern medicine, of course. If modern medicine is threatening the future of mankind, it ought to be stopped. I wanted to arouse public outcry over this. Ambitious, I suppose. Then, at the clinics, I witnessed absolutely unbelievable things. There was indeed a hundred-percent fail-proof method. Do you know what it is?"

He asked me like a police investigator. I thought he was glaring at me. I couldn't move a muscle. I wanted to protest but could not utter a word. His eyes were fixed on me.

"I felt a fear of God. The fail-proof method was murder of female fetuses! A precise, scientific, and perfectly planned murder of fetuses just because they were female. Modern medicine diagnoses the sex of a fetus and gets rid of it. Until the conception of a male child, female fetuses were repeatedly slaughtered. That was the doing of advanced medicine."

"Please stop. I can't bear to hear anymore. Abortion is not new. In my mother's day, some women went through seven or eight abortions, I've heard. Otherwise, our population would have gone out of control."

"Sure I know of those days when one added mouth threatened the survival of the entire family. Contraception was uncertain, too. Therefore abortion in those days was a kind of justifiable defense in contrast to the scientifically planned murder of females. In olden days, people wanting a son would probably steal a red pepper from the prohibitive sacred rope hung across the door of a house where a son had been born. Such thievery was understandable, but there was nothing redeemable in the murder of female fetuses. I had never known so distasteful and painful a job as covering the most disgusting people I met then. Finally I went to my editor and tried to beg myself off the story. I didn't feel like writing the story, but I gave him a different excuse. I told him my original purpose was to warn our society about the ecological catastrophe it was going to face if we persisted in this artificial rearrangement of sex ratio, but I changed my mind because I feared that some people might want to imitate those murderers. Since our magazine is respected for its dignified treatment of ecological problems, we decided to scrap the story."

"Please don't hate those women. Desperation drove them to it, I am sure."

"I didn't say they did it without their husbands' knowledge. All their husbands were willing accomplices. Oh, I'm sorry I talked too much," he said and hurriedly walked out of the room.

The word "accomplice" whirled around in my head as I tried to find some rational words to say. Now I've come to understand the uneasy, unpleasant feeling that nagged and oppressed me all this time was caused by my living with an accomplice. The calm river surface had small ripples on it. The river didn't freeze maybe because of the unusually warm weather or water pollution. So, there will be no ducks to carry off the frozen river. Unless such a time comes, I will never see the man again. Giving him up for good left me desolate.

Did he say he was researching for that story last year? Oh, God, more than ten years ago, I was stretched out on a surgical table, clenching my teeth, to have my amniotic fluid drawn out. At the head, my mother-in-law and sister-in-law stood watching. It was so long ago that he couldn't have seen me, but I felt as if I had bared to him my ugliest and most miserable secret.

The waiter came to ask me if I could share my table. I stood up and came outside. It was cold and I was lost. When the uniformed man brought my car around, I smiled and tipped him 1,000 *won*, just as I had observed others do.

Instead of going down and straightforward to my home, I made a left turn away from downtown. It was my first drive out of the city. I didn't have any place I wanted to go to; I simply wanted to get as far away as I could from my home. My sense of direction was atrocious and I had to stay close to the River. Like a long string to lead me back home, the River would guide me back home.

However, when the highway went around a mountain, I would lose sight of the River and become nervous and anxious. As long as the River was on my right, I didn't have to think about which way I should turn. Between the River and the road, there were riverside soccer fields, vinyl hot houses, and small villages. I didn't have to worry about falling directly into the river even if I should drive off the road. I fantasized about crashing. The traffic was fairly heavy but still lighter than in the city. I drove on smoothly with the traffic flow, feeling quite happy and proud of my driving.

At the first fork, though I didn't have to decide which road to take, I spied a left road, obviously a new one that seemed to have thrust its way between two halves of a hill. On both sides, raw red earth was exposed on the sloping cut. The redness of earth gave me shivers. The two sloping cuts looked like two widely spread legs of a woman in a hospital stirrup. No head, no torso, but two open thighs covered with blood. Through them lay the new road filled with cars coming and going. I was being sucked into the raw crotch. I was scared stiff, then nauseated. Oh my God, what a shameful sight, I could die of shame.

In a desperate struggle to get hold of myself, I turned my car at a 90-degree angle and managed to get onto a wide un-paved road on the right.

All the cars in the next lane had to slam on the brakes to avoid me, but they were not real in my half-delirious state. My car was unscathed, but I vaguely thought I should get out and apologize. The air was crisp and cool. Immediately my ears were assailed by curses and swears from the drivers who stopped in a fury. One got out of his car and made obscene gestures toward me while others stuck their heads out and hurled every curse and insult at me. I was "a crazy bitch." But their invectives were as refreshing as the cool breeze. I breathed them deeply in. Since I wasn't given a chance to apologize, I just stood there looking over the peaceful little riverside village. I might have even been smiling, which apparently made them think I was truly insane.

The man who looked ready to pounce on me and throttle me got back in his car and all the other yelling heads drew back in. As if nothing had happened, the cars began to move. As I watched the cars leave, I felt abandoned, as if they all had decided to ostracize me. Underneath the rumbles of the road, I could hear the lowing of a woeful moan. From deep inside me, a wail gushed upward and I wanted to cry to my heart's content. Cautiously I turned my car toward the village and parked alongside a lane. I hugged the steering wheel ready to cry, wail, and lament as much and as long as I wanted. But neither a sound nor a tear came out of me.

Am I really living with an accomplice? There is no evidence that my husband was an accomplice. Did he ever say he missed having a son? Just once he said he was envious of men who go to baseball games with their sons. He never said it again. Then, why was I so deeply hurt? Was it because he acted so sad when he said it? He didn't care for baseball that much, but that day he sounded crestfallen as if he had been turned away at the ball park gate because he didn't bring a son. Why couldn't I tell him that it was possible daughters could enjoy baseball and sons didn't care for it? What is baseball anyway? But baseball is important because I had killed a daughter in order to present to my husband a son to take to baseball games.

When it became known that I was pregnant with the third female baby, a murderous air began to fill the entire extended family. Was my husband a part of it? Was he coolly detached? Even if he were, I don't think I could ever forgive him. He is not only my husband but also the father of a living being whom everyone wanted killed. How could he have been detached? He couldn't have been. Then, is he an accomplice? Is the nagging anxiety I have lived with so long from living with my accomplice?

I recall with a fond heart the man not as a briefly-met stranger but as a long-lost old lover. It saddens me deeply that I'll never see him again. I wonder what his wife is like? I am envious of her. When I heard his argument, I was shocked by it and yet I agreed with him. Looking back now, I find what he said wasn't anything exceptional. I had the kind of vague ambivalent feeling about his argument as when I heard a research paper read by someone who had not thoroughly digested its content himself. The argument might be mere common sense wrapped in erudite words.

However, what was very important was how much thinking he had put into his argument, solely to convince himself that he wasn't disappointed with having two daughters. It was definitely a result of his earnest effort. Consequently he had succeeded to expand his love to embrace not only his daughters, but also the daughters of other people. His love was sure and well-founded.

Had my husband ever put that much effort and thought into it? This is the cause of my envy of his wife. Was I too gullible? Was I too uncritically receptive of his argument? He was the first man to raise suspicion of my husband's complicity. On the other hand, I myself might have held it inside me while trying to suppress it. Yet, could I make my husband an accomplice without compunction? Partners in crime are bound to undo each other. They shouldn't live together. As has been shown many times in movies, crimes can be clearly executed by a lone culprit. Then movies will no longer be interesting; that is why there is inevitably a witness or an accomplice. Partners in crime will have it out eventually, that's unavoidable. I believe I know their psychology.

After the horrible feticide, I turned into a cold, insolent person, unlike my former self, a polite daughter-in-law and congenial sister-in-law. I fought them over every little trifle and my hostility gave my life vitality. Every time my husband and I visited his side of family, I was hard and impolite. I openly disliked my mother-in-law's visit to my home. She would bring me my husband's favorite dishes, fermented bean sauce or a special kimchi, which I resolutely refused to serve him. I would leave them untouched till they spoiled and made it sure that my mother-in-law saw them.

My sister-in-law and I had been classmates in college. We were acquaintances majoring in different subjects. Since my marriage, however, we had become bosom friends, and with my mother-in-law's permission, we didn't have to use mutual honorific in-law titles. We helped each other in obtaining our first apartments in the same neighborhood where we used to go grocery shopping together, baby-sat each other's children and cleverly manipulated our husbands into participating in shared outings and picnics. My sister-in-law had been my constant helpmate throughout the abortion and the birth of my son.

After my son was born, suddenly I couldn't stand the sight of her, so I moved my family to a new place. I even schemed and succeeded in estranging our husbands from each other. When my husband and I visited her family, I made it a point to wear the most expensive dress, eat and speak as little as possible. I was determined not to call her by name as I used to, but use her correct title. When she brought cookies and snacks on her visit to us, I'd disdainfully push them in a corner of the pantry, leave them there for weeks and then discard them in a garbage can, always pointedly in my husband's presence. At times I thought I was committing a terrible sin, but never felt guilty. I was merely sorry I wasted so much good food.

My in-laws knew that their obedient and congenial daughter-in-law had turned into an ogre after my son was born. On occasion, they would attempt a frontal attack by saying, "Now that you have a son, you think you have suddenly become a queen?" I didn't care, though. The haughtier I got, the more respectful they became. I was indeed a queen, I had nobody to fear, because I bore a son. I gave them an heir and I could be as grand as I wanted to be. In fact, I became a man. My son was my newly acquired male organ. When I thought of my son, I found myself invincible.

Then, why did I assume such arrogance and such aggressiveness? Being male couldn't mean an incessant impulse to attack, could it? Why did I so detest the sight of my mother-in-law and sister-in-law? Wasn't it because they were partners in my crime? Whenever I saw them, I shivered, remembering their faces watching me on the operating table. The room where I was to have my amniotic fluid drawn was not called an operating room but an injection room. Against one wall, a medicine cabinet stood, against another, a wheeled stretcher. The doctor, a friend of my sister's husband, called in both of them as if he were going to show them a magic show. When the doctor pulled my panty down to the pubic hair, my sister-in-law untied her scarf and covered me. The doctor's cold hands touched the surgical scar of my caesarian operation, which induced a sigh and lamentation from my mother-in-law. I couldn't plug my ears, so I closed my eyes.

"Please listen to me, Doctor, if my girl, my daughter-in-law were able to bear babies easily, I'd not have asked you to do this. I know there are people who would be thankful to have a girl, and if my daughter-in-law keeps having babies, she may someday bear a son. But as you can see here, she is unable to. Since this third pregnancy is her last and if it's a girl again, I don't think I'll be able to live or die in peace. I stay up nights thinking about the dire fate of our family. I didn't know about recent medical advances, and worried and worried myself sick."

I could hear every word of her long lamentation, including the final, drawn-out sigh. Her calling me "my girl" felt like a disgusting worm crawling over me. The doctor's unctuous voice answered, "Madam, you really were in the dark, weren't you? Who in the world gives birth to two girls in this age? At the second time, everybody goes for an examination and deals with the problem. People who want only one child do it even at their first pregnancy. We try to dissuade them, but they are adamant."

The doctor began to rub some evil-smelling liquid on my lower abdomen. I opened my eyes to see the doctor's face, but, instead, the two tense faces of my in-laws loomed above me. I wasn't yet anesthetized, but their faces seemed floating above, disconnected from their body. Beyond their faces hung a milky white florescent light. The doctor's cold hands pushed a small lump inside me to one side and I could feel the lump desperately resisting his push. All my nerves concentrated on the doctor's pushing and the lump's resisting when I suddenly felt a piercing pain. Screaming, I tried to sit up but my two in-laws held me down from both sides. It wasn't the pain but my fear for the life inside that caused me to scream. "My poor girl, there, there. It's just a syringe," my mother-in-law said. Yes, I will try to endure the pain, but how can I control my maternal instinct? Tears streamed down my temples. "Tut, tut, tut. You are too soft for your age," my mother-in-law mumbled. The doctor didn't draw any fluid because, he said, not enough of it had been formed. I caught sight of the huge empty syringe. Oh my God, how could he attack a pea-sized life with that humongous evil weapon?

I was released that day with no more ado. I had to wait two more weeks, during which I was on edge day and night worrying about what harm might have been meted out to the tiny baby. I couldn't eat or sleep.

The sex of the baby wasn't known yet. It never occurred to me that if the aborted fetus was to be a girl, I wouldn't mind. Definitely not. I felt infinite sadness for that small life. I had never had such tender love for the baby at my first or last pregnancy.

Despite my innermost sadness and attachment, I was dragged back to the clinic. This time the doctor succeeded and told us the result would come out the next day. Like high school seniors waiting for college entrance notification, my mother-in-law was so nervous that she stayed at my apartment. The next day, my sister-in-law informed us that the aborted fetus was female. The three of us hurried back to the doctor who was known for his expert abortions. "Don't we live in wonderful times? In the old days, you would have produced another girl," my mother-in-law exulted. She was elated and in awe of modern medicine. She even hinted that I ought to be grateful to her and her daughter for accompanying me.

"Abortion? That's no big deal. I had it done three times without my mother-in-law knowing about it. I had the operation in the afternoon, came home and cooked dinner. I whined a little to my husband at night but he never said a comforting word. He wasn't that kind of man anyway. I don't know whether because we had no recreation of any kind, we kept having babies. A glance at each other, presto, I was pregnant," my mother- in-law happily chatted.

To speak the truth, I had an abortion once and she didn't know about it. A hundred days after my first baby was born, I found myself pregnant, when my husband had just quit his job with no alternative plans. We were at the end of the rope. A truly lucky stroke descended on us and I found a job. It was a teaching position at a school opened by a business firm. The firm was run by a relative on my mother's side.

In those days labor unions were so ideologically conscious and aggressively demanding that business firms competed one another to open company schools to give the laborers a chance to get an education. The pay was higher than that of the teachers at regular schools, but there was no job security. It was before the days when maternity leave rules were made. On top of it, my mother was already taking care of my first baby. I discussed the matter of aborting the second baby with my husband. In order not to humiliate him, I pretended to be cheerful when he went with me to the doctor. He was very tender toward me, and one night I found him sobbing alone. Whether because it was absolutely necessary or because I discussed it with him, when I recall my first abortion, I don't feel guilty. Rather, the fear of poverty looms like a haunting spirit.

I don't know why I didn't talk about it with my husband beforehand when I had the second abortion just because the fetus was female. Did he have an inkling of what I was going through? At that time, I myself was resigned to its inevitability, as if I had caught the family's contagious lethal air. Otherwise, I wouldn't have gone so docilely to the clinic. The main cause of my weakening resistance was my sister-in-law. Her poisonous whisper that the seaweed soup, a traditional postnatal dish to new mothers, tasted different after having a son from after having a girl, must have infected me. She had a boy and a girl. She told me a more shocking story to drive in her point. It was about a handsome, admired and respected professor at our college who lost his wife. He was also known as the loving husband in a very happy marriage. I had seen the pictures of the elegantly aging couple in several women's magazines. I had been sure that he would live out his life alone with memories of his dead wife. My sister-in-law, the gossip, however, shattered my romantic picture. The widowed professor remarried within a few months of his wife's death. Moreover, his new wife had been his mistress for more than ten years. He had two daughters with his wife, but the boy born of the mistress was already in middle school. The boy was the very image of his father, handsome and tall. My sister-in-law's gleaming eyes were piercing me through the heart. She was unusually animated when she gave me her last thrust. "The professor's wife didn't die ignorant of her husband's infidelity, but rather of a heartbreak that had eventually developed into a cancer." The story chilled me.

My mother-in-law began to nag about the necessity of a grandson soon after my father-in-law passed away, leaving her a rich woman. When I was married, my father-in-law was a bedridden invalid paralyzed from a stroke. The old house was falling apart, and the family barely made a living by renting out several rooms. The house had a spacious yard, though, and when a wide street was built in front of the house, money began to roll in. With advance payment from future renters and a bank loan, my father-in-law had a sizable building built. The whole undertaking, shaky in the beginning, became a successful business venture. My mother-in-law used to iterate that she would never depend on us in her old age if only she owned a small house. Now, a rich building owner, she asserted herself confidently and demanded a grandson. She made it a habit to grab my husband and insisted that daughters were absolutely useless. If he, her eldest son, refused, she would think about bringing her younger son back from America. He had emigrated when the family were desperately poor and managed to get a permanent residenceship after years of hard work running a small business. He and his family were making a fairly decent living, but in no way comfortable.

I could sense how insulting and threatening his mother's nagging was to my husband, who was expecting to inherit her property. His mother proclaimed that she would not leave her earthly possessions to her son unless he had a son himself to carry on. She used the ownership of the building as if it were a throne. In other words, the carrying on of the family name only meant property inheritance.

My two in-laws watched over me as I lay on the stretcher ready to have my third daughter murdered. What devotion to the family! They looked like two angels of death waiting to make sure the murder was complete though they were saying soothing words to me.

The moment I decided to hate them started then. I thought my hatred would be a way of mourning for my daughter. There was nothing else I could do. As I slowly went under anesthesia, I forced myself to keep my eyes open to etch the images of my in-laws in my mind.

In the incubator, my baby is wiggling. She is as small as a thumb. I call her Princess Thumb. Poor little thing. If I don't watch over her, someone may try to carry her off. I pinch my thigh to stay awake but I don't feel any pain. Suddenly my mother-in-law and sister-in-law, both in black, bring in a big fat baby. The room fills with people in white and my in-laws demand that the tiny baby be removed so the big baby can be placed in the incubator. No, no, please, the tiny one will wither away if taken out, I want to shout but no sound comes out. Those in black and those in white begin to haggle over the price of removal, upping the price higher and higher while they snicker and cackle like fiends. I desperately thrash my body to stop them, but I am absolutely immobile. In a minute Princess Thumb is gone. Evaporated like a drop of dew. My sorrow means nothing to them. They laugh and guffaw. I am dangling on top of their laughter. I want to jump down but can't. I want to throw up. Their laughter changes into a noise like that of metal wheels scraping over a pebbly road. Unbearable noise. The noise invades my head. I writhe and thrash. I was wheeled into the recovery room.

"My girl, are you all right?" My in-laws bent over me. Their faces again floated above me. I closed my eyes. I heard her asking the doctor whether I'd be able to conceive again. Later I learned that the operation had been difficult because the fetus had grown a little beyond the right size for abortion. That was why my mother-in-law asked the doctor about the next conception. I had merely served as a human incubator very briefly for my Princess Thumb.

Probably because of the tonic herb medicine my mother-in-law fed me, I conceived soon after. Even if it turned out to be a girl, I was determined not to go through the horror again. But, the fetus was a male. I received congratulations and attentive care from everyone. I bore a son, but secretly I wanted to show my family and friends that I would become a different woman.

I heard children's voices. Schools must be out. Several boys were looking into my car. They might have been uneasy seeing a woman bent over her steering wheel. I grinned at them to show them I was not drunk or dead. The red-cheeked boys grinned back and dispersed. A woman was walking toward me with a basket on her head. Nowadays city people rarely see a woman carrying a thing on her head. The basket held some green vegetables. Posture experts in fashion magazines said that the best walking posture was an arrow-straight posture as if someone were pulling your head upward. With the heavy basket pressing down, she had to hold her head straight to balance the tension, and her posture was perfect.

I thought about my own mother. She used to say that your husband was like a load on your head. By my observation of my parents' marriage, I interpreted it that your husband was somebody lording over you. Now it occurs to me that because of the load on your head, you learn to stand straight, resisting but with confidence. That may be a woman's fate. My mother knew what she was talking about. She was always in awe of my father. Her backbreaking daily work meant little to him and she received my father's not very large salary in gratitude and humility. She seemed to consider herself an undeserving mouth to feed, a burden to my father. There were two boys and two girls, but my father didn't discriminate against girls; rather, it was my mother who humiliated us girls. At table, my mother would not permit the girls to look at good dishes, let alone eat any part of them. When my father gave her tuition money for the boys, she accepted it with dignity whereas when she got school tuition for us girls, she was servile and anxious. Later, she made it a point to tell us that she felt so guilty about getting money for the girls.

At times of marriage, she was again two-sided. When my brothers married, she was a perfect picture of dignity and pride to the in-laws, but when we girls married, she acted cowardly and nervous as if she were selling damaged goods in underhanded way. I was hurt. Moreover, she acted like a guilty sinner when I had girl babies. I pleaded her not to, but her answer was, "nobody tells me to act so. I just do it naturally."

Therefore, I was exceptionally happy when my sister had a boy because my mother didn't have to humble herself so much in front of her in-laws. At the birth of my first daughter, my husband and I were proud and elated. I don't know how my mother-in-law felt. While I was recuperating at my parents' home, my husband moved in with us, for he said he missed the baby. Without a thought, I changed the baby's diapers and sometimes asked my husband to do it. One day my mother happened to see my husband changing the baby's diapers. After he left the room, she scolded me.

"My goodness, you senseless girl, how could you show a girl's ugly lower part to your husband?"

"It's okay if the baby is a boy?"

"Of course. A boy's little pecker is something to be shown proudly."

So, my mother raised us in the same manner. It was her life philosophy, her fundamental ethics, and her habit.

Now that I look back on my past, I was indoctrinated from my diaper days to serve as an incubator without raising a question. However, I must change for the future. My husband, too. Not to show other people but for ourselves. We committed the most horrendous crime, and we have not even felt guilty or remorseful. Unless we clean our soul from the lingering unease, we will never be able to feel anything. We will never be wholly human. I got out of the car to breathe the fresh cool air.

I began to drive. Since I could not make a left turn, I had to drive away from the city. There must be a U-turn somewhere. It wasn't important. The city and my home were falling far behind, but I felt refreshed and rejuvenated.

At the Sundown

by Yoon Jungsun

"Isn't the sun wonderful?" the old man asks.

"Yes. It's bright and warm," the old woman answers.

"Look at the sparrows. They chatter so cheerfully."

"Don't you think they are singing about us, a grandpa and a grandma? Maybe they are admiring us, how loving we are to each other."

"Do they have time to pay attention to us? Looks like they are too busy among themselves."

"Like our children?"

"Everybody has a life of his own."

"I know, but...."

"My youngest daughter-in-law is expecting her first baby."

"Congratulations. When is the baby due?"

"Autumn."

"You will be very busy then, being a grandma and all."

"Well, its not the first time. I already have two grandchildren."

"And still you have lived alone?"

"My son wanted to marry her on the condition that I live with them. But I declined."

"Why?"

"Because I didn't want to be a burden."

"But aren't you lonely?"

"Either way it's the same. I'm old and can't be of much use to them. I thought if I became lonely while living with them, it would be worse. I have my own work. I like the way things are."

"But, don't you sometimes feel afraid?"

"Well...someday...I...I am unable to move around without help...I don't even want to think about it...because it is absolutely terrifying."

There was silence.

"Aren't you alone, too?"

"Once I lived with my eldest son, but being a widower father-in-law was too difficult. Besides I missed this old land."

"I thought you'd never return."

"As they say, as I got older I found myself wanting to be buried in my homeland. It seems to me that death is going back to your origin."

"Yes, like fish that go back to their birthplace to die."

"Yes, like fish."

"Don't you miss your grandchildren?"

"Of course I do. They are wonderful. The boy is a strong determined young fellow. He can do pretty much anything he sets his mind on. He is a leader at school. The younger one, a girl, is so smart that she can sing along every word in all TV commercials. She called me Grampy and followed me around. They send me pictures. They have grown a lot. Oh, I'm sorry I carried on."

"No, no. When my friends got together, we used to talk about our daughter-in-law and brag about our grandchildren. But now that we are much older, we tend to complain how our children mistreat us...and how useless they are after all the years of hard work we'd put in in raising them."

"Is there anyone who hasn't felt betrayed by their children? But, if you look at it closely, such resentment comes from expectation, which is another form of selfishness or...."

"But, if you can be free of such resentment, you are no longer a human being."

"You are right."

"I thought I was trying not to be a burden, but my feeling lonesome itself may be a burden on them...so life becomes doubly difficult."

"As the saying goes, children want their parents to live quietly and die quickly. A friend of mine, a widower, once told his sons that he wanted to remarry...but what horrible insult he had to face...."

"How?"

"All the children rose up in protest. They said their father had lost his marbles."

"A few days ago I read in the newspaper that a man in his 70s stabbed a friend in his 80s."

"I saw it, too. Apparently they were rivals for the love of a widow."

"The reporter implied that it was a foolish love triangle...of two demented senile old men."

"The general tone was so condescending."

"As if they were talking about silly monkeys."

"Yes, cackling monkeys in a zoo."

"A long time ago, I read an article. I can't remember whether it was about Sweden or Norway; anyway, it was a Scandinavian country. Some advertising agency used a love-scene of a couple in their 70s. I vaguely remember the advertisement was about insurance or a social welfare system. Anyway, if you wanted to have a healthy life in your old age...something like that...But, the advertisement caused a storm."

"Why?"

"People said it was dirty and ugly. Overt sexuality was acceptable only with the young and healthy."

"Aha."

"At that time I thought I was still young, but I felt deeply about this. My concern was not about the countless people who found the scene dirty but for the couple. How shocked and saddened they must have felt that people thought them dirty and ugly. I am sure they were proud that they had kept their love both in mind and body through their old age."

"Right."

"People are...well, life is so cruel."

"But don't you think it strange that everything that's nearing death looks ugly?"

"I guess it's the instinct of the cosmic life force. To preserve its life by pushing away death."

"You may be right. To a buzzard, carrion is the most beautiful object."

"Likewise, to a seed, a decomposed leaf feels warm."

"And yet, human beings lament and weep over the flowers withering, leaves falling for winter."

"Don't you think human beings would be much happier if they didn't have the power of analogy?"

"Yes. They wouldn't get so sad in anticipation."

"Nor would they torment themselves."

"But you don't seem to have aged that much."

"Actually you are amazing. I used to think you might not live long because you were so fragile when you were young."

"I thought so, too. There were times when I had to hold onto something to support myself.... At times I was afraid I might die young, suddenly."

"And here we are about to greet a new spring."

"But as an old granny."

"To this old man, you are not."

"I am as wrinkled as the E. T."

"E. T. ?"

"Yes, E. T."

"Ha ha ha. Don't be so sure. In the current expression, don't brag about your wrinkles in front of a pupa."

"But, I do feel like a pupa."

"Which means you are going to fly away someday."

"I wish."

He gazes longingly at her.

"Why are you looking at me like that?"

"You are as beautiful...as this spring."

"Not as the fall but as this spring?"

"No, not as the fall nor as the winter. Just like this very spring."

"Like this spring when all those flowers are sick with love?"

"Yes."

"Your eye-sight must be bad."

"True. My eyes have weakened. But as long as you look beautiful to me, you are beautiful."

"It must be because you have a beautiful heart."

"Means the same to me."

"You don't have to comfort me."

"Do you know Sartre said Beauvoir was beautiful when she was over sixty. He also said she was still beautiful."

"I know Beauvoir kept vigil at his death-bed. His eyes were protruding like a frog's and his skin was rough as a lizard's, but she caressed him all the while in his last days. Now they must be rotting together in their grave."

"Have you ever heard Sartre's voice?"

"No. How could I?"

"There is a disk. A friend of mine brought it from Paris. His voice was so raspy that I didn't like it at all."

"Really?"

"A gray man's blabbing voice."

"That's funny. The man died, but his voice was copied and reproduced by electricity with his unique voice intact...."

"He wasn't a very cheerful man. But he lived his life on the power of her love. When I was young, I read about the two of them and thought it flattery, but later I have found it true. He was being honest."

"Whether you intended to comfort me or be honest, I am glad to hear it. It means much more to me now than when I was young.... I guess that means I've become weak and unsure. My self-confidence is so much needed now."

"I think weakness is a premise of love. Love is for people who are lacking in one thing or another, in other words, for people who will someday die. In face of death, what else can a living being hang onto besides love?"

"I guess love is the only way to extend one's self."

"People who are nearing death can have deeper love. In that sense, being old can be a blessing."

"But getting old is a sin. People become ugly and feeble. I don't think anyone deserves such a curse. Everyone gets old, weak, ugly, and sick. Old people seem to be unpardonable sinners, garbage of the living world."

"Please don't be so cynical. Some poet said a decline in the body brings on wisdom. Beauty and ugliness are not necessarily superficial.... Anyway, sneering at other people is a sin, but sneering at oneself is also a sin. Despair is a bigger sin."

"But do you know there is often despair behind true love?"

"I do. I might not have understood it when I was younger."

"Once I went with a friend, a psychology major, to meet a gay person. He, no, she, he had a transsexual operation, so it was she.... She told us her love was the truest because her back was against the wall of despair. There was no room for her to step back, so she loved her lover from the depth of her soul. Her surgically-made sex organ didn't give her bodily satisfaction, but she said she felt spiritual orgasm from her partner's sexual pleasures."

"In other words, the more alienated one is, the more desperate one's love becomes."

"As much as the world laughs at her...."

"In that case, old people in love are kind of gay lovers."

"Yes, like empty bottles and empty jars."

"But I still feel full by just looking at you."

"Your old face is a reflection of mine...but somehow you are always young to me. I have kept you in my memory and that 'young you' must have cast a spell."

"Then, why don't you become young with me?"

"Like those children over there?"

"What children?"

"Over there. They have been in an embrace, whispering to each other all this while."

"Right. Maybe we can become younger than they."

"To them, we must look...."

"I don't think they see us. We are no more than these rocks and grass."

"You are right. When we are young, we don't see anything, even our own selves."

"Voltaire said 'if only youth knew, if only old age could'."

"Isn't it sad we spend our youth knowing nothing then become old and can do nothing? I find it hard to accept. Someone said being old is like a shipwreck, and while saying it, he really did struggle for breath."

"Shipwreck!"

"Yes."

"Can this be a life boat?"

"What?"

"Someone was passing this out in the street."

"'Be joyful, believers in Christ. The time has come'."

"Your eyesight is good."

"The letters are so big. Anyway, religious believers are happy people, I think."

"But do you think people will suddenly turn to religion by this kind of thing?"

"To me, the most unbelievable thing is death. People who believe in death are believing the most unbelievable thing. So, why wouldn't they turn to religion?"

"You may be right. In everyone of every culture, there is this unceasing hope for afterlife. At the same time everything in this life tells us we are going to disappear. There's no avoiding it. It's enough to make us schizophrenic."

"How can I accept it? I mean, the inevitable fact of our eventual disappearance. We think, we feel sad and happy, and even a pin prick hurts us terribly. Then, we just disappear suddenly like a whiff of air? Can you believe that? Does it mean that our existence has never been real but a mere lie? Can you believe that?"

"That is why man has filled museums from time immemorial. It seems ancient Egyptians lived on this earth only to prepare themselves for the other world. Life on earth was merely a passing illusion."

"People in India and Tibet are the same."

"If you believe in transmigration.... And yet, is there any corner where the eyes of death don't reach?"

"People die too soon."

"They don't if compared to gnats."

"For creatures with such amazing brains, human beings die too soon. I was told they use only a fraction of their brain cells before they die. Even Einstein spent only fifteen percent of his."

"Because of his enormous contribution to science and humanity, his brains cannot be put to rest. Scientists weigh them, slice them, dye them, poke them...."

"If human soul is in his brains, Einstein's soul will be an eternal prisoner of a science lab."

"Sounds like science fiction. If one is buried and slowly turns to soil, I wonder what it would feel like."

"You know, among so many possibilities in life, we are each given only one."

"What do you mean?"

"I could have been a composer, a painter, a scientist, a doctor, a diplomat, a nun...or a prostitute."

"I don't like the last one."

"Prostitutes are as good as the men who seek them."

"Anyway, this world demands specialization," he said, ignoring her comment. Modern men therefore live a much narrower and more fragmented life than the ancient people. Our life is torn into parts, specialized.... Now that I look back, Lao-tzu was right."

"From my girlhood, I have always believed that men should live at least 300 years."

"What a grand dream. Three centuries!"

"I know it is my preposterous greed. Sometimes at the table, I look closely at the fish roe, thousands of them, and think about their infinite possibilities and their infinite desire for procreation, and suddenly feel sorry about frustrating them."

"Well, we don't know when the life cycle may end, but it will end eventually. If one dies soon, maybe one is spared of more suffering and pain."

"You know the big sea turtles. They crawl to the sand risking their lives to lay eggs. Then at last the day comes for the eggs to hatch. Thousands of tiny baby turtles march toward the sea. They are marching to a new life but the march becomes a death march because birds are waiting to eat them. Millions of birds darken the sky. The black birds of prey."

"To the baby turtles, it is a day of fear, but to the birds, it is a day of feast."

"I saw a similar scene in a movie when I was a child. I couldn't get over the shock."

"Then, how have you survived all the other shocks until today?"

"It's a miracle."

"Think it over. How much we have benefited from nature."

"You mean it's a privilege to get old?"

"Someone once asked why we have to get old before we die, and the answer was we would be too resentful to die if we died young. You know, our life is a table made for us by our fate. We must take it as it is."

"A table prepared by fate...."

"Do you remember what we ate the first day we met?"

"Chinese spaghetti."

"Right."

"In that shabby little eatery. We didn't even ask...."

"There was no menu to ask for or choose from. Only tasteless noodle soup and raimyon. We chose the best."

"You ate it well...but I couldn't. I was afraid of smearing my lips with the dark sauce."

"You were in love with me the first day?"

"No."

"Then, why were you afraid? I wasn't able to take you to a nice restaurant and ask you like a gentleman what you'd like to order. I was a nobody."

"I was angry."

"Why were you angry? I bought you tasty food."

"Tasty? Phooey."

"Oh, oh, you are angry."

"Yes, I am, because you regarded me so lightly."

"That's not true. At that time I didn't know what to do for a woman. What, how, nothing. I didn't even know how to approach and speak to a woman. I was dying of love for you.... It was a live-or-die situation for me. But I had no money...."

"Really?"

"True. You knew that."

"But I enjoy hearing it again."

"And later we went to a tearoom called Zarathustra."

"By the way, that professor died a while ago."

"Who?"

"You know the philosophy professor? One day he was talking about Nietzsche when he got excited and cursed, 'the blasphemous Nietzsche, the Satan's son, got syphilis and died raving mad.'"

"Oh, yes, that professor."

"He fell far short of being a philosophy professor."

"Did he die of syphilis, too, I wonder."

"You are too much."

"Maybe of AIDS. Philosophy professor and AIDS. That sounds fitting."

"Come to think of it, the most aggressive minds of all ages seem to die of the worst disease of their time. Is it because they were too arrogant before God?"

"Not really. Modest people get leprosy, like Job."

"But he was the only one cured."

"Leprosy, pest...All the geniuses and beauties once died of tuberculosis."

"Syphilis was indeed Baudelaire's Flower of Evil."

"In our time, syphilis gave way to AIDS. Few people die of syphilis anymore. Michel Foucault, wasn't it, AIDS?"

"Who?.... My God, you are committing a terrible slander."

"Rilke was said to have died of a thorn prick, but really it was tetanus. Anyway, we don't choose our disease. Disease chooses us."

"Leprosy, syphilis, and AIDS.... the one extreme end of life, a holy curse."

"Have you heard about a woman who injected herself with AIDS-contaminated blood, so she would die with her lover?"

"A suicide of love."

"A double suicide."

"What happened to them?"

"I don't know. Maybe both of them died. Death from AIDS is not quick but prolonged. I cannot imagine what they might have gone through."

"I thought there was no one who would die for love in this age."

"You are wrong. But, do you know what Schopenhauer, the admirer of suicide, said on his death bed?"

"No, I don't."

"Oh, 'I.... I can't die. I have too much to do yet'."

"That's interesting."

"Ironic, isn't it?"

"What do you think of all the religions objecting to suicide?"

"I think religions in general disapprove of man's arrogance. From that point of view, suicide is the most disrespectful act committed by the most evil man because he refuses to accept his share of pain. He is like an actor who quits the stage just because he doesn't like his role. Suicide is man's final act of vanity."

"But it is unspeakably cruel to judge suicide as an act of vanity. The man might have been besieged by a pack of wolves and decided to refuse a horrible fate."

"In that case, what do you think of euthanasia? Do you approve of it?"

"If death is unavoidable and one honestly wants it, shouldn't one be given the right to refuse further pain and preserve one's dignity?"

"It's not that simple...by the way, how in the world have we come to talking about suicide on a fine spring day like this?"

"We were talking about Zarathustra."

"Zarathustra doesn't exist anymore."

"I miss him."

"There are very few things that stay on for us."

"Especially in this country. Everything is being dug up, cut off, and...."

"In our time things were better...."

"We did go around a lot to so many places, didn't we?"

"And never felt tired."

"When I ride a subway, I always look down at people's shoes. Old and weary-looking shoes, cheerfully healthy sneakers, shiny and nervous leather shoes.... I don't have to look up at the wearer to tell the hard-up from others. Old men's shoes are the easiest to tell."

"How are my shoes?"

"They look like moles."

"Moles?"

"Yes, they are covered with dirt."

"That's a good sign. I went hiking this morning."

"I remember you carried me on your back once."

"Yes, while we were traveling."

"In a lane in the wood."

"You were light as a feather."

"I liked your broad back."

"Why didn't you tell me that?"

"Lest you like it too much."

"So, you took several decades to tell me that, didn't you?"

"It seems like yesterday to me."

"It does to me, too. The country scene and...."

"Yes, on the thatched roof, there was a huge gourd and a thin thread of smoke was coming out of the mud chimney."

"In the summer night, we saw a shower of shooting stars, do you remember?"

"How could I forget?"

"Those stars were truly beautiful."

"They say that every time a shooting star falls, someone dies. I've always believed that. So, somewhere in the universe, all the dead persons are living with their looks and voices still the same as they were."

"You may be right."

"I wonder what our soul looks like."

"Well...."

"I hope it will not look like our death masks. Will it?"

"Do you believe souls live on, loving and hating?"

"Only loving, I hope."

"If you erase hatred from yourself and pass away with only love in your heart."

"I believe so."

"By the way, what are we doing here?"

"Loving."

"Are we doing it? That's wonderful."

"Yes, we are. We are making passionate love."

"Yes, passionate love."

"I love your smile."

"Did you like it in the old days, too?"

"Of course."

"Then, why did you leave me?"

"I didn't leave, you did."

"Makes no difference. I...didn't like all those women hanging around you."

"But my eyes saw only you."

"I thought you didn't love me enough because you weren't desperate anymore."

"Good heavens!"

"And other men were."

"You made me lose my confidence. You seemed to say, 'you are not good enough to make me happy. So, get out of way.'"

"You were such a coward!"

"You used to say that to me."

"I didn't know then how to love. Perhaps, I haven't learned it yet."

"Please, just be there before me. Don't cast me away."

"After all these years?"

"After all these years."

"I regret deeply all the years that have gone by."

"Nonsense. Are you going to regret the past and let this golden present pass by?"

"You are right. We are alive, aren't we?"

"And isn't it just terrific, we are greeting another new spring?"

"How many springs like this can we have in our lifetime?"

"I'd rather think about how many springs we have left in the rest of our lives."

"But we have already been blessed so much. Look at the bright sunlight between flowering trees! This overwhelming blessing...how many times have we embraced it wholeheartedly?"

"Even if spring came to us always."

"Yes, it was in the field."

"And outside our windows."

"But, tall buildings, noise and dust hid the spring from us."

"Yes, the most unimportant things took our spring away."

"Such as our stupid ambitions."

"And yet, spring always brought us brilliant flowers."

"Come to think of it, you used to send me your poems."

"I did."

"They were not love poems, though, but rather philosophical discourses, more like pseudo-philosophical...."

"I never said I was a poet. I just jotted down a few words.... I didn't know a thing, but pretended that I knew a lot. Now I think I can write real poetry of love."

"I think everyone's life can be a poem."

"I agree. Perhaps you are a true poet. Our life is a work of art we've created ourselves."

"Are you satisfied with your work?"

"That's the hardest question I've ever been asked in my life."

"Did you ever know I despised you?"

"Why did you?"

"Because you ran away from me."

"I told you I did not."

"You settled in an easy worldly comfort. How could you have written poetry?"

"You are right."

"So, I hated you. It took me quite some time to find peace of mind. I thought someday you'd be abjectly defeated, not completely destroyed though, and yearn for me. Then, one day we'd happen to run into each other in a cafe or some place...I'd turn away in contempt and you'd follow me, reeling and hoarsely calling my name.... then, I'd...."

"You'd turn around?"

"To tell the truth, I have always hesitated at that point. Turn around or not? I spent long nights pondering over the question."

"Did you love me?"

"From the first moment."

"On my part, I was extremely jealous of the man you chose."

"I didn't want to choose but be chosen. I wasn't honest with myself, I am ashamed to admit. It's funny but the word 'jealous' makes me happy."

"Occasionally I thought about kidnapping you to an uninhabited island."

"That would have been a crime."

"Yes, it is, but is there anyone who hasn't imagined of committing a crime at least once in life? Even as an adult, I had such a dream once in a while. You know, even when I lived and had children, I secretly hoped that news of my love affairs would reach you somehow. I knew I was living a meaningless life and despised myself. It was remorse. Our life seems to be a succession of guilt and shame."

"God teaches us guilt and shame."

"I was ashamed of myself and our society. I've fought against it and found it nearly impossible to overcome it. And the famous line of Yoon Dongjoo's poem, 'Till the day I die, no spot of shame I shall have,' sounded too much. So are Mencius' words. Is it possible to have no spot of shame for a person with conscience? Unless he be so obtuse as.... What is life anyway? Every day we eat the flesh of other creatures. By eating it we usurp someone else's happiness."

"Are you going to rail against the society and the age as you did when you were young?"

"No, that's not what I'm trying to do. Do you want to hear the truth? When I was with you, I felt ashamed of myself for wanting to conquer you physically. And when I wasn't ashamed, I'd yearn for you while despising my cowardice at the same time."

"Now that I've heard it, I feel strange. This is so confusing. I'm uncomfortable with the idea that for all these years I've been a torment on your conscience."

"What a misinterpretation!"

"Let me tell you about an old relative of mine. She had been married less than three years when the Korean War broke out and her husband was kidnapped to the north. Raising her posthumous son and waiting for her husband, she grew old. When her son became a businessman and obtained an American citizenship, he went to North Korea to meet his father. The father in the meantime had married another woman and raised a family. Though he was a poor old laborer, the son was happy to meet him. When they parted, the son asked his father if he had anything to say to his old wife. The father replied, 'I am a sinner, what can I possibly say except I am sorry.' He felt guilty, sure. But his wife who had grown old after years of loneliness and yearning, fell ill after hearing her husband's news. What a life! She said she wouldn't have felt so betrayed and so empty if he had written her a short note, if not a tearful letter."

"Why are you telling me this?"

"And the daughter of my high school classmate. After her mother died of uterine cancer, her father married the woman who had taken care of her. Her own mother had been so frugal that she would not even eat a whole egg, but the new woman cooked sumptuous food. The daughter ate the food but was literally sick in the stomach because of the guilt."

"...."

"Why is life such an endless cycle of love and hate, betrayal and guilt?"

"Wait a minute there. Are you now accusing me?"

"Maybe."

"In that case, let me recite a few tragedies of life. A friend of mine had his ear drum torn apart in a fist fight with his wife. Another friend was driven out of his home after squandering all his money on a young mistress. A couple became paralyzed of a stroke, simultaneously. Other friends have lost their minds; one of them, a high school principal, came to a reunion party without his pants on. Finally, a Christian minister cast a curse upon his family at his death-bed. Shall I go on?"

She said nothing.

"See? You instantly get depressed."

"No, no. I am all right. I realized long ago that we think we live, laughing, crying, playing, but, in truth, we don't live. We 'are lived' by some power. As you said, we are forced to eat only the food on the table, prepared by our fate. Just like the children who have to do their homework; we do our homework, it's called life."

"Our life is what we make of what's been given to us. If we become better at solving problems, our homework becomes much harder."

"In this life of ours, what is really true and what is not?"

"I don't know. The older I get, the more confused I am. Whatever it may be, all I want is...to be free of all the things restricting me. Really I want to be free, completely liberated! Is it possible? After all the years of pain, I think we deserve it. There's nothing more important than life itself."

"Then, where do I stand? And your meeting with me?"

"You are standing right in it."

"But don't you know love binds you?"

"All right then, let it. I want to be simple. Simplicity itself. After all the years, I've finally realized I want to live, simply live with no frills, however long my remaining days may be."

"And you still want something new?"

"Yes. Even if I had only one hour left to live, I'd want it because that's the principle of life."

"You are alive, living, like this, beside me."

"Yes, here and now."

There is only a sweet silence.

"Ah!"

"What?"

"Look at them?"

"What?"

"Beautiful flowers in gorgeous bloom!"

"Shall I get them for you?"

"Oh, no, no. Leave them be. They are exquisite."

"Indeed they are."

"What are you gazing at so intently?"

"The sun. It's gorgeous."

"You are exactly the same as before."

"In what way?"

"Falling into sentimentalism whenever you see the setting sun."

"It is bright but soft."

"And a little sad."

"I always see tear drops in the setting sun. It almost hurts my heart."

"Because it has done its day's work and is about to fade into darkness."

"The evening sun looks like it's lying down slowly in weariness. Every time I see it I am moved."

"I guess, everything is melted into it.... But getting teary-eyed at it...aren't you a little girlish?"

"Do you think we ever get past our childhood?"

"I guess not."

"As old as we are, I don't think we will ever grow out of our childhood."

"That means you are still young."

"You are laughing at my childishness, aren't you?"

"Of course not. The minute we lose the heart to be moved, we are dead."

"At the center of all the things that had moved me was you. You still move me. If I stay at your side, I'll always be young. My love for you is as natural as my breathing."

"May I...kiss you on the forehead?"

"Please do."

"Not in public."

"Too shy?"

He coughs.

"Goodness, you are coughing."

"Are you cold? Shall I give you my jacket?"

"Thank you. Now, I'm fine."

"Let's go before it gets dark. Aren't you tired?"

"No."

"Really?"

"Really"

"Shall we go to a restaurant?"

"Yes, I would like that. With candles. I'm not well enough to eat at a restaurant, but I'd love to look at you in candle light. I wish the soft warm candle light would restore us to our youth."

"But I'd rather choose now than my young days of sorrow over losing you."

"Really?"

"Yes."

"Look, the setting sun is truly beautiful."

Tears begin to fall from her eyes.

"Are you crying?"

She turns her head away from him.

"Why are you crying? Did I say something wrong? Tell me, please."

"Oh, never mind. It's nothing."

"How can you say that? You're crying."

"It's nothing."

"Nothing?"

"Life is so achingly beautiful that it's sad."

"That's nothing to cry over."

She can no longer hide her tears.

"My, you are sobbing."

"So what?"

"You are right. So what?"

"Ha, ha."

"Are you laughing now?"

"I'm laughing because you look so cute when you cry. I'll give you my handkerchief. Wipe your tears. Oh, er, where's my handkerchief? Surely I had it. It must be my amnesia."

"In more learned words, geriatric dementia."

"You are cruel!"

"Oh, here it is. Look, this is a magician's handkerchief. Madam, what do you wish for? A dove? A rabbit? A goose? Or, a young man? See, you are smiling now."

"Is this handkerchief clean?"

"Of course, it is. My grandchildren call me 'Clean Grampy.' I wash things quite well."

"Really?"

"Yes."

"Did you wash this, too?"

"Yes. Remember I used to be a self-sufficient working student? I even ironed it."

"Yes, you were always hardworking and diligent. Look. You dropped your memo-book."

"Where?"

"Here."

"Thank you. My reflexes have dulled."

"Do you still have the habit of scribbling in your memo-book?"

"Yes. Do you want to see what I wrote yesterday?"

"What kind of writing?"

"It's nothing to speak of."

"You just asked me if I wanted to see it."

"Oh, it's really nothing."

"If you don't read it to me, I won't budge from here."

"Then, you read it yourself."

"Well, I need my glasses."

"Ha, ha."

"What's so funny?"

"A young girl wearing thick glasses."

"Don't make fun of me, just give it to me."

"Umm, it's really nothing."

"Here we go.

I hear the wind.

I hear the curtains flapping,

Window panes rattling,

I hear the wind swishing.

The wind crashes into things,

Things crash into the wind.

Their sound is the sound of resistance.

Is the wind crashing into things or

Are things crashing into the wind?

Makes no difference.

Then, why do I sit here trying to tell them apart?

Probably because I see an analogy in the relationship between the wind and Time.

But Time does not exist at standstill.

If change is a flow,

We are flowing, not Time.

But we say Time flows.

I am getting nervous as I watch my clock,

As if Time existed in the clock.

I hear the wind.

I hear people, like waves.

I hear the universe, like Time.

As if they had a place to go.

As if...."

You didn't finish."

"As you know, our life itself remains unfinished. Who on earth dies after putting a period to his life?"

"Who knows whether we have a place to go to."

"No one."

"Then, won't you put your arm into mine?"

"My arm?"

"Yes. Let's link our arms, then our shadows will merge into one."

"Yes, our last shadows."

My Wife's Boxes

by Un Heekyong

I go into my wife's room for the last time. The light blue wall paper, the German-style desk and an easy chair against the wall, and the indescribable fragrance floating among the furniture and, of course, the boxes. My wife has many boxes. One box holds in it an embroidered tablecloth she made and another a bundle of letters. All of the letters were yellowed with smudged ink spots. I have never seen a recent letter addressed to her. One box contains an infant cotton shirt that a friend of hers sent her prematurely when my wife became pregnant. She miscarried the baby in the third month and has never conceived again. But she kept everything as if her boxes were containers of her life's scars. People remember their pain by the scars on their body, but my wife seems to preserve all of her scars in her boxes.

I open the box on top and see a cheap necklace of seashells. I remember we bought it in a seaside town on our honeymoon. I also remember the blue sea mirrored in her eyes and her singing laughter, so lovely that I wanted to scoop it like sand in a basket.

She is gone now. She does not exist anymore. As her desk drawers are tightly sealed, her yellow pencil with the eraser tip is irretrievably lost. My wife is gone.

Tomorrow the movers will pack everything neatly in their boxes, then my wife's room will also be gone.

The landlady said, "Why move now when the rent is going up? Your lease won't be up for quite some time yet. Oh, perhaps something wonderful has happened to you that I don't know of?" I had nothing to say to her. Now that I look back on

167

it, I must have decided to move because I knew how painful it would be to wait for my wife's return. If her room is emptied and gone, will it mean that I don't have to wait for her anymore? Of course not, but I felt I just couldn't sit and do nothing. I had to do something, anything.... The first thing I must do would have been to curse her. I had to hone my knife of vengeance, so I would never, ever forgive her. I had never thought I would use a knife against her. When I whet the knife against the stone, vile dark water will seep out, dampening the gray stone, and seep into the earth. I will splash the stone with clean water and inspect the shining silver blade. I will watch it and relish the moment. How will I ever forgive her?

Slowly I walk to the window. As I move, that indescribable fragrance rises again. It smells like an insect repellent long forgotten in a drawer or a cheap foreign perfume splashed on artificial flowers. It is certainly not the smell of my wife.

Beside the window sits her easy chair, the only furniture besides her desk set. She used to take long naps in the chair, which she said was deep and comfortable, like a grave. With her knees drawn up to her chin, she slept like a worm snugly nestled behind a large leaf.

I remember all the nights when I could not enter her tightly-balled body. "Listen, we are man and wife. This is a very natural act." Then, she would kiss my cheek and whispered, "I know. I really want to be good to you." But her body was still closed and cold. In order to warm up her body, I had to rub her breasts, ever so carefully. After a while, I would enter her. "I love you," she whispered weakly as she held my shoulders in her arms. Her eyes would be wet. And then what did she do later?

I pace around the room. I stomp on every part of it. Last week I left her there. I couldn't bring myself to kill her, but leaving her there was pretty much like killing her.

I decide to come out of her room. As I go near the door, it dawns on me what the smell is. There on the inside of the door hangs a dried-up wreath with a small pack of potpourri. That's where the smell comes from. Like a body after the spirit leaves, the wreath is a shadow of time, a taxidermized flower.

Her room is a tomb. I step out. She is gone. Even her shadow is no longer there.

It was March last year when we moved to this new suburban city. We had been living in an apartment south of the Han River near an infertility clinic. Since the rent was cheaper in the new suburb, we could get a three-room apartment and my wife was very happy to have her own room. The apartment was clean, so was the air, and we could even see the trains go by. But, the truth was that she was happy about not having to go to the infertility clinic. All in all, the new suburb seemed to offer us a change and a less bleak life.

In the beginning, my wife made quite a few plans for our apartment, new curtains, new plants, new shelves....

"What color of curtains would you like?" she asked one night as I was just changing TV channels with a remote control. A group of dancers faded away and the next scene was that of a man sitting in a rose-patterned sofa and the same rose-patterned curtains were in the background.

With my eyes glued to the TV screen, I said, "How about rose-patterned fabric?"

I pushed a button and there appeared an office scene.

"How about blinds? They look so clean."

"I don't like them."

Her tone was unusually decisive, so I glanced at her. She was peeling an apple with her head down; her slender neck caught my eye. I turned back to the TV and suddenly realized that my wife didn't like anything that reminded her of a hospital. When she handed me a piece of apple, her face was placid enough, and we both watched the last news.

The news anchorman's lips went up in corners in a smile while the words "Sweet Rain" loomed up. The man went on to say that the whole nation was anticipating "a shower of goals" in an international soccer match to be held that night. He was doing a good job associating the weather and the game. Then the man looked down to read his written script, and when he looked up, his expression had turned grave to fit the nature of the next news item. In the right corner of the screen was the title, "America Plans to Remove the Three Kims." "In 1980, under the direction of the American government, Mr. Shin Hyunwhak had led ..." were the lead part of the news. The newscaster emphasized that the news was his broadcasting company's spectacular scoop. But the next moment, President Y. S. Kim, one of the three Kims, appeared and gravely announced that he would try to be an "Environment President."

"All three presidents I have known spoke in the same tone and manner. The minute I hear such manner of speech, I automatically think the speaker is a great man," my wife said. I picked up another piece of apple without a word to her.

The next news item was about badgers and cuckoos. They were taken care of in the winter, then returned to the Demilitarized-zone in the spring. "Protection of Wild Animals" was the title.

My wife began to talk to herself, ignoring me.

"I am not sure if my memory is correct, but I think I read somewhere that animals should be released into the wilds in winter when there is no food, so they will learn quickly how to survive and be wild. And where did I read about an American man who was arrested for killing a rat for eating his tomatoes? It must be in one of those overseas news snippets. Animal protection people were up in arms against the man. Anyway, he wasn't released until they passed a law that an animal which has caused damage was to be exempted from legal protection."

I didn't say anything but thought to myself that those rich Americans had nothing better to do than get excited over a dead rat. I turned my attention to the news about stock markets.

I turned off the TV, grabbed a weekly news magazine and went to bed. My wife washed the plates and came into bed. I pulled her cold hands inside my pajama crotch. She smiled. I loved her. I thought I knew everything about her.

She had finished a two-year secretarial course at a junior college, but she said she didn't remember anything she had learned. Originally, she had wanted to go to an art school. All through her high school senior year, she went to a small private art institute situated on the third floor of a small wooden building. The classroom was very cold. Because of the coal fume, a window had to be open even in winter. She sat beside the window, her right cheek burning from the steam of the boiling water on the stove, her left cheek freezing from the cold air. Despite all this, she sketched and drew. She gradually got used to the fume. Sometimes, she would place a cup of hot water on the window sill and wait for the water to cool. Then she took her headache pills with the lukewarm water.

As in every year, the college entrance exam day was freezing cold. Her mother had knitted a turtleneck sweater for her to wear that day, but her mother's ineptitude had made the neck too tight for her head to go through. When she finally managed to put it on, she felt as if someone were choking her. She couldn't move her head. All her blood seemed to rush to her face, but her mother seemed happy.

In the exam room, she began to paint in watercolor when her headache became unbearable. She heard water dripping

171

somewhere. In fact, at the end of the hall outside the room, there was a row of faucets. All the examinees would bring in water from there to use for watercolor painting. She kept hearing dripping water and decided that someone hadn't turned off one of the faucets tightly enough. "May I go out and stop the dripping water?" she finally asked the proctor, who nodded at her with a doubtful expression on his face. No faucet was dripping, though. She came back to her seat, but the noise continued to bother her. At the third time, she didn't even ask the proctor, who kept staring at her. She rushed to the door and began to pull at it. The door wouldn't budge. The proctor, his face full of pity, said, "The door is open," but instantly sensed what was happening to her. He patted her shoulders gently and whispered, "Now, now, try to relax." He then led her back to her easel and helped her resume her painting. Suddenly, she flung her brush down and screamed, "Stop the dripping water!" She clawed at her sweater neck. "Please, somebody shut off the faucets!" "Please, close the door, please."

She later woke up in a room at the hospital of the college she had applied for. "Entrance Exam Stress" was the doctor's diagnosis and she was ordered to rest in bed for several days. She slept most of the time and woke up to take more sleeping pills. For days, she slept and woke surprisingly at the pill-taking time. She had once mentioned a novel called "Bell Jar" whose author's name she said she couldn't remember. A man was conditioned to salivate at the sound of a bell like Pavlov's dog.

My wife said her failure at the exam didn't much affect her life. She finished a junior college, got a job in a small trading company and earned a comparably low salary fit for a lowly office girl. She saved a little money, met and married me. She was a completely ordinary girl. I, too, was an ordinary husband in every way except in food. I was a little finicky. My wife was not an imaginative cook, but good enough to make the bean sauce soup just right without a fish smell from dried anchovies in it, to grill fish crisply without burning, and to make egg rolls soft. She was neat, too. Reserve batteries, brushes, and tools were always where they should be. Fluffy towels were placed in the bathroom and ice trays without food odors were in the freezer.

She didn't care for going out or having people come to our place. My parents had moved to Canada to join my older brother the year I married. For her, having no in-laws to meddle in our life was a boon. She had two friends, the one who had sent a baby shirt prematurely and another, an insurance saleswoman. There were occasionally people who had the habit of showing exaggerated friendship to anyone and those who had an ulterior motive, to visit her. But, after we moved, she didn't give our new telephone number even to her two friends.

Alone in the apartment, she would do household chores or read newspapers and magazines. She liked reading in her room at her desk, and she read indiscriminately. Her reading wasn't particularly to improve herself because she remembered very little of what she read or she often misinterpreted them to suit herself. And she seemed to know this. As when she mentioned "Bell Jar," she always began uncertainly, "I am not sure my memory is correct...." She would put the finished books in boxes and shut the lids over them instead of keeping their contents in her head. The rest of free time, she slept.

Occasionally, I would call home from office to get no answer. "How can anyone sleep so deeply, huh?" I would ask.

"When I look down from our veranda, I get sleepy," she said.

Everything in sight was always the same, she said, the neat square windows, the picture-perfect playground, benches, lined parking lots, and trees. Even people looked the same, wearing about the same clothes and carrying the same vinyl shopping bags. The sky had about the same uninteresting color and the air smelled the same. In this new suburb, there were no pedestrian roads because they were blocked by tall apartment buildings. "When I go out for a walk, there is no road to walk on, so I came home," she used to say. "Going back and forth on the automobile road tires me and makes me sleepy."

She slept unusually deeply. She slept when she was sick, when she was worried, or when she was angry. One Sunday several days before we moved, I got angry at her when I found the economy and finance section cut out from the Sunday paper. She said she needed the story on the back of the section and made no attempt at apology. "Shut up," I shouted. I had just been appointed the head of a new project and was unusually nervous. I had no room to be tolerant. Without a word, she began vacuuming and I snatched a wind-breaker and rushed out.

I saw a beauty shop sign and went in to have a haircut. Feeling better, I bought some eclairs, her favorite, at a bakery before coming home. I rang the doorbell, again and again, to no avail. My keys were in my coat pocket. I rushed to a public phone and called, but there was no answer. I ran back and rang the next-door neighbor's bell, so I could climb from the neighbor's veranda to mine. I found, however, the gap between the two was too wide to jump over. I called home several times from the neighbor's living room, but there was no response. My heart began to pound and my hands shook as I called the key store. While waiting, I dialed home repeatedly. The key man said he couldn't unlock and asked me if it would be all right to smash the lock. I was then about to dash to the veranda to make a death-defying leap. I could have plunged to death from the eighth floor. After all the hullabaloo of smashing the lock, kicking in the door, I dashed in, only to find my wife sleeping soundly on the sofa, balled up in fetal crouch, a few steps from the door.

Since then, whenever I see her sleeping in her easy chair, I think of that day. The way she slept beside the tightly closed boxes reminded me of her refusal to open herself to the world that had hurt her.

One morning, she complained, "Everything dries up in our apartment!" She was holding a bowl of rice so dry that the rice grains were hard as sand. The soy sauce had evaporated leaving black salt granules in the small bowl. Apples get wrinkles overnight. "I think the cement walls suck moisture out of everything, including me. In the morning, I feel my bones rattling for lack of water in my body."

"Maybe because we don't air out our apartment often enough," I said by way of consoling her, and suggested that we get an aquarium with a few tropical fish in it. My wife jumped at my suggestion. "You are right. I saw on television that an aquarium loses one hand-length of water every day in an apartment. Cement walls are not walls really but water-suckers. They will suck water out of even water pipes."

On a Saturday I bought a vaporizer, but my wife didn't bother to open the box, because, I knew, it reminded her of a hospital. I was disappointed but said nothing. Some things are better left unsaid to make family life less irritating.

My wife had the habit of telling me trivial things in which I had no interest. "You know that kindergarten beside the supermarket? For nature studies, they raise a rooster and hens, but the rooster crows in broad daylight instead of at dawn. I was stepping out of the supermarket when I heard the crowing. I was so surprised. Our ecological environment had changed so much that even cocks don't have to wake up early, it seems. They say dogs and cats now get along as well." I would nod a couple of times to her such prattle without taking my eyes from the television news or a weekly news journal.

Our life went on more or less smoothly. My wife's daily routine seemed to have changed little from before. There were yet no curtains for the windows as spring changed into early summer, but I didn't complain. It was about this time that the woman moved into the empty apartment next to ours.

One afternoon I came home and was surprised to hear a dog barking.

"New people moved in today," my wife explained.

"The husband is stationed in a foreign country and the wife lives here with their two sons."

The dog kept barking.

"It's going to be noisy around here."

My wife hung my coat and pants in the closet and handed me a well-ironed cotton slacks and a polo shirt.

"The dog has been barking ever since you came home. The sound of the elevator seems to make him bark."

My wife didn't seem to mind the barking. She had never paid attention to anybody or anything in the neighborhood, but after a visit to the next-door apartment, she began to change.

"We had a neighborhood monthly meeting today, and afterward the woman invited me to her place for a cup of tea. You know, that apartment is so packed I couldn't see how they manage," my wife said.

"Really?"

"Right from the foyer there were an umbrella stand, a letter holder, a key rack...then in the living room, a sofa, stools, a rocking chair, a corner cabinet, a home bar, and so on. The rice cooker was covered with an embroidered coverlet. There was no empty space on the walls, either. Wicker ornaments, bread ornaments, clay dolls. She must have gone to all those hobby classes."

"She must like to decorate her home," I said and turned on the TV.

"She said it was her nature. She can't stand empty space."

"Really?"

"Yes. She has already signed up for massage and swimming lessons. She said she keeps those dogs for the boys because she goes out often." My wife suddenly fell silent and sat there pressing the sofa corner with her fingers. Then, she looked up, her arms crossed in front of her as if to protect herself.

"Both of the dogs are little puppies."

"There are two?"

"Yes."

"She said she got them when they were only three days old. The boys tied them together with a long iron chain to the door knob. They did that because the puppies spilled milk and had to be punished. The dogs were so tightly wound that they couldn't budge an inch."

My wife went on to say that the frisky dogs were so playful that they didn't know they were tightening their own chains even more until all they could move were their heads. I imagined the hyperkinetic dogs and found it rather amusing, but my wife's face turned sad.

"They loved each other so much that they were choking each other's necks," she said. According to her, the dogs were very different. One was plump with shiny fur while the other was scrawny and its fur was patchy. When my wife went near them, the plump one wagged its tail happily but the thin one sidled away a little and finally bared its little teeth. At that moment, one of the boys, a fifth-grader, came out with cookies in his hands. The happy dog immediately tried to move to him whereas the unhappy dog was unwillingly dragged by its pal, resulting in getting its chain digging deeper into its neck.

Cookies were thrown in front of the plump dog, but the thin one still resisted. The boy kicked the contrary dog and said, "You unpleasant cur, if you want to live, try to change your attitude." Then the boy went in his room and slammed the door. After telling this story, my wife covered her face with both hands as if in pain.

I tried to console her.

"Boys are boys. Don't cry over such a small matter."

"It's not that."

"Then why? Because you feel sorry for the dog?"

She shook her head, stood up, and went to the kitchen to prepare dinner.

That night she gently pushed her hand under my pajamas and began to rub my stomach and my nipples. Immediately I began to warm up, and my crotch got heavier. I threw down the news magazine I was reading.

But, her body remained cold, as always. Her arms around my neck had strength in them but her lower body felt cold and unresponsive. The minute my hand slid sown and touched her inner thigh, she urgently whispered, "I love you." Her eyes were closed, her eye-lashes wet and tangled. She urged me, "Please come inside me, please." Her skin was soft but her vagina stayed closed. There was no wetness. Once I entered her, however, she was warm and inviting. She said later she was happy to see me satisfied.

When I came back from the bathroom, she blurted, "You haven't given up on babies, have you?"

We had been avoiding the subject. It was the first time she herself brought it up. She had gone to the infertility clinic and done everything she was told to. But it had never occurred to me to ask her whether she wanted a baby. In fact, I had never asked myself, either. I simply assumed that life would be better if one had all the necessary parts.

"I thought about why I have failed to conceive," she said, looking up at the ceiling. "I know why."

She knew the reason? Even the specialists couldn't find it out. Without a word, I lay down beside her. She began to tell me about an American movie she had seen more than ten years ago. As always, her story began with her customary "if my memory is correct."

The story goes like this. There was a family. The father was a wanderer. The hard-working bitter mother raised their three children. One day the mother died and the children were sent to an institution. The father learned of the news and came to claim the children, but he was jobless and drunk. The manager of the clean and well-run orphanage despised him and said in a cold correct manner that the children would be better off at the place. The father loved his children and was willing to give up his freedom such as it was. He began to fight back. Though his efforts were doomed from the beginning, he continued to try to get back his children. He tried to reform himself by getting a job, though each time he was fired very soon. After several years of bitter struggle, he at last emerged at the door of the orphanage in a neat but threadbare suit and a cheap tie. But, alas, it was too late. The children had been scattered everywhere. No one knew of their whereabouts. The father was crushed. He begged every concerned office for some documents or clues. He was kicked out of many orphanages. Finally, he "found" his children who had run away to no-man's land. One had been beaten to death by his foster parents. Another became an autistic, completely lost to the world.

"The third one was...castrated at a boys' home."

"What a horrible story," I said half-heartedly, at a loss as to how this story was connected to her infertility. I sat up and lit a cigarette.

"I was castrated, too," my wife said quite sharply. She blinked her eyes at the smoke.

"The boy was castrated in order to cut off the bloodline of a criminal. So was I castrated because of my bad blood."

"At a boys' home?" I couldn't suppress sarcasm. My wife was not logical enough to carry on a long debate, but she tried to explain herself.

"That's not what I mean. According to the theory of natural selection, people like me are made to be weeded out. Only people with superior genes survive and prosper."

Filled with pity for her, I touched her breast, but she pushed my hand away.

"Those puppies next door, I think the weak one will die of hunger. It will hang onto the plump one and harm it, too, by not dying soon enough. The shameless cur! Why don't dogs kill themselves?" Her tone was so unlike her.

A short quiet minute later, she stood up and went to the bathroom. She looked like a sleep-walker, her steps accurate but empty. When she returned to bed, her eyes were red. I thought she had always put away her pains in her boxes, but she apparently had not. Perhaps she needed a change, I thought, and decided to let her associate with the frivolous woman next door.

The woman had a car. In a suburb where there was no road for pedestrians, to own a car proved that the woman was "superior," at least according to my wife's theory. The woman took her to department stores, discount outlets, lunch counters and noodle shops in the basements of shopping centers. As the weather warmed, their visit to "week-end farms" became more frequent. One Saturday, they came home later than I did. I had done my night shift overnight and came home later than usual.

I took every other Sunday off. Even on the Sunday when I stayed home, my wife went off with her to the opening of a new department store and came back with things we didn't need. Those things were fad products or cheap imitations my wife used to look down on. She said the potpourri was the woman's present.

"Why did she give you a present?"

"There's no reason."

I remembered the heavily made-up face of the woman who drove a more expensive car than mine.

My wife's answer was naively simple to my sarcastic question. To me, there was no such thing as "a gift for no reason."

"You are the one who gets favors by riding in her car. You ought to give her a present."

My wife stopped fingering the gift and stood up.

"She likes me. Isn't it reason enough?"

"She likes you?"

"Yes."

"Why?"

My wife bit her lips and started toward her room. Then she turned around and spat out, "Because she is lonely."

She seemed so desperate that I couldn't say anything. Holding the cheap gift in her hand, she glared at me, as if expecting some sort of contrary response from me.

"Are you lonely, too?"

"No."

Her answer was definite. She went in her room to hang the potpourri and came out triumphantly. She began to peel potatoes as if not to rile me further. More than ever, I realized she needed something, anything.

The next day was a drizzly Monday. Standing in a crowded subway, I seriously searched for something to fill a void in her life. First thing I did when I got to my office was to call the infertility clinic and my wife who, to my surprise, acquiesced meekly. I was quite pleased with myself for having found a pretty good prescription for her.

The day of our appointment at the clinic, I took the day off from work and left home with her. It was an invigorating spring morning in May. Light green hills were dotted with white and pink flowers in the translucent sunlight. I used to see them on my way to work, but I felt different that day.

Out of nowhere a brand new white sports car cut in in front of me. I stepped on my brakes when another car, a red one, plunged in. Both cars had young drivers in their early twenties. They wore bright new modish clothes and so did their young mates. They slid in and out of lanes, finally occupying a parallel lane each and slowed down.

The red car window opened. A light green blouse sleeve stuck out amid long wind-blown hair. The woman seemed to toss something to the white car. A woman's bare arm came out of the white car and shot something back to the other car. In a minute, I could see that they were shooting a water gun at each other while the male drivers drove on playfully. All four of them were giggling like little kids. On top of the cars were ski-racks, and I assumed there would be in the trunks ice-boxes of beer, fruits, and picnic foods.

Every morning I drove my car in a hellish traffic jam on this same street where these two sports cars were playing as if they owned the road. I drove every day as if forcibly dragged by an unknown hand while these young people danced to their own music.

I was amazed at the street being used this way. At the next signal, they made a left turn and entered a grassy side road leaving me on the hot asphalt. Then they disappeared behind a bushy clump. There were flowers all around the bushes.

I glanced at my wife who was intently watching the two cars until they were no longer visible.

"I'd like to go down that road someday," she said.

Her voice was tinged with despair as if she were excluded from such privileged people who could drive on such a road.

Glancing at her, I said, "We will do just that one Sunday."

"Before the spring goes by."

"Okay."

She was quiet for a while before she breathed a deep sigh.

"I've always wanted to go there whenever I passed by it."

"Have you been near here before?"

"Once in a while. If you go further in that direction, there is a building called The Central and South American Cultural Center."

She said ruefully that she had never gone into the place. Apparently the next door woman wasn't interested in such places. Past the Cultural Center, there is a Buddhist temple, in front of which stands a traditional restaurant where, she said, the woman and she had lunch a few times. Then, they drove on past Kwangtan and had coffee beside a man-made lake. I almost blurted out if there were only the two of them, but my wife seemed to sense my intent.

"If you go to a suburban cafe, you see many middle-aged women."

I didn't say anything.

"They call home by cell phone to tell their children to do homework, talk about the books they read, their health clubs and jewelry. Some complained about the many ancestor worship services they had to prepare for, others said they made a lot of money because of the real-estate boom. And still others talked about some college professor's lectures that moved them to tears."

I glanced at her uneasily and found her expression unexpectedly forlorn.

"You know, sometime ago, the next door woman scraped a man's car in a department store parking lot. Though the scrapes were quite bad, the man said it was okay, but she insisted she wanted to buy him lunch and asked me to go with her. I didn't. She said she saw him several times, because he listened to her."

My wife looked more forlorn.

I remained silent. I needed will power to suppress my curiosity. Later, I found that my need for such a lot of will power was because of my suspicion. At the clinic, neither of us spoke. When her name was called, she answered meekly like an elementary school girl and walked to the doctor's room. Before she went in, she turned and gave me a look full of helplessness and desperation. I stood up, rubbed out my cigarette and drew a cup of coffee from a vending machine.

At my wife's ovulation times, I came home early, if at all possible. She seemed to find it hard but followed the clinic's instructions and accepted my semen calmly. One night while making love I found her eyes no longer got wet nor did she wind her arms tightly around my neck. Furthermore she no longer gave me such excuses as having cold symptoms or failing to take a shower beforehand. At a moment when my thrusting had gone into a frenzy, she had sometimes pushed me away and rushed to the bathroom like a pregnant woman with morning sickness. She no longer did that, either. I interpreted these as an indication that she was somehow regaining normalcy.

As the consequence of a personnel reshuffle at office, I had to take on heavier responsibilities and became much busier. I had little time to spend with my wife except when I had to meet her ovulation times. Gradually I adjusted myself to getting sexually aroused at regular intervals. In a word, I was a very adaptable type.

My wife seemed to get adjusted to our new routine. The next-door woman didn't seem to go out so often as before since her husband had returned to the Seoul headquarters of his company. There was no barking noise of the dogs, instead, I heard from time to time shouting of harsh words or some heavy things smashing into furniture. And yet, the next morning at exactly 7:10, I could see from afar the woman driving her husband to the subway station.

As the season turned into fall, my wife spoke less and less, her illogical statements becoming fewer, too. Our apartment was always neat and quiet. She would read at her desk, then take long naps in her easy chair.

The number of boxes containing her books remained the same, so I asked her why she hadn't bought any more books. She said she was now borrowing books from a neighborhood book-loaning store. In the meantime, magazines such as *Geo* and *Readers Digest* piled up in her room, their paper wrappers unopened. Apparently, she took longer naps.

Uneventful days went by slowly. I was increasingly trusted and given more responsibilities by the company where I had to face daily problems, not major but still stressful. When I came home, however, everything was in its proper place, my wife included.

There had been some small troubles: several nights in a row obscene phone calls bothered my wife so much that she cut off our phone cord; the decorative candles her friend had brought as a gift accidentally burnt our wedding picture; during one night somebody punctured the tires of my and some other people's cars, an incident that offered a chance meeting between me and the next-door husband. The man, with protruding cheekbones, didn't like the new suburb. He said he was astounded by the appearance within a few years of a brand new city with all the public facilities, even a man-made lake.

He said it was unthinkable in Europe. When he asked me how I liked living in the suburb, I told him I liked its quietness.

Besides these trivial incidents, there was one that was a little more serious. My wife suffered a burn one day when she spilled boiling water on herself. The burn was not serious but there were watery sores on it for several days, so I could not get near her. To my relief, it healed quickly.

One morning she handed me an all-weather coat to go to work. At the traffic signal, I sat in the car and felt suddenly how far the fall season had crept in.

It is spring again. Last week my wife and I passed by that road we had promised to travel last spring. There were light green leaves and white and pink flowers just as last spring. But I found myself glancing at my watch.

My wife, on the other hand, looked oblivious to the fact that soon we were about to go our separate ways.

Last winter was excruciating to us. From that dreadfully quiet November night, she has gotten much thinner. Once in a while I observed my wife sleeping soundly, all crunched up in her easy chair. She seemed to have gotten much smaller, but.... I had to send her away. I had to.

The last day of November was a blustery, drizzly day. I came home about nine o'clock and rang the bell several times before I opened the door with my keys. I looked into my wife's room but she wasn't there. The easy chair was empty. The entire apartment was sunk in heavy darkness. My wife must have gone out before dark, for there was no sign of anything being cooked in the kitchen. It was rare for her to do so, but there was no reason why she didn't have an emergency outing. I understood. I washed my hands in the bathroom, watched TV, and resolved to myself that even if she should come home late, I would understand her. But she didn't return even after eleven o'clock.

When the clock-hand passed 10 o'clock, I went onto the veranda several times to look down. At 11 I stood outside and smoked more than a few cigarettes, before I realized I should call someone or somewhere. I was stunned that my wife had disappeared and yet I knew no one to call. I went into her room where everything was in place as usual. On her desk was her lone yellow pencil, without so much as a piece of note. My wife used to tell me that she needed to hold the pencil in hand when she read books because it helped her understand them better. I had never seen her write anything with it, but it had somehow become much shorter now. Her boxes were neatly stacked according to size. Nothing was changed except for the barely noticeable layer of dust on the cover of the top box. It wasn't like her to leave dust on her things. In every room, there was nothing, no sign whatever that suggested any change in her inner life. In other words, any woman could step into this apartment now and live without causing a disruption. There was no odor of my wife anywhere. She vanished without a trace, but I knew absolutely no one to call who might give me a clue. What in the world gave me the idea that I knew everything about her?

I went out to the parking lot, as it was the only place I could think of going. The lot was full. I squatted down near a flower bed. A thin drizzle fell coldly on my head and shoulders but I didn't want to get an umbrella. A car was coming in. In the hazy headlight, the slanting rain drew clean lines. A man got off the car. It was the next-door man. The moment he recognized me, he asked, "Why are you out here, sir?" I mumbled, "Oh, uh," and stepped aside when his wife came into light. I was very happy to see her, but she averted her eyes as if she were afraid and on guard.

"My wife hasn't come home yet. Do you by any chance...."

The woman glanced fearfully at her husband and hurried into the building without a word to me. I knew there was something in her rude and unnatural behavior, so I walked slowly home and waited for her.

The woman came to me in about five minutes. She propped her door open and I did mine, too. She seemed terribly concerned about my wife; perhaps she needed such a facial expression to justify to her husband her visit to a man alone in the middle of the night. She sat on our sofa and dialed a number quite rapidly. It must have been a familiar number, probably a cell phone number. Several dialings, but no answer. More than ten minutes went by before she stood up. All I could do now was call the police station and hospital emergency rooms. But I didn't want this to go on some public record but end in a private mishap such as too long a visit with a friend, a late night movie, or even falling asleep in the last bus.

At first I didn't quite catch what she was saying because I was so desperate. In the middle of leave-taking, she suddenly stopped, closed the door, and said, "Please, please don't let this get to my husband."

"What? What are you saying?"

"At the front gate, turn left and you see a by-pass road. Go down a few blocks and you come to a bridge. Cross the bridge and turn right and go on, then you'll see a big neon sign, "Green Park." It's the corner room on the third floor. There are many bars and motels around there, so you won't have trouble finding it." I listened to her as I would to a savior and thanked her. She asked me again to make sure what she had just told me never got to her husband. It was a kind of a deal. I assured her, too relieved to resist or raise a doubt. She grabbed the door-knob, then turned around. Her eyes full of dread, she said, "It was all my fault." Her voice trembled. Her dread and anxiety were palpable. All of a sudden the word "Park" flashed its meaning to my consciousness and I grabbed her shoulders, so hard that my nails must have cut into them.

The by-pass was buried in eerie silence. An occasional car coming toward me lit up the wet road. As she said, the motel was easy to find. After I crossed the bridge, I saw high up in the air a red neon sign with a spa symbol. It looked like a red hot branding iron about to burn into the rump of a cow. I gritted hard. I wanted then and there to take it down and sear it into the white bosom of my wife. A scarlet letter on her.

The next-door woman had told me that the room was a special suite occasionally rented by someone. She didn't say she had used it herself. "Your wife doesn't have a car and the place is tucked far away from the main road. I was so worried about her. I had to tell you. It was my fault. She was dragged into it because of me. Just once she went with me, but he kept calling her. He bothered her so much that she cut off her phone cord.... Before you go to the room, please check the basement restaurant. She may be still there. She is not the sort...."

I went straight to the room. The door was open. It was dark inside. The empty TV screen cast a hazy moon light upon the bed. My wife was asleep alone. Her shiny hair spread seductively, her face pale white, she was in deep sleep. I snatched back the cover. She was naked. The darkness outside looked in leeringly on her naked body.

On the way home, she trembled uncontrollably and fell ill. It was a terrible cold. For days she lay in bed without swallowing so much as a drop of water, but I paid no attention. As she got a little better, she began to do cleaning and washing. She was almost transparently thin. I signed up for an early morning health club and an evening English class. Late at night when I opened the door, all the light would be on in the deserted apartment. Then, like a ghost, she would emerge from the kitchen or her room. Looking at her, I felt a searing anger and remembered her remark, "Why don't dogs kill themselves, I wonder."

We rarely spoke to each other. What gave me the idea that I knew her? I hated her. I didn't want to know what really happened that night and I hated myself for it. Her sleep became deeper. I suspected she took sleeping pills, but I said nothing. Once in a while, I would put my ear on her door to make sure she was only sleeping. Her breathing was irregular but went on. I wanted to seal her room completely to cut off light and air. Seal it with paper and industrial sealant.

Once in those long months, I really looked at her. As always I came home late, but my wife was nowhere. I knew she would be asleep in her room. I washed myself, changed into pajamas, and was about to turn on the TV when I abruptly decided to check up on her. As expected, she was sleeping, utterly lost to the world. I shook her violently. Her body on my finger tips felt like a skeleton, almost paper thin and airy.

She opened her eyes. By the light coming from the living room, she recognized me and gave a crooked grin. She got up and passed by me like a ghost toward the kitchen. She rinsed her hands and began to prepare dinner. She made my favorite bean-sauce soup with tofu, scallion, and made an omelet. She brought out cleanly dressed swordfish and grilled it. Her actions were accurate and orderly. She was completely oblivious to my close observation of her.

She set the table. She placed two full rice bowls, one each for me and for herself. She sat down and began to eat.

I saw how serene she was. She acted like this only when she wasn't herself. Serenity belongs to the person who is looking on the surface of the water because underneath it some fish may be gobbling up struggling shrimps.

She ate enthusiastically. Finishing her share, she stepped to the refrigerator to bring water. When she brought the full water cups, she looked at the table and stopped herself in surprise.

Picking up her empty rice bowl, she whispered, "When did I eat this?"

Indeed, last winter was very difficult for us.

The day we were to leave, she washed her hair. The telephone rang but I didn't pick it up. It kept ringing until my wife came to answer it with a towel around her wet hair. "Hello," she answered dryly. After that, she just listened. The towel got loosened and her long black hair cascaded down her back. She squeezed her hair with her left hand and sprinkled the water over a small plant beside the phone. She put down the receiver while intently observing the soil dampen slowly.

"Who is it?"

"A joke call."

y wife sat beside me. I helped her with the safety belt. She smiled as if we were going to the clinic. We drove on into a bright spring scene of green hills, farmers' fresh vinyl tents, and children playing. She watched all these, especially the two barred trucks, full of chickens. The chickens were so jammed up together that they couldn't move at all. A light spring breeze blew a few chicken feathers into the air.

She looked at everything with interest like a child on a field trip. Her pale thin hands were on her lap, looking like a pair of white gloves left on a theater chair. As if sensing my intense gaze, she turned to me. I pretended to look straight ahead. She looked down and slowly turned her eyes out of the window. At this moment, out of the blue, she let out a horrible scream. I grasped her shoulders.

"What is it? What?"

She calmed down. As if coming out of a nightmare, she blankly stared at me, then, at the truck in front of us, and mumbled, "All the chickens are gone." True, the truck was empty. "The chickens are all gone." But it was no mystery. There were two trucks, but the front one didn't carry any chickens from the beginning. She had seen only the loaded second truck. The trucks had changed their places.

No matter how much I explained the situation, she didn't seem to believe me. Silently, she rubbed her neck and grimaced as if in pain. In a little while, she dozed off.

She opened her eyes when we arrived there. As soon as she perceived that we had arrived at a strange place while she slept, she began to show extreme anxiety. She was like a kidnapped girl waking from a drugged, blind-folded stupor. She remained calm while I went through paper work. The sanatorium, situated deep in the forest, was a gray building like the suburban apartments and the infertility clinic. The sanatorium was more calming because it offered no false hopes. My wife would no longer be hostage to false hopes.

I drove out of the place following the tire marks I had made going in. There were red flowers all around. When I lowered the driver side window, a woodsy smell rushed in. I breathed in deeply. Ever since we arrived there, my wife hadn't met my eyes even once. "I didn't know there was such a place as this so near," she mumbled to herself.

On the way home I passed by the scenic country road I had promised to take my wife to, come spring. Could we have gone back to the way we were then? I shook my head.

Back home, I impatiently pushed the buttons on my remote control. Time dragged on. There was one short report called "The World Now," in which a man narrated a story of scientific discovery.

"On last Valentine's Day in a California biology lab, a male fly and a female fly had a fierce fight. The male fly kept approaching the female to copulate, but the female would butt him in the head. In the end, the female went so far as to kick the head of the male. Even after the male sprayed its semen, the female didn't conceive. The reason was found to be due to gene mutation. The research team found that the mutant gene affected the nerve system. The team called the mutant gene 'Dissatisfaction'."

My wife would have liked the story. I remembered our burnt wedding picture and the burn on her waist.

I went to bed before the final news came on, but didn't sleep well. Next morning I called a real estate office to look for a vacant apartment I could move in right away. I also called a mover.

The movers arrived right on time at 9 o'clock. One man put on his work-gloves, whistling a bright tune while another man asked me for my new address and my office number. Later I regretted that I hadn't looked around my wife's room for the last time. As I started up my car, I looked ahead and saw the next-door woman washing her car.

I began to drive out of the suburb but I felt nothing. The familiar green hills came into view, which reminded me that I had really left the new city. I was still numb. I drove into the left lane to make a left turn. There were only a few cars on the road. At the left-turn signal, I turned left and got on the grassy country road that my wife had so wanted to drive through.

The road was bent sharply, rough and dusty. My car shook violently, so I thought of backing out, when, out of nowhere, a huge mountain emerged. The mountain was covered with graves in eerie silence under a low sky.

I didn't stop. Sweat gathered in my armpits. There stood a signpost at the fork where the lane to the crematorium and the lane to the village met. I abruptly veered into the lane to the village and drove on. Only rows upon rows of graves stretched out to no end. Now, streams of sweat dampened my shirt and ran down my face. When I opened the window, dust rushed in. My car was reeling drunkenly.

Yes. I did everything for her. But how did she repay for my devotion? She is probably sleeping now. She will wake up for her medicine-time and go back to sleep. Awake, she does nothing but wait for me. She won't be allowed to leave the place without my consent. She is fine. By waiting for my visit, she shows her loyalty to me.

Today her room disappeared.

Far ahead, to my relief, I see an opening, a long, clean paved road.

The Unbearable Sadness of Being

by Kong Jeeyoung

I was fired. I had been informed of the decision a month before and cleaned out my desk last week. The entire process was carried out exactly as planned. The sales graph of our company had been dipping gradually and, finally, hit the bottom because of the general economic slump. It was decided that the company should adopt a more exotic brand name and produce a line of clothing befitting the name. Immediately a new generation of young designers, pageboy haircuts, shiny hairpins, miniskirts and long boots, marched in as we old timers with perm-harassed dull hair straggled out of the back door. In this field where fresh original ideas were the very lifeline, 30-year olds did indeed belong to the older generation. We the oldsters had been given a rather ambiguous title of "nonregular design consultants," which in truth meant part-time contractual employees. Strictly speaking, I wasn't fired but let go after the contract expired.

I went to the Accounting Office, presented my work sheet, a couple of days short of a month, and waited. A long-haired young girl, obviously a new graduate of a commercial high school, counted some paper money and coins to put into my pay envelope.

I entered the company soon after graduating from college, which means that I had been working there for nearly ten years. And those years have come to an end with the clinking of a few coins. Ten years. In those years, the fabric of all-weather coats changed from wool gabardine to silk, from silk to shiny metallic cloth. My first designs were produced with the label of "Shindo" which has now changed into a foreign label. I watched the young bookkeeper as calmly as I could. Though there was no mirror, I was conscious of a change in my facial expression caused by a sudden jab of pain in my chest. Absurdly, I thought I might be jealous of the girl. It was not for her young hair that looked like it had never been assailed by a permanent wave lotion but rather for her simple labor requiring no professional training.

The excitement and pride I felt when I first got a job, of making my own money, of being called a fashion designer, has slowly ebbed away. But when I was at her age, I used to say that I wanted a creative job. Now I was standing here waiting for my last pay. The inner creative core that made me what I was seemed to have seeped out. I had been to many overseas fashion houses and shows, read every fashion magazine available, all of which drummed into me just one motto, "forward into the future." I was like a person chasing a ball that always rolled one step ahead of me. I was panting but I kept running after the ball. Then, one day someone came and whispered to me, "Stop running, dear. The ball has gone up in the air. Now we need new people with wings." I was stunned.

The girl pushed a white envelope into my hand. An utter sense of loss enveloped me as if I were all alone in the world. It whipped through my empty heart. I hadn't felt this way even when I was divorced.

Holding down a desperate sense of loss, I counted, but not really counted, the money. The girl looked up quickly. I wondered about what I should say if she spoke to me, "You will drop by once in a while, won't you?" or "What are you going to do now?" but I was wrong. She merely tore off the receipt from the computer, handed it to me, and turned right back to her computer.

It was I who almost blurted out, "I'll drop by once in a while." But I knew I would never do that. The ball had gone high up in the sky and I was too heavy to fly. I had a child to raise, and a mother who had been hinting that she wanted to spend her last years with me.

I was a 33-year-old single mother with huge responsibilities, no career and no means of support. It was the last thing I imagined when I was a fashion student at university.

"Thank you," I said. The girl gave me a quick shadow of a smile. I left the Accounting Office and walked into the lobby. It was too late for lunch, too early for dinner.

The envelope with coins in it felt heavy in my coat pocket. All of a sudden I realized that the coat I had on was the same one I had worn on my first date with him two years before. The art gallery where we were to meet was closed, so I was standing outside when he arrived a little late. He looked at me up and down and around, and exclaimed, "This coat looks great."

"I designed it. I'll have you know that hundreds of women stand in line at stores to buy it," I proudly told him. That I might not be able to design anymore had never occurred to me.

After he had left me and we no longer kept in touch, I used to call him at the office, pretending to be a much younger friend, just saying hello. Then, a man, perhaps sitting in his chair and holding his telephone, hesitated a little and said, "You apparently don't know it. He is in Peru." Occasionally, the same man asked me if I wanted his telephone number in Peru. "No, no, it's not necessary. I just wanted to say hello. Thank you." On such afternoons, I had to struggle with a mysterious toothache in my love (wisdom) tooth. So, Peru became my toothache. Though I took four pain-killing tablets every two hours, the toothache didn't subside.

Outside the window, a ripe autumn filled the air. The gingko trees had already shed their leaves, covering the street with a thick golden carpet.

Mid afternoon and I had nothing to do. I had never had such uncomfortable leisure. On the street, in the subway, wherever

I happened to be, I used to closely observe what people wore and note the subtle changes in people's fashion preference. At times they were ahead of professional fashion specialists while at other times they were practically dragged on by a new fashion trend. To me, therefore, seasons changed with hiking skirt hems or widening of pants legs.

Time was not a flowing river to me, but rather a cascading torrent. Today, however, I stood on the street really looking at the autumn leaves as if the day were the first fall day I had ever encountered. The gingko leaves did not signify a new fashion direction but were just leaves. Blankly I turned my eyes to the few movie posters nearby. Since I had no intention of seeing any of them, I felt nothing.

Suddenly I had a strange awareness that someone was watching me. Perhaps a man I had loved millions of years before had come back to haunt me. I couldn't resist the overwhelming pull of the feeling and turned around. Among the rows of gingko trees, one tree caught my eye. It was an ordinary gingko tree but its spell was so powerful that I couldn't take my eyes off it. It seemed to say, "It's been ten years. I've been standing on this spot for ten years watching you, but you have begun to notice me just now." As if in response to my sudden awareness, the tree, though there was no stirring air, began to drop its leaves by the armful. I stood still and gazed at the falling yellow leaves. The figures in the movie posters began to come alive and move toward me. I couldn't move a muscle. The tree was giving me, me alone, armfuls of yellow gifts. Someone bumped into me and said "sorry" as he passed by me and entered a glass door. I was jolted out of my reverie.

Despite the dreary cold of autumn winds, I knew I'd never stoop to falling in love with a gingko tree. It was simply a fall season and trees were losing their leaves. It has been like this from time immemorial. Gingko trees had lived with dinosaurs.

A love-stricken gingko tree never sprinkled its leaves for a dinosaur, I was sure.

I began to descend the dark stairs toward the parking lot. To me, life had always been a steep downhill. After the divorce, I realized for the first time how awesome it was to make enough money to live for the next month. My child was growing fast and I had no other place to go to. There were only so many designers' jobs, only four seasons in a year, and people wore more or less similar kinds of clothes. Every year bright young designers were pouring out of colleges by the thousands.

Being over thirty made me feel like someone sitting at a table in a crowded cafeteria where everyone in line was practically expecting me to leave. But where else could I go if I stood up and left in hurt pride? I was so afraid of being fired that I refused to think about its possibility. I comforted myself that such a dire fate would never come to me. Like the legendary match-selling girl who had held onto three matches, igniting a match at a time, never counting what's left in her hand, I turned a blind eye to my eventual professional demise.

I wanted to stay with the company for a long time. Once in a while I felt like quitting for one reason or another, but when I thought of the old-age pension and forced savings plan, I knew I would be better off by staying on. Compromise, compromise, and I'd get old within the company. My talents would deplete, my eyesight would dim, but I would still hang on, struggling to keep up with young trendy consumers....

"Can you take care of my child's kindergarten tuition and my mother's dental bills?" I asked him long ago. I knew we would eventually end up doubting our relationship within a few years. Our love would have cooled. We would look at each other with unwashed sleep-laden eyes, and you would think of running away, away from everything. I used to make these ominous predictions and argue with him. I never let him get into my private life. I was the breadwinner of my family, and he was barely able to pay his own ever-rising rent. On top of that, he had a mother and younger brothers to support. That was why I asked, "What is Peru?" when he brought up the matter of going to Peru. He burst out laughing. Was Peru a magic kingdom where you could hide yourself? Besides, three years of overseas work there? Okay, let me make concessions here, and marry you. Then, you, my child, and I would travel to Peru pretending we had been a family from the beginning. You have your work there, but what about me? What can I do there? Can't go to an English language institute in Peru. Can't learn to cook Italian food in Peru and hope to open a restaurant some-day in the future. Furthermore, your mother and my mother would write us long sad letters always adding at the end a request for more money.

Three years of hiatus would put an end to my designer's career. I'd lose the touch. I've seen many of my older friends who followed their husbands overseas. When they came home, they had no jobs, nothing to do. I wasn't going to follow in their footsteps.... Peru? It was too far from here. He didn't say anything while I went on and on. He smoked up a whole ciga-rette without saying a word.

"I think I'll age quickly," I said. "When I get the first pay-ment of my pension, I'll buy a rocking chair and spend the whole day in it on my veranda. I'll see how slowly time goes.... Then I shall think to myself, what was all the hurry when things will end up this way anyway? I'll laugh at my youthful ambi-tion. But, until then, I'll cherish my dreams and go on. Maybe I'll become the head of my design department. I may even come to own my own brand."

He listened and quietly replied, "Life does not offer many things. Youth. Time. Love.... Life does not give you many chances at these. If you miss a chance at any of the three, for whatever reason, you are very foolish. You and I must open our eyes to the deeper meaning of life and nurture whatever little we get. Do you know how many people struggle with tears in their eyes to get a piece of happiness? What is most frightening to me is being swept on without knowing where we're going. In that rocking chair of yours, you'll someday weep over your loss."

I stopped myself briefly, but pretended to look out of the window, rather nonchalantly. I was the second daughter of a weak incapable father and have already experienced the steep downhill of life. My hesitation, or rather resistance, was not because he was a bachelor and I was a divorcee with a 2-year-old daughter. It wasn't because of social stigma, either. I simply hated the idea that he could, without consideration of my position, lightly ask me to go to a distant foreign country. Ages ago when I married my husband, we both thought, because we were young and in love, we would be able to work out anything we might face in life. We were naive, and this man now has the same kind of naivete that scares me.

Life is made of many scars. The color of a scar does not depend on money, and the shape of a scar is as varied as the faces of people. I knew this, but I acted contrary to my understanding. "Money seems the only important thing to you. I don't like that," he used to say. I knew that, too. I knew there were many things more important than money, but the truth was they were precious few. I had learned the value of money early. And lest I should forget, life gave me some hard bumps to remind me of it.

My marriage, too, eventually ended with an argument over money. We fought over the alimony and child support. It was far more naked and fierce than our fight over whether we should get a divorce. For the first time, I found how money-hungry my husband was. If I hadn't divorced him, I would probably have told my friends that my husband was indifferent to money.

My lover sat before me, talking about traveling, weaving hopes and dreams in a beautiful pattern. He scared me, because such a life might become possible only when I am old and gray in a rocking chair after years and years of making money. I thought I was too old to commit myself to love. I had no use for sentimentalism and sympathy. He told me about his unfulfilled college romance and his subsequent five years of foreign life where he said he dwelled long on his lost love. When he made the confession sorrowfully and shyly in a small shabby bar, I felt like yawning.

If he had married the woman, he might have enjoyed the five years of freedom, perhaps dancing happily. Love, marriage, it's no big deal. Eternity exists only at the moment it is pledged. I couldn't help giggling and nearly spilled my drink on my coat, the same coat I am wearing now. So I was undisturbed after he left.

"Every existence has its own sorrow," he insisted. "Every being has to shed its share of tears before it can really see what life is. You are not the only one. Nobody can stop your tears, but at least we can wipe each other's tears. We need someone who will wipe our tears for us. I want to be that tear-wiper for you," he said as he sat beside me in my car.

"I have too much to do to wipe your tears," I answered coolly. I didn't cry. For a moment I felt tempted maybe out of fear. It had occurred to me a few times that I might find some happiness if I went with him. Once a long time before I had gone to the appointed cafe and seen him from the door. He was poring over a newspaper, utterly oblivious to his surroundings. His serious profile was so attractive that my heart thumped. I felt I wanted to have his child. I quietly backed out of the cafe and walked around till my cheeks turned red in the cold wind. I went back much later than I had originally promised to meet him. I lied to him how busy I had been, too rapt in my work to notice time. I lied more animatedly than necessary.

I went down to the dark parking lot. It suddenly occurred to me that I should call my mother who was baby-sitting my daughter. I wanted to tell her I would be very late tonight, not because I had to hunt for a particular button, an unusual zipper or lace, in the East Gate or Kwangjang Market, or to survey in a department store what class or generation of people preferred what brand of clothing, but because I wanted to have this evening all to myself, and not to think about my child or my mother. My daughter will try to stay up for me, but she will have to go to bed. If I close my eyes, I can see her nagging her grandmother about a missing Lego piece (it was missing from the beginning). She will insist that she not go to bed until Mommy comes and will stand in the cold veranda. As the evening deepens, however, her eyelids will droop and she won't be able to hold them up. She will crawl into our empty bed. She will gradually learn that an empty space is a part of life. Also, the person you wait for doesn't necessarily come back as you wish. No matter how much Mother and Child may miss each other, their wishes sometimes don't come true.

I took out my cell phone. It must have been the loss of my job that I was confused enough to try to call from this underground parking lot. "No Service Area" showed up in red letters. Of course. From this subterranean cave, no one could communicate by cell phone. Unless wires are physically connected as in above ground phone system, cell phones are useless underground.

My life has become a "no service area." I have no place to escape to. My cell phone will be the first I may have to sell unless I get a new job right away or open a store of my own brand in South Gate Market, or marry a rich man. Next will be my car, parked right over there, followed by my daughter's first birthday gifts, her gold bracelet and gold ring.

I may have to move from a two-room rented space to a single room, then inevitably to a half-basement, dark and dank. Since he knows only my cell phone number, the only connection he has with me will be gone. The part of life where we tentatively tried to hold together will always be a "no service area." Then, in the end, I will have only myself to...sell. Haven't I been selling myself all these years?

I have tried to create, mix and match innumerable colors and shapes to find something new, something eye-catching, and something to satisfy the consumers. At first I wanted to become a designer to be happy, but as time went on, I did that in order to keep the title of designer.

Even when I watched a movie, what caught my eye was what the actors were wearing. On TV music shows, I only paid attention to the clothes the singers had on. I wanted to study the subtle advances in fashion in the clothes of the entertainers. I had become a designer in order to make a living, but now I live in order not to lose my designer's job.

"New," "Newer" were old words to me. In the first few years I was awarded a citation every year for designing clothes that sold well. Then, out of the blue, someone came to whisper to me, "Stop running. The ball has gone up in the air. These days balls sprout wings." And my career came to an end.

As I walked toward my car with my keys in hand, I saw a bright light sliding to the direction of my car. In an instant, I heard a crash. I didn't know what happened. The minute I saw a man get out of a car, I realized what had happened. He had crashed into my car. Oh, my God, now my car won't be worth one month's living expenses. Good things come one at a time, but bad things come in pairs and triples.

Slowly I approached my car and found its front part crumpled. I turned my face to the man and, to my astonishment, burst out laughing because the man had the looks of a gingko tree after all its leaves have blown off.

"It's nothing. A little bit creased," I said, pretending to be the most generous woman in the world.

"Look, the door opens. See? It's nothing."

"The floor was so slippery," the man said, faltering and incredulous at my reaction.

"Yes, the floor is slippery. I myself almost slipped," I emphasized by pounding my high heels on it.

I couldn't believe this sense of liberation I felt at the moment. I felt released and wanted to be as generous as I could be.

"It's nothing. Nobody died. It's all right," I wanted to reiterate loudly and repeatedly. It was a strange feeling.

"Shall we take care of this matter now, if you are not busy? Fortunately there is a garage nearby that I know well," the man said. He looked truly remorseful.

"No, I am not busy."

The man looked over at me and stood still in a frozen moment. I had an eerie feeling that I had had a similar experience before.

"Oh, that's good. Please follow me then."

The man might be a little over thirty. He began to drive and I followed him. When he turned on the right-turn light, I did, too; when he stepped on his brakes, I did on mine; when he gave a left-turn signal, so did I.

My car had many scratch marks, now with a crumpled door that still opened. Since I had begun to drive, I had traveled in numerous streets and back alleys, leaving as many varied marks and scars on my car. The first time someone had scratched my brand new car during the night, I was furious. The second time some unconscionable man had pushed my front door in and fled without leaving so much as a note, I took my car to a car-care center and asked tearfully to have it restored completely regardless of cost.

Other small accidents followed, but I no longer bothered to take the car for repair. I resorted to cursing whoever did damage to my car to get equal treatment from someone else. As days and months went by, I lost track of which scar was caused by whom, didn't care and didn't curse either. During all those years, I might have scraped a car or two and left the scene of crime. I knew the irate owner would have cursed me during sleepless nights.

I wouldn't have been surprised if the man had suddenly sped up or in the few seconds between an amber and a red light he had accelerated to shake me off. On the wide Kwangwhamun Street, however, he gave me insistent signals every time he changed lanes, which assured and comforted me. It was an overcast autumn afternoon. Under the heavy gray sky, the yellow of gingko leaves looked brighter. I found the one gingko who had given me an eye earlier. It was easy because there were more leaves piled up under it than under any other tree. I wanted it to ogle me one more time, but, alas, it was cool and indifferent. Embarrassed and out of spite, I drove slowly over the pile.

The man in Peru used to tell me that spring and fall were seasons of movement. One moving toward consummation, another toward enrichment. That was why in spring girls get restless whereas men become so in fall. Now that it is autumn, is he restless? In Peru, does he think about the darkening field of fall?

Along the stone walls of the Duksu Palace, white dressed brides and tuxedoed grooms were lined up for outdoor photo sessions. It would be a perfect place for a ball if there were waltz music. Next to them, kindergarteners in canary-yellow hats with canary-yellow backpacks sat in rows, looking up at their young teacher. Behind them, the wall, and above the wall, I could see beautifully colored leaves fluttering. Overhanging them all was the heavily grayish sky.

The man's car drove into a narrow side-street along the Palace wall, past the former courthouse, and stopped in front of a small car-care center. I stopped, too.

"Would you care for a cup of coffee while the car is being repaired?" the man asked. I was surprised and a little suspicious because usually the party that was responsible for the damage would pay and leave.

"Well, don't take it wrong. I am sorry for detaining you like this and I feel I shouldn't just pay and go."

My life-motto had been "everyone must have a way of their own" and this congenial man momentarily helped me put it aside. I went along with him, for there was nothing to do while waiting. If he lives his life like this, he is bound to be fired from his job. Maybe he was already fired. A man, who shows such an apologetic manner for a small error he makes, cannot survive in this world, I thought. He ought to learn how to stonewall small mishaps.

As for tonight, he could have blamed several things, the slippery floor, my car parked kind of sideways, the darkness in the basement parking lot. We walked toward Kwangwhamun and found a café named "The Tears of Being." When he read the menu he squinted a little, perhaps a myopic, and ordered "Machu Pichu," a cocktail. The word gave me a small pain in my heart, but I said, "same for me." He rubbed his hands as if embarrassed at sitting with a strange woman. I took out a cigarette and he seemed relieved to have something to do. He lit his lighter for me.

"Is it Du Pont?" I asked, eyeing the lighter.

"So, you know it," he said, a little shrug of his shoulders showing pride.

"I don't smoke but I like the sound it makes when I light it," he said. He sounded apologetic even about not smoking.

For my lover's 33rd birthday I had given him the same lighter. It was a day when an unusual snowfall paralyzed the entire city traffic. We had to cancel our plans to dine at the riverside. Instead we managed to drive to his apartment. Snowflakes covered his head. After a long kiss, I was in his arms and watched the snow on his head melt into dew drops. I knew I had snow on my head. I wished achingly to live happily with him till another kind of snow covered our hair. The memory still hurt. Who taught us that marriage was completion of love? Cinderella? Chunhyang? And....?

I let him light my cigarette. He had nothing to do again and just watched me. My man in Peru didn't smoke, either, but he liked lighting my cigarettes with the lighter I had given him.

"Have you by any chance been to Machu Pichu?" the man asked me.

The drinks in dark tropical jungle green over plum-colored velvet red were brought to our table.

I shook my head.

"I arrived here only a few days ago from there," he said.

I decided to leave the café even if the car repair wasn't finished. On the day I was fired, I didn't feel like talking with a man from Peru. On this gray fall afternoon, I had been thinking of selling my child's first birthday gifts, my cell phone, and now my crumpled car. Why do I have to think about Machu Pichu and Peru?

My lover sent me one postcard. It had a picture of Machu Pichu. He said, "I came to Machu Pichu to spend my short break. It is about an hour's flight southeast from Lima. From here about sixty miles northwest in the rugged mountains stand one "Old Peak" Machu Pichu and a "Young Peak" Waina Pichu. Where these two peaks meet, there is the "Lost City" one can see in its entirety only from the sky. It once held about 10,000 people, but no one knows how it was built and when the people left it. Everything remains in a legend."

I tore the postcard into pieces and threw them into a wastebasket. I didn't want to know why he went to Machu Pichu. The Old Peak and the Young Peak, the city one could see only from the air, a ghost city where no living person lived. Why did they build such an elaborate city? Where did they go?

Perhaps he was touring and bought off all the cheap trinkets from a girl. He would sit her in his lap and braid her hair. He was that kind of man. Once when he was at the Tongkin branch office in Vietnam, he bought up the entire stock of useless knickknacks from such a girl. He said he felt such pity for the girl that he had to do it. At his apartment, there was a pile of such trivia. I fished out the torn pieces and tore them into smaller pieces. If you can't face it, try to avoid it as best as you can. That was the lesson I have learned in my thirty odd years.

"Er.... Are you married?"

"Yes. I was. I'm alone now."

I guessed I added the unnecessary part because I was about to leave the café. The man sat still as if slightly confused, then began to laugh out loud.

"I'm sorry I shouldn't have asked," the man said, again apologetically.

I looked out of the window. There were no pedestrians in the windy street. A few gingko trees stood forlornly dropping a leaf or two. I wanted to make eye contact with one of them, but it was no use. It was like trying to speak to someone who absolutely refused your approach. I looked around. We two were the only patrons in the café. The hostess had disappeared after placing the drinks in front of us. Complete silence as inside an aquarium.

"May I ask why you divorced your husband? Oh, oh, I'm sorry to ask such a.... You see I have never been married."

I rubbed out my cigarette and looked at him. It wasn't the first time I had been asked.

"Well.... I married him because I thought I would die if he weren't beside me. After a time, I felt I would die if he stayed beside me," I said, smiling slightly. The man didn't smile back. He took a sip of his drink and made a grave face.

"That is strange. A woman told me the same thing when we met for the last time before I left for Peru about a year ago."

The man smiled sadly. I didn't. It occurred to me that my old boyfriend in Peru might be saying the same thing to a woman there now. A jab of pain tore at me inside, and I became angry. Then, all of a sudden, I wanted to get to know this man better.

"It was very hard," the man said, slowly turning his cocktail glass.

"It must have been," I tried to be a little more friendly.

"Do you really think so? What pained me most was that it might not have been so hard for her, and it was just some relationship that ended." The man's lips trembled.

"I don't know. A friend of mine once came to me on a rainy day after losing her man. She sat in my room, just watching the rain. When I tried to console her, she said, 'We are still under the same sky. The rain I see, he sees, too. That is comfort enough for me.'"

I looked at him, asking wordlessly whether he understood me. But his eyes said no. Just as my boyfriend did, the man seemed to ask me to speak in plainer, easier terms.

"Since you were leaving for Peru, she must have felt completely at a loss. Do you know such a feeling of loss, being adrift? She would never know whether her man was seeing the same rain she was. While it rained here, it might be dry and sand storming in Peru. When it snowed here, people in Peru might be swimming in the ocean. While we were enjoying a fine weather, birds might be dying in a violent storm in Peru. It's not like Japan, America, France, or Germany. Peru isn't included even in our international weather report. Can you understand? He may be having the same bowl of noodles as she is, but she doesn't know that. She can't have the comfort of knowing that he is listening to the same music she is. She may go back to the street where they used to walk together, and ask herself, does he also think of this street once in a while? If he is in Peru, she cannot even guess. It is always harder for the person who is left behind. The one who leaves takes his body away, but the one who stays is apt to find one strand of his hair at a time in everything he touched. His chair, his coat hanger, and his.... All of his things insist on testifying his absence. The same scenery, the same place, but the empty hole where he used to be. Only memories remain. It is unbearably hard."

The man nodded ever so slightly. However, he didn't seem to be comforted. I might have talked too much, unnecessarily.

"When I see a smoking woman I think of her, though there are so many smoking women in the world." The man looked down in the hazy smoke from my cigarette. He fidgeted with the hem of his coat, deep in thought.

"Life or rather living is just.... You brood when you see someone smoke, you brood when you look at the Nam Mountain, but, you know, neither the cigarette nor the mountain has anything to do with it."

The man looked up, incomprehension in his eyes. I grinned. He wouldn't know that my man's apartment was under the Nam Mountain and the Nam-san Tower loomed right in front of his windows. At night the tower glowed in its multicolored brilliance like the crown of a Persian prince. He had given me his T-shirt for my overnight stays. I wore it on Saturdays and Sundays and drank coffee and watched TV movies in it all day long. By the way, did he take it to Peru? The old faded T-shirt had become soft as silk after repeated washing. Every night as I put my child to bed, I missed its soft touch on my arms.

The apartment of the faded T-shirt is still there, where some strangers must live and look in wonder at the tower. The dark steep alley where we hastily and thirstily kissed and the mussel-soup shop we used to frequent are still there. As there are smoking women everywhere, the Nam Mountain is visible from any corner of Seoul. It can be seen on the highway long before one arrives in Seoul. I am a Seoul native, but I never knew the tower could be seen from afar and from every direction. It is the head that retains memory, but it is the heart that holds remembrance. And my heart is frightened by the tower.

"I used to call her from Peru," the man said.

He had the look of not comprehending the connection between the Nam Mountain and Peru. He was sunk in his own thought.

"When she answered my calls, she became so cold that I called her after work hours when nobody would be in office. Can you understand how I felt when I called her to her empty desk?" The man, no longer hesitant, looked at me straight in the eye. Our eyes met and I turned away. The ringing telephone in an empty office, calling her while knowing she wasn't there.... I looked out. The empty alley...a few gingko leaves, more yellow in contrast to darkness, were scattered in it.

"She wouldn't believe that there was someone with a warm heart who could share sorrows of life. At times she sounded like she was going to put an end to everything. And yet, I kept two tickets to Peru because Peru was a no-visa country. She didn't come to the airport. My cell phone said "no connection."

Today I called her at office and was told that she had quit. In fact, I was in that parking lot to make a telephone call. Her office is near here. After I left for Peru, she must have moved. I don't have her new number."

About a year after he had left, my man did call me once. I couldn't believe he was calling from Peru because he sounded so near. Like a secret agent informing his contact, he began his call with, "Write it down." And gave me a long code-like number. I was sketching a new dress. I didn't copy the number he gave me. Who said marriage was completion of love? My sketch was that of an impossibly proportioned woman existing only in dreams. I scribbled in big blocks, "Finished" over the sketch, as his telephone number evaporated into the air, gone inexorably. I wrote "Finished" "Finished" over and over again on the skirt of the woman's dress I created.

"One of my colleagues gave me a hint. He said a woman with the same voice called me several times. When he was about to give her my Peru number, she hastily hung up. I suspected it was my girlfriend.... Are you all right? Is my story too long?" the man asked.

"No, no. I'm fine."

I wasn't fine. I had a pain in the pit of my stomach. Hoping the alcohol in my drink would anesthetize the pain, I drank it. I felt better immediately. I had another sip. I wanted to feel light, lighter and lighter, so I could fly. The cocktail, made in the shape of the Machu Pichu temple in green and red, had now melted into a formless mix.

"Birds fly to Peru to die, I've heard, do they?" I asked.

No longer did I feel that I had to escape the café. I merely wanted to change the subject. The man smiled a slow smile as he rubbed his well-shaven chin.

"You're talking about Roman Gary's novel. Birds die anywhere. And baby birds are born anywhere. Do you want to know more about Peru?"

"No. I know nothing about Peru."

"You don't want to know, I see. Lest you may die there?"

He laughed. I didn't. I took up another cigarette. He lit it with his silver lighter. The man's cocktail had melted, too, but mine seemed to be rebuilding itself inside my stomach, into bright green and red tiers. There was no one in the café, not even the hostess, there was no music, either. The place felt like the inside of a tomb. My watch told me the car repair time was almost near.

"There was a book that once impressed me deeply. Its first sentence begins 'there is one unchanging truth in the world and that truth is that everything changes.' That reminds me of what you said. At first I thought I couldn't live without the truth, but now I feel I cannot live with the truth. The book was right. Everything changes. I believed everything in the book except its first sentence. I believed foolishly that the truth in the book will remain true. I hoped that there was at least one thing in the world that would not change. Be it love, a person, truth, or myself. I guess I wanted to lean against it. By nature a being wants to stay on. That is why I went to Peru."

"I think the car is ready," I stopped him.

He was obviously disappointed.

"I'm sorry my story must have been too depressing. I'll leave in a minute. It's time I left. I want to stay on but I can't. If you don't mind one more word...."

The man gave me an appealing look. This man is strange. If his story should drag on, I'd just up and go.

"I'm sorry. The minute I saw you, I wanted to say this. 'Love is not something to be completed.' Nor is revolution or life. Nevertheless we have a tendency to want to see the end.

We want to see and touch the end product. If not, we feel as if the thing itself did not exist at all. But the middle, the process, exists, and life is no more than a process. Life cannot be completed. I think I hated her as much as I loved her for her hasty rush to see the end of everything. Just as I hated and loved my hope, my endless hope. I guess that's why I could leave for Peru."

I stood up. The man hesitated and then rose to follow me to the counter where he paid. It was indelicate to watch a man pay, so I turned around, to be suddenly assailed by a dark blue shape. High above on a rocky ridge loomed a man-like shape, slowly melting down. It wasn't clear whether it was a man or a woman, facing me or the other way. The shape, a being, stood in air with no footing. It seemed to be enveloped in a black and dark blue whirlwind. From nowhere, the word "death" flashed through my brain and my lower abdomen caved in in one painful swoop. The layers of drawers of my life, all tightly closed, began to open one by one for the first time. In them were writhing all my bloody internal organs as if being salted. A heavy blow of pain straightened my back rigidly upright.

"I'm afraid I have to leave," the man said.

I glanced down at the yellow leaves he was standing on. His once clean shoes now covered with a thin layer of dust, the well-ironed pants legs, and the neat navy blue coat came into my sight. Above them all sat his face, a very sad face, seeming to submerge into eternal silence.

"Please, don't live like that. If you live the way you do, everything will be hard for you," I wanted to say as I might have said to a younger friend. The man patted me lightly on my back. Like a shy virgin, I stepped back, nodded to him and walked away.

From the moment my inner drawers began to creakingly open, my fingers started their demand, which I decided to comply with. As I had been generous to the man who did harm to my car, I wanted to be similarly generous to my fingers. For a long time, my lips had been misused, so I was going to give my lips a chance, too. I took my cell phone out of my pocket and called my man's company in Seoul.

"May I have his number in Peru?"

"I don't know what to say to you. He had been missing for nearly a week. He said he was going on a short trip, but he hasn't come back. His apartment is empty. He is not the kind of person, but he has vanished. Where he went, we heard, there was a terrible storm. After the storm, all the survivors came back from the mountains and the sea, but him. The Peruvian police and our embassy there began an intensive search, but haven't found him yet," the man on the other end of the line said, often fumbling for words. He sounded as if he were responsible for his disappearance.

I couldn't cut off. I couldn't talk, either. I hurriedly searched for the man who had just left me. There was no one in the alley. I began to run after him. He was gone, vanished. Cars roared by. The kindergarteners were boarding their school bus. Their photo session over, the grooms were escorting their brides, wide grins on their faces. You are full of hope now, but someday you'll walk this same street in despair. Only hope will lead to hopelessness. Be on guard for the unexpected turns in life. One day the music will stop, and only silence will reign around you.

I had the feeling that I was standing in absolute silence. It was in my company's underground garage that I first met my man. He scraped slightly my then unscarred car. Like other people who disfigured my car, he could have fled, but he waited for me. "Your emergency light was on, so I knew you'd show up soon," he said. I appreciated his thoughtfulness but couldn't shake off my feeling that he was the kind of man who would live a hard life. It was two years ago. I had on the same coat that I am wearing now. The coat was crisp and new, and the lights in the garage weren't so dim as now.

Two years later, here I stand in my frayed old coat in an unbearably oppressive silence. The man is gone. Where has he gone? I remember the electricity I felt when his neat all-weather coat touched mine and his hand patted my back. Did he fly from Peru because he had become lighter? No, no, that's not it. Did my encounter with him really happen? I cannot hear. I only feel a deafening silence.

Through the pudding-thick silence came to my ears the noise of thousands of birds flapping their wings on their ascent into the air. From the open drawers of my life, birds began to fly out in a neat pattern. The birds will continue their way over the wide ocean, past the Lost City, collide into the Old Peak Machu Pichu and die. Mounds of fallen dead birds....

Do the birds remember the first time they tried flying? The glory of their first flight? After a long time, they will come to the moment when their wings shiver in defeat. Such a moment proves that death is also a process of life. Birds die and new birds are born. On this gray fall day, in a spot in the field, some bugs will wither away while a pile of clear eggs will wait for their birth. In far Peru, a man has vanished. An award-winning designer has been fired at 33, a city built for a millennium disappeared along with its ten thousand people. All of these are possible. But, how could he, how could he bear to disappear like that?

I remember the play we saw together first. Its title was "Nobody Will Disappear." Did he take me to the play so he could disappear? So, he would someday leave me the memory of those words? Can't I pray at least that he be alive in some little corner on this earth? It doesn't matter where, even Peru, as long as he is alive. But it is no use anymore. I am standing all alone on this oppressive dark day. My hand holding the cell phone is damp and sticky. I put it away in my bag and rub my hand on my coat. Even if flocks of birds fall dead and dinosaurs walk with gingko trees, I will never, ever want to go to Peru. The birds of my heart that have held a secret dream to fly to Peru have flown away. But, what am I to do when new birds are born in my life's drawers, with eyes made only for distant places?

I must go home. I will sit in my veranda in my rocking chair and braid the gossamer hair of my little girl on my lap. I will think about the man's words—the only unchanging truth is that everything changes; it was the first sentence of the book that I took as my life's guide; I believed everything in the book except its first sentence; I hoped against hope that at least one single thing in the world would not change, be it love, a person, truth, or myself. I wanted to lean against it because a being by nature wants to stay on. Over on the Old Peak Machu Pichu, among the birds eternally settled there, one bird who flew over the wide ocean in search of Life and the Lost City, sits alone. One drop of tear hangs quivering at his slowly fading eye. It is too late. I cannot move. I'm so, very, very sorry. I believed at least Time would be on our side. Slowly I put out my trembling hand and wipe his tears.

There was before me a street where yellow leaves were slowly whirling downward. It was a street as silent as a tomb.

Nostalgic Journey

by Han Kang

"Never forget
the season of the wounds
and the land where
even the sleet felt warm."
-- "Yosu" by Kim Myungin

Yosu. The rusted rail tracks on its ocean front might still be wailing in a wounded voice. The cool currents of the Yosu Bay might still be whirling around the green isles as if wrapping in comfort some sore spots of bruised flesh.

On every pier, naked bulbs would glow in dull orange. Between the temporary sheds, the sun would set in its bloody red. The salty sea wind would upend people's umbrellas, women's skirts and hair.

Where am I?
Raindrops keep sliding down the window panes of the train, ceaselessly, like the tears of a grieving woman. Thunderbolts crack. The train wheels explode, like a demolition boom. The shussing noise of raindrops reminds me of the sobbing of a woman, her wound never to be healed.

Under the overcast sky, trees thrash in their struggle to survive. Wet branches bow and twist on the verge of breaking. Yellow and red leaves like sparks give themselves up in the wind. Trees and the soil seem in death throes. Slanting rain poles hit and hurt my eyes as they crash into the window panes.

My watch pointed to four o'clock. Two more hours till the destination Yosu. I let my hands drop and leaned against the seatback that smelled of cheap nylon cloth. As I hadn't slept for days, my eyelids drooped immediately, but my nervously palpitating heart would not let go of my consciousness. Into my closed eyes swam a few small goldfish. Within the small confines of a fishbowl, there were a few blades of green seaweed and one, two, three goldfish swimming round and round.... Suddenly I jumped upright. Those fish had died. Yesterday morning I scooped up the sixth and the last dead fish and threw it in a waste box outside the door. For four days after Jahun had left, the fish died. One or two a day.

I fed them and changed the water exactly as she had done, but I could not stop them from dying. I took the empty fishbowl and poured out the water into the sewage hole. I cleaned its slippery inside with soap, dried it, and put it on a shelf. At that very moment, I felt an oncoming nausea. With a groan, I threw up over the hole and put my fingers deep into my throat to dredge up whatever was still there. Blue and yellow pills and capsules, not yet dissolved, came out in the greenish stomach bile. Looking at them made me sick again, so I pushed them down the hole.

Every time I threw up, I was invaded by a sense of resignation and remorse. I twisted the faucet open and rinsed out my mouth with the chlorine-smelling water. Crawling on my knees, I climbed the steps to my room and collapsed onto the floor. I didn't want to recall Jahun's voice at a time like this, so I shook my head and pounded my forehead on the floor. No use. Her disembodied voice had already come into my ears.

"Why did you do a thing like that?"

It was the question she asked me the first time I induced vomiting by sticking my fingers into my throat. Jahun had a surprisingly beautiful voice, but her face was entirely indistinctive. Her eyes, nose, and mouth were all so unremarkable no one would remember a single feature unless one observed it on purpose.

"If you put your fingers into your throat, even a healthy person will get stomach spasms. Does your doctor know about this?"

Jahun asked me as she put her arms around my shoulders. Ignoring her, I put my mouth to the faucet and rinsed off my tongue.

"Never mind," I blurted out, gasping. "It's so dirty, dirty. I cannot stand it." That evening, I washed my face and hands repeatedly till my fingertips swelled in bloated stubs. Then, I threw up again.

"What is so dirty?"

I didn't answer her. Nausea assailed me again. Pushing her off, I ran to the sink and vomited. Tears ran down my scrubbed-raw cheeks and neck. Through my tears, I saw Jahun's bare feet on the tiled floor, nervously fidgeting.

"No more. That's enough," she whispered as she gently rubbed my back. When her cool fingers patted my feverish forehead and cheeks, I pushed them away. She let her ten fingers hang in the air for a while and mumbled quietly.

"It's all right now."

As if ocean tides had receded, her voice slowly subsided. Into the small rented room we shared, the late autumn sun poured its warmth. On the oil-paper floor, I lay and turned on my side, when a pain assailed me in the center of my chest. In the quiet air, countless dust motes flew around, which, I thought, were beautiful. Those motes reminded me of snowflakes that used to fall gently on the ocean. The flakes of Yosu.

The train was rushing onward amid the rainstorm. Presently the station-master's indistinct voice announced the

Namwon station. Two or three persons in raggedy clothes stood up to bring down their bundles and umbrellas from the overhead rack. There are yet many stations from Namwon to Yosu. Jahun's name sounded peculiar, and people asked her what Chinese characters her name had. She would simply say, "It is 'hun,' meaning joy, happiness," and give an entirely joyless smile. I myself asked the same question expecting some traces of a uniquely sad life. Hearing her simple answer, though, I burst out laughing and she joined in. To me, Jahun's rather indifferent and tired smile had a tinge of unbelievable darkness, too dark for a young woman of twenty-six, two years younger than I. I drew my own conclusion that the dark shadow of hers might be a sign of her intelligence. But now, I realized that it was only her loneliness. It was also the kind of expression that only someone who had long endured something could have. It was an expression one could see in the faces of people waiting on a platform, of passengers on a late night bus forlornly looking out at neon signs, and of those cheekbone-protruding haggard faces in early morning subways.

"It means joy." Jahun's quiet and serene voice contained the sum of all those people's longings.

The day I met Jahun for the first time was a sweltering summer day. I was then looking for a roommate to share the monthly rent of 300,000 *won*. The room had been occupied by a younger classmate of mine who had to go to the army. Since then, I had been paying my rent into his mother's bank account. I had had a series of roommates, every one of whom left within a couple of months.

My last roommate was a friend of a friend of mine, who was working for her master's degree. She had so many books and magazines that half of our room was buried under them. I myself owned quite a few books, and visitors joked about our "mini-library." Coming home from work, I would fling open the door and be assailed by the odor of old paper and mold. The odor was unbearable. In order to get rid of it, I would get up at dawn and dust and clean every book. I didn't care that I might be late for work. My roommate seemed unnerved by my obsession for cleanliness and my repeated washing of face and hands. One early morning, she was shocked to see me, in my pajamas and with my hair disheveled, dusting books, piece by piece. I must have looked like a malevolent witch to her.

I was relentless. I had to clean every book. I went so far as to fish the thin poetry books out of her bookbag and dust each page of them. It was before dawn when I opened the windows to let out the stale dirty air. I mopped the shelves and window frames and washed the rags, pounding them with a washing club. Still I wasn't satisfied. One day I asked her if she minded packing some yellowed old books in boxes and putting them outside. Alarmed, she stared at my nervous eyes.

"I think I'd better move out," she said, after a few seconds of silence.

On Sunday the following week, she did move out. She packed her books in boxes, tied them with cords, and had them loaded on a small moving van.

"Don't take it hard, please. It seems to me you need medical attention," she said, still uneasy and slightly angry.

I was devastated until the afternoon I met Jahun. My obsession with cleanliness was already known, and the series of roommates I'd had surely spread gossip about it. I never held malice toward any of them, and yet, all of them left without so much as a kind word. None of them bothered to call me, let alone visit me, which hurt me deeply. I couldn't hold my head up to those who had introduced them to me. It gradually dawned on me that I might soon lose all my friends and acquaintances. I finally decided to get a total stranger as my roommate.

On that afternoon I made flyers by writing in black ink on pieces of white paper:

"Looking for someone to share a small room. No key money. 150,000 *won* per month." I added my telephone number and a simplified map. Since the neighborhood was a small one, three would be enough, I thought. If there was no applicant, I would put an ad in the newspaper.

The afternoon sun was scorching the earth when I stepped out with the flyers and a pot of glue. From a house there came an odor of clothes being boiled in an open pot. Children's voices floated faintly from the playground. I was pasting the first flyer upon an electric pole when I felt that I was being watched. Turning around, I found a woman, a stranger, staring at me from the doorway of a house. At her feet stood two big travel bags and she held a bundle in one hand.

I was startled as I didn't think there was anyone out in this sun. How could I have missed her with the bags and the bundle for all to see? I walked on. Suddenly I felt as if someone were tugging at me and looked back.

The woman wasn't looking at me. With the bundle under her armpit and the two bags in her hands, she made a few steps out into the sun and flung them all on the street. In her unseasonably heavy coat, she was perspiring profusely. She seemed to have no handkerchief and rubbed away her sweat with her not very clean hands. She was so absorbed in the act of rubbing her perspiration that she seemed to be erasing all the features of her face, maybe even her own self. Her rubbing motions reminded me of someone trying to core an apple with a dull knife.

After I had pasted the rest of the flyers on the side of a public phone box next to the neighborhood supermarket and on the movie bulletin board, I trudged home. The moment I stepped through the half-open door of my landlord, the grandmother of the family, who was trimming sweet potato sprouts, looked up and asked me.

"Did you put up some advertisements?" I was surprised at the speed of the effect of my advertisement and smiled rather sheepishly. Then I noticed a woman heavily rising from beside the old lady. She was the very woman I had noticed standing in the street. She sat there so self-effacingly that I hadn't noticed her.

"This girl says she saw your ad." At this, the girl nodded and gave a smile almost idiotically naive and sweet. I could see how tangled and disheveled her hair was. The buttons on her heavy winter coat were misbuttoned, so her coat-front hung askew. Her brown shoes, nearly half of each sole gone, were so worn out that when she walked, her naked toes protruded.

Despite her unusual attire, she didn't look strange; I guess it was because of her serene expression. She looked extremely tired. Her fatigue was the kind one saw in the faces of those just coming back from a long trip. The shadow of fatigue somehow made me feel close to her and even willing to wash her clean, the heavy coat and all.

"Are you traveling?" I asked.

We stepped into my room, but she simply looked here and there as if she hadn't heard my question.

"There is no fishbowl," she mumbled. Those were her first spoken words. Her voice and enunciation were clear and pleasant, belying her poor appearance.

"I like a fishbowl in a house," she said and giggled. Her giggle instantly brightened up my desolate room as if it had been repainted in a brighter shade.

We introduced ourselves to each other and I explained the terms of rent. Each would donate 100,000 *won* per month plus the rent, for taxes, food, heating, etc.; if we fell short, we would chip in more equally; if, by any chance we had money left-over, we would put it in a piggybank and divide it equally when we parted. As soon as I finished, she took out a white envelope and counted out twenty five 10,000 *won* bills which she handed to me and said, "Now, can I live here from today?"

She took off her heavy coat and flung it down on the floor. Flopping herself beside the coat, she sighed, "Aah." Her eyes brightened as if waking from a depressing dream. Suddenly, she straightened up and blurted, "Give me some water, please. I'm thirsty."

As the train got nearer to south, the mountains became gentler and the rain thrashed harder. The empty rice paddies stretched far toward the autumn-colored mountains. The scarecrows in the paddies suffered silently, their rags flapping in the wet wind.

The middle-aged woman beside me said she had a three-hour nap when she found an empty seat. Finally she was asked to leave the seat by the last ticket-holder and came back to her seat next to mine.

"I had a nice nap. Why didn't you have some shut-eye while I was gone?" she said smiling broadly, then she fell asleep again. She seemed to be having a bad dream because she moaned audibly once in a while. I could see on her face deep creases and wrinkles, traces of her life-time suffering. From the sleeve ends of her faded beige blouse, I could see parts of her shabby white undershirts sticking out.

"When I took the medicine you gave me last time, I had nausea," I said to the doctor. I went to see him yesterday afternoon after I had thrown up while washing out the fishbowl. I had a stomach spasm that brought on a throbbing headache with heavy pressure on my eyes. The doctor in his late fifties had brown spots on his bald head.

"You shouldn't have nausea after taking the medicine. This time I'll prescribe you a milder one," he said, smiling primly.

He wrote a prescription on a piece of paper. Those scribbled words would relieve my chronic pain at least temporarily.

"You are overworking yourself, aren't you?"

He said decisively as a fortuneteller would.

"Take it easy and eat soft gruel for a while."

At the doctor's order, I lay down on the bed and soon felt the cold touch of his stethoscope. Then his expert fingers pressed here and there on my stomach and abdomen. In spite of my efforts not to, I groaned.

"I'm afraid it's gotten worse. Today I'll give you two shots. Can you come back tomorrow?"

I sat up and put my blouse on. The sunlight pouring in between the slats of the window blinds was brilliant. "Today is Friday, the first day of my break." I had succeeded in squeezing out three days of rest from my busy schedule. At the time I was in the doctor's office, I should have been out of Seoul on the 7:30 train to Yosu.

"I'm afraid I can't," I said, trying desperately not to groan again. "I am having a break. It begins today. I have to go...."

"I see. Then, come back on Monday. My prescription is for three days."

The doctor gave me the prescription slip and said in a business-like manner, "Have a nice holiday." I had been seeing him for three years, so he knew all the insides of my head and my organs, yet he remained as impersonal as at the first time. It was in the middle of deep winter. When I first went to him, I was beside myself with pain and fear. My face was covered with sweat and tears, and his expression betrayed momentarily a tinge of unease. Trembling violently, I began to scream at him.

"I don't know how many times I've had this. It attacks just when I am sure it won't, then.... Look at me, please, I'm young. I even had a stomach fiberscope test at a university hospital and they told me there's nothing wrong with me. Is it possible? I mean I have terrible pain."

I had never confided to anyone about my pain this way and my heart was pounding. But the doctor paid little attention to my appeal while busily examining me. Then, as always, he said, decisively.

"You are overworking yourself, aren't you?"

The inexpressible coldness in his matter-of-fact voice awakened in me a realization that I was indeed fatigued from overwork, and this strangely comforted me. Indeed I had consulted numerous doctors, but his manner and the comfort it gave me made me settle on this one, even though his office was on the second floor of a shabby little building at the entrance of a market alley.

The doctor sent in a nurse to give me the shots on my behind. She had a very fair complexion and a cold neat mouth. I climbed down the dark stairs and came outside to find snowflakes whirling down. Icy air bit into my coat collar and white flakes lit lightly on my eyelashes when I looked up.

Yesterday afternoon when I came out of the same old dark building, the alley was filled with brilliant autumn sunlight. The two shots I'd had continued to hurt and I had to walk slowly and awkwardly toward the subway station.

At the entrance of the subway, I rested for a moment taking in the wedding outfit rental shop where a half-clad mannequin stood with one arm missing and a restaurant whose signboard was girded with a long string of dust-covered dead colored bulbs.

In the subway filled with the jobless, students, and middle-aged women, I felt the effect of the injection spread rapidly through my veins. My throbbing eyeballs calmed and my rigid stomach became malleable.

Last night I didn't believe my pains would ever subside, as one doesn't trust night will ever turn into dawn or winter will bring on spring.

The subway train was going through a tunnel. Watching the faces reflected on dark windows like some silhouettes, I stood completely lost. Do I have to go back to that dark room? I had left my room with just my medical insurance card and my small purse.

Will I have to make rice gruel in that lonely kitchen-wash-room and try to push it down my throat? Must I swallow the medicine every hour on the hour? Will I be able to go to Yosu? Yosu, the place I left more than twenty years ago? Do I really want to go there?

With my fists balled tight, I stared at the darkened windows.

Jahun and I were like oil and water. Once a visitor mentioned that Jahun and I looked like sisters, which, I think, might have been caused by our equally fatigued look.

One thing I could not stand about Jahun was her attitude to money. She had the habit of putting her possessions anywhere handy; I used to find money beside the sink, on the make-up table, or on the door-step. When we shared the room, she was jobless and had no money, but her habit persisted. About a month later she got a job in a sewing shop, and things got worse.

On many occasions I complained about it to her. I was a neat person who didn't like things scattered around. I had been taught not to treat money carelessly. At times I would ask her if she didn't care about her possessions, or if she would become more cooperative on this matter. Sometimes I even scolded and pleaded. To all these, however, she would merely nod and smile, and that was it. There was no change at all in her ways.

There was more. Despite her thin small body, her behavior was oddly rough and careless. At times I thought she was angry because she would slam the door or shut the rice-cooker lid so hard that I resented her. But it didn't take me long to realize that her behavior was not out of ill temper or malice but out of her carefree temperament.

Jahun was careless even about her own body. Whenever she changed clothes, I would notice bruises on any part of her body. At the sewing shop, she constantly pricked herself so that there were band-aids on all her fingertips.

On our weekend shopping trips, I saw her bumping into people far more often than usual. She also hit her forehead and knees against glass doors. It was not unusual that she was absorbed in herself that she didn't hear the horn of a car or a motorbike. I nearly had heart attacks many times. Whenever we went out, I was busy watching out for her, so she would not get run over by a car or fall over something in her way. But, to my chagrin, she would walk around, carefree and serene, as if she trusted some power above to protect her.

For such a careless girl, there was one thing she cherished dearly, and it was goldfish. On the third day after she moved in, I came home from work to find Jahun beaming at a fishbowl. Several small goldfish were peacefully swimming around in it.

"Aren't they pretty?" Jahun asked, quietly grinning.

Jahun was the kind of girl to tape a torn hem rather than sew it, but she doted on her goldfish. Twice a day she fed them generously and every two days she changed the water. When she happened to run out of the feed, she would dash out, no matter how late, to the market and bring home a huge bag of fish feed. Bread crumbs and the part of custard that stuck on its paper wrapper went to the fish. She would watch them devour the crumbs. Once, she mumbled to herself, "All the water in the world flows to the sea, and the sea inevitably mixes with the sea of Yosu."

When she found out that I was from Yosu, she was so ecstatic that she wanted to talk about it whenever we had some leisure time together.

"As a matter of fact, I don't like that place. I don't care to talk about it," I said. But she wouldn't listen. I also told her that I had left Yosu when I was seven and lived in Suwon ever since with my maternal grandparents. Suwon was more like my hometown. But Jahun asked, "Even so, how can you change your hometown?"

My father died when I was five and my mother passed away when I was seven. I had never gone back to Yosu since then. Jahun, however, continued to talk about it, with her un-usual black eyes gleaming in her animated chatter.

Did you ever see the night light of Yosu? Did you ever walk over the Dolsan Bridge? Do you remember the azure blue sky above the shores of the Dolsan Island? Did you go to the Odongdo Island? The camellia blossoms in Odongdo looked like tear drops falling on the boughs, I remember.

One day I put a plateful of "komak" clams with a pot of red-pepper dip on our dinner table. No sooner had Jahun seen them than she began to sob loudly. "These look like Yosu, my Yosu is crying," she whispered.

I finally decided to ask her where her hometown was, but she hesitated as if I'd invaded a private part of her life. She blushed and turned away and remained quiet for a long time before she answered it was Inchon. Then, she changed it to Chonju, no, Namwon, eventually all the way to Samrei, Koksung, and Sunchon.

"No, actually it is Yosu," she said, watching my incredu-lous face.

"Where in Yosu did you live?"

"I don't know really. I was very young when I left."

I left Yosu at the age of seven, but I remembered neighborhood names like Mipyong and Yosuh.

"Then, how old were you when you left?"

To this question, she merely evaded my eyes. I thought I might have pained her deeply and decided not to pursue it.

"Except for Chejudo, I've lived at least one year in each of the provinces," she said. This was her story: Her father died when she was eight. Her mother and she moved to Chungmu to open a small eatery. Several years later, her mother remarried. She lived with her mother and stepfather in Taegu for about a year, then went to Sokcho to live with her mother's parents. She finished high school in Sokcho and moved back to Taegu where her mother got her a job in a small bookstore.

"I even fell in love with someone there," Jahun volunteered this information.

"The bookstore was a tiny one. And there was a college student who used to come there and order 'deep' books. I couldn't even understand the titles. Many a night I stayed up all night reading the books he had ordered before he would come to pick them up. Every one of them was about Man's fate, death, and loneliness. When he picked them, my heart went out to him. He looked about twenty-three or so, and a young man like him didn't have to read such gloomy books. He had the gloomiest face. I kind of disliked him, but he seemed to grow on me. Alone at night, in a backroom behind the store, I began to think about him.

"I wanted to hold his hands, pat his shirts, stroke his cheeks. I dreamed about him lying beside me. I thought I would be so happy if he were beside me.

"Sometimes I repeated like a mantra, he is with me, he is with me, before I fell asleep. Of course, he wasn't when I suddenly woke up in the middle of the night. I became so desperate that I couldn't take it anymore. I would dash into the store and mumble to myself all the book titles that came into my sight. In the morning I found my pillow wet with my tears."

One night Jahun decided to tell him of her love next time he came. But when he showed up a few days later, he was with a young woman. He didn't look gloomy. He stammered whenever the woman said something to him. She looked "doll pretty" but that was all. After a long agonizing scrutiny, he picked out a book, wrote his name on the inside cover, and gave it to the woman. It was a recently translated collection of English and American love poems. Jahun read the remaining copy of the same book and cried.

"I still remember the first lines. O Love, thou art everything my soul craves."

Jahun smiled bitterly and said, "Am I not foolish?"

Soon after Jahun quit the bookstore and got a job in Changwon as a book-keeper of a small trading company. The company's bankruptcy, however, forced her to roam here and there, living a hand-to-mouth existence. From early childhood, she had moved around so much that her wanderlust became a habit. She couldn't stay put in one place more than a year. Eventually she ended up in Seoul with all her possessions—two travel bags of old out-of-season clothes, the last pay and bonus she had received from her workplace in Chonan.

She wandered in Seoul till she somehow ended up in this poor neighborhood at the far edge of the city.

"Of all the places I have lived in, Seoul is the coldest and cruelest place. I don't think I will stay here long," she muttered. Suddenly it dawned on me that she had no future.

I didn't know what or who stole her future away and pushed her here and there, but I knew one thing clearly, and that was that Jahun was exhausted, not just from twenty some years of wandering but from what seemed like centuries of roaming.

However, there appeared a strange smile on her face from time to time. The smile seemed to say that, though she was tired of everything, she had not yet lost everything. The smile miraculously erased the dark shadow off her face. Watching her, I wondered how a person could be so hopeless and at the same time so positive about life.

For instance, Jahun and I would be watching the 9 o'clock news on TV, and I would shout, "Oh, those dirty dogs!" "Oh, those shameless pigs!" Then, Jahun would simply giggle and improvise a tune, "dirty dogs, dirty pigs...." as if my swear words were nice lyrics. She hummed them in the room, in the washroom, while standing and sitting. I thought she was making fun of me and I couldn't take it after a while.

"Stop it!" I shouted and looked around at her. I was surprised to see no trace of a smile on her face, but a shadow of complete serenity. "Dirty dogs, dirty pigs" seemed to be lyrics for a lullaby to her. What kind of a woman, no, what kind of a human being she is, I wondered to myself. I merely stared at her.

Her reactions were always in that vein. When I had a stomach spasm, she would lay me down and gently rub my stomach. Her palms were warm, full of concern and sincerity. She pushed my hair neatly behind my ears.

"What did the doctor say? You are too young to have such a chronic condition."

"That is enough. Thank you. I feel much better," I said.

"Oh, good. I'm so glad. My hands have a healing power," she was elated. "Why don't you have a short nap?"

For my recurring pain at night, I had some sleeping pills in my desk drawer. As soon as Jahun fell asleep, I got up and gulped down a few of them. These pills worked better than the doctor-prescribed yellow and blue tablets.

Suddenly, I found myself shaking terribly for no reason.

How have I come to this point? I wondered, placing the water glass on the desk and burrowing back into my cover. Jahun was sound asleep breathing regularly in the predawn darkness. Her face was so peaceful that all the pain and resentment in the world seemed in deep sleep in her pure soul.

I saw such an expression on her face from time to time. She fell asleep as soon as her head hit the pillow. Once she told me proudly, "I can sleep anywhere if my head is placed on a solid surface."

However, when the alarm clock rang and the dawn light seeped through the window, I would often notice her lying with her eyes tightly closed, sweat breaking out on her forehead. I would turn on the light and get ready for work; then, she would sit up, eyes still closed, and stay that way. Her hair hanging every way down her ashen face, half covering it, with patches of psoriasis covering her cheeks so that she looked like a badly made-up puppet.

After a few minutes, she moved on her knees to her desk and pushed the play button of her tape-recorder. The music was always the same dance music from the opera *Carmen*.

Even if you don't love me
I still love you.
But if you love me,
Come to me now.

In contrast to the lyric and light rhythm, she slowly and uncertainly twisted herself up. As if her bodily batteries had been recharged, she began to fold her beddings and put them in a wall closet. The passionate aria seemed to whip her shoulders and waist, and she moved listlessly as if spurred by the whips.

At such moments, she looked so lonely and gloomy that I could not believe any human being could be so unhappy.

Then, suddenly she would look up and give me a dazzling smile. Her surprisingly white teeth gleamed in the fluorescent light. Her face lit up, unbelievably.

"Well, it's morning again," she said in her sweet gentle voice. I couldn't tell whether she was happy, sick, mystified, or pained to face another morning. At the table, she reverted to her old tired self, picked at her food and left for work.

One day, having gotten sick of the same music, I complained to her. "Can't you change the music? You seem unable to move unless you have that same song." Pushing up her hair, she replied reluctantly, "If I were back in Yosu, I wouldn't need the music."

The train began to move again after a three-minute stop at Kooreigu. The dark blue water of the Sumjin River stretched through the pouring rain toward the black clouds. The whipping gust stirred up the yellow mud and scattered it like mist. On the train windows, I could see the blank staring faces of passengers.

"What's the matter with you? Are you sick? Why the sudden departure?"

A colleague in my office asked me on the day I got the permission to have Friday and Saturday off.

"I knew you were going to get sick. You were just too damned conscientious, doing your work over and over again, when it looked all right to us. How can anyone take such a workload? If you abuse your body when young, the stress will assail you later all at once," my colleague went on. I couldn't tell whether it was out of good will or malice. I smiled helplessly.

"Why don't you take it easy? No one lives forever, you know," she added pointedly, looking down on her desk.

But I worked till late at night to make up for the lost hours. Stretching my neck and arms, I noticed the empty chairs sitting forlornly facing their fellow desks.

As mumbling or sighing would surely intensify my loneliness in the office, I kept silent. I did my work without making any noise or looking up. Finally I finished, turned out the light, and groped down the dark staircase. Suddenly I thought I saw Jahun's face. She was quietly gazing at me with imploring eyes, while ruefully regretting that she couldn't tell me why she was imploring.

"What are you so afraid of?" she asked me quietly.

One steamy July evening, Jahun and I were sitting in a small subway police station. We would have been at a movie directed by a Polish man had Jahun not lost her purse to a pickpocket. Jahun often came home with red and swollen eyes after watching a movie. That night, we would have cried together, bought some bread, and come home happily together as sisters. But....

"I was just stepping onto the platform to catch the Number One. I think the pickpocket must have put his hand in my open bag and took my purse. I felt a cold sensation as if someone were going to hurt me and looked into my bag. The purse was gone. There were so many people in the car and I couldn't do anything," Jahun said.

Two police officers, one young and another in his forties, sat dozing off at their desks when we entered the station. Jahun was so flustered that she didn't even thank the officer who offered her a chair.

"Please sit and calm down," he said.

"Can I get it back? Can you find it for me?" Jahun kept asking.

I had tried to dissuade her because I knew it would be of no use, but Jahun dragged me here.

"So, you lost a black vinyl purse with your ID card, 45,000 *won*, and your room key. Is that all?" The police officer wrote them down on a yellowish paper, and yawned till tears came to his eyes. The cash, 45,000 *won*, was an overtime pay she had received for working last Sunday. It was special to her, but it seemed nothing to the officer, who asked again in a bored tone, "Is that all?"

Jahun fidgeted awhile but calmed down. Realizing that she would never get her things back, she had the look of complete resignation.

"And, there was a train ticket," she whispered.

"To where?" The police officer looked up with a modicum of interest, watching her face. Jahun began to rub her forehead, then her nose, mouth, and cheeks, just as she had done on the day I met her.

After a long silence, she finally placed her hands on her lap and said, "Yosu."

I felt in my heart a delicate glass breaking in pieces. I had never paid much attention to her chattering about Yosu nor believed her word that Yosu was her hometown. I had never dreamed that her obsession with Yosu was this strong.

"For what day?"

Jahun hung her head. I didn't know what went on in her mind; I only saw the shadow of her intense yearning on her face.

"Tomorrow night. 10:35 p. m."

On our way home, I asked her why she hadn't told me, who was in Yosu, for how long she'd stay, but she refused to answer any of them. After we washed up and got in bed, she whispered, "My mother in Taegu, she is not my real mother."

I sat up, shocked. It was near midnight and I thought she was already asleep. The street light was dimly coming through the window. Her dark eyes seemed to draw and embrace everything in their sight.

"I heard that I was found in a train. I was about two. When nobody claimed the crying baby, the train master took me to the police.

"Yosu may not be my hometown. It was only that the train was from Yosu going to Seoul. So, I vaguely guessed that I was from Yosu. Even when I heard Yosu casually mentioned by someone, my heart would skip a beat."

The two-year-old Jahun was shifted from one foster home to another for a year or so, then sent to a municipal orphanage in Inchon. She was soon adopted but sent back to the orphanage when her foster parents found that she couldn't speak even at the age of five. They were worried she might need special education.

About three months after she returned to the orphanage, she suddenly blurted out her first words. She was always teased and tormented by other children who called her an idiot. One summer day at the playground, a child pushed her down a sliding board and Jahun fell hard into the sand. When the orphanage teacher rushed to her and touched the scratches on Jahun's knees, Jahun whispered distinctly, "Hurting too much," with tears welling up in her eyes.

The following year she was adopted by a well-to-do couple, but within two years, the father died and his business collapsed. Soon afterward, she followed her "mother" to Chungmu, as she had already told me. Her "mother" took care of her and sent her up to high school. Ever since she left her, she sent a small gift to her mother and the mother's brother in Sokcho and called them once in a while. Lately, she felt that neither of them wanted her calls. They always said, "come see us someday," at the end of each call, which, Jahun said, sounded more like, "Don't call us anymore." From the moment she was found in the train, she seemed destined to wander, she said.

"My hometown is nowhere. Every town I lived in was just a spot for temporary stay. Every morning I opened my eyes, I felt lost. Every day was hell for me until I went to Yosu," Jahun said with a wry smile.

"But it is different now," she said, suddenly serious.

"It doesn't hurt anymore," she said, lying on her back and staring at the ceiling.

That was all she told me that night. She simply looked at me as if she had talked too much. Her face betrayed no joy nor pain.

I turned away, feeling as if I had seen something I shouldn't have. Only, all the veins in my body, every bit of them, seemed on fire.

It was an unbearably steamy summer when murders and gang fights frequently occurred in back alleys. The heat wave lasted more than a month. In order not to lose my new roommate Jahun, I had to grit my teeth not to show my obsession with cleanliness, but the heat and humidity unraveled my determination.

All kinds of eye and ear diseases traveled through subways and buses. Just to avoid skin contact, I walked three or four blocks. The pavement was like an inferno, probably over 110 degrees. Sweat poured out from my forehead, neck, armpits, between the legs, and even from each toe. Yet I walked on, sticky and breathless.

The minute I got home, I washed every part of my body squeaky clean till the skin became raw. I could not stand stickiness. If at all possible, I wanted to cut out all the sweat glands from my body. I heard the news every evening that cholera was rampant in Southeastern countries, and I began to suspect whether every fellow subway passenger was back from one of those countries, perhaps, contaminated. Maybe some passenger had a family member or a colleague who had returned from that area.

I was so overwhelmingly seized by a fear of disease germs that I couldn't concentrate on anything either at home or in the office. To aggravate my condition, Jahun was careless about hygiene. She would keep her dirty clothes in a pile to wash them on weekends. I couldn't stand the sight and smell of them, so I washed them for her. But the intense humidity caused wet clothes to give off an odor I could not tolerate. I ended up turning on the furnace to dry them. It goes without saying that Jahun and I had to sleep on the tiled floor of the washroom, the room being too hot.

Finally, I became a neurotic about odors. I could smell the rotting flesh of my hands, the rotting paper of books, and the sewer water of the washroom sinkhole. The tap water, the wooden spoon, the plastic bowls all emitted stench, to my nose.

I would not allow Jahun to come anywhere near the cooking board. At first she seemed grateful, but gradually she came to sense my excessive fear and loathing. If Jahun didn't wash her hands before she touched the door-knob, I washed it with soap. If she happened to touch me, a cold shiver seized me.

Above all these, however, what bothered me more than anything else was the odor of Yosu emanating from Jahun's body. Her wet hair when she came from the bath house smelled of the salt water of Yosu; from her hands and mouth came the odor of rotten fish on the shore; on her face was the shadow of the bloody twilight of Yosu.

From the fingertips of Jahun seemed to come the heart-rending songs of the barmaids on the shore, the weeping and suffering sounds of the unhappy. I remembered the horrifying, hacking coughing of my mother, a small woman, minutes before she died.

One night I screamed at Jahun, "For God's sake, don't touch me!" She quickly withdrew her hand from my shoulder and retreated. On the gas stove was a pot of soup boiling and the rice was almost done.

"What did I do to you?" Jahun stammered. I hastily turned off the burner knobs and took off my apron.

"Don't even talk to me in my face!" I screamed and added, "because it is so dirty!"

Since that night she had attempted to talk to me, but I turned my back every time, without so much as a word. Jahun swallowed back whatever words that might have been on the tip of her tongue and sighed a painful sigh that got on my nerves.

The heat wave went on.

Our old electric fan made a scratching noise at every turn. We practically stayed up all night, far apart from each other. We sweated in our pajamas as it was impossible to dry the sweat. A sickening tepid breeze stirred once in a while through the window. Without exchanging one word, we rolled about on the sticky floor, trying to stay away from each other.

Jahun became noticeably depressed. The air in our room seemed stuffier without her innocent laugh. Coming home early from work, we would sit, each in our thoughts, and the only thing that moved in that stifling room was Jahun's fish. This way, the hottest summer in fifty years trampled over our bodies and spirits.

The rain filled the window panes of the train as if someone were pouring water from a hose. Leaves were broken off the trees in the wind. A farmer in his shiny blue rain gear and black rubber boots was struggling to go against the wind. He looked like he was fighting a giant.

The woman with the wrinkled face and good-natured grin got off at Sunchon. The train continued its way to Yosu, about 30 minutes away.

My heart began to constrict. I had never thought that I would voluntarily go there. I vaguely guessed that someday I might happen to or be forced to go there, and see the sky and the sea of Yosu. Just thinking of Yosu was more than I could bear.

The train quickly passed by the Sunchon harbor, past the red flower dotted hills, wet fields, and the flapping wind-driven trees. What would Jahun have seen in these? What mysterious thoughts would she have thought?

"Okay, I promise I won't go there," she said to me.

The next day she left. There were reminders of her stay: One pair of clean white socks dry on the washline, a few long hairs stuck on the washbasin, the yellow toothbrush back in its place, the broken useless hairpins in the desk drawer, and the old cassette tape, used so often that the tenor's voice was no longer the same.

Jahun had quit her job at the sweatshop around early autumn when the summer heat was noticeably losing its grip. I came home one night to find her key stuck in the lock. I opened the door and nearly fainted when I stepped on something soft. It was Jahun.

I could not even scream. I turned on the light and dragged her to the stepstone. She was unconscious. On her face, arms and legs were blood and bruises.

On her way from work, she crashed into a bicycle coming at full speed in the dark. She couldn't see the man, but he felt like a teenager. Scared, the man dragged her to the front of a house and ran away. Jahun didn't remember how she had crawled to our room. She said she had felt so relieved at reaching home that she let go of herself.

Next morning I took the reluctant Jahun to a clinic and had her X-rayed. Waiting for the result of the X-ray, we sat side by side on a bench. Once she looked up at me. There was in her eyes no hatred, bitterness or resentment, but, oh, such indescribable loneliness! Though we were sitting close together, we might well have been miles apart.

The middle-aged nurse called Jahun's name. I stood up too to help Jahun limp into the doctor's office. The young doctor, with his hair cut short and neat, pointed, in an obviously lackluster manner, to the X-ray pictures on the light-box and said no bones were broken.

Every night Jahun put hot towels on her legs. Weak and in pain, she trembled and clenched her teeth when she tried to squeeze dry her towels, but she wouldn't let me help.

It took her almost a week before she could walk without pain, but she didn't go back to work. She didn't turn on the music tape, didn't get up when I left for work in the morning. I would find, upon returning home in the evening, that Jahun hadn't touched food all day long. She crouched instead in front of her fishbowl muttering to herself.

Days went by. The early autumn sun was warm and dry. All the bruises on Jahun's body gradually faded, but the wounds in her heart seemed to get worse. I was not any better off. My fastidiousness subsided somewhat as the days became cooler, but I began to feel desolate as if after a drunken spree. The sewer filled with every desire, pain, and frustration seemed to have dried in the open sunlight and the resulting dust began to blow into my face.

As Jahun once said, every morning I felt lost. When the day was over, every day, I wished all would just end. Moreover, it was a torture to see Jahun collapsing a little day by day.

Weeks passed this way before I finally broke down. After dinner, Jahun crawled back into her bed and I sneaked out to wash the dishes. All of a sudden, I threw down the dishes and flopped on the floor.

"Father, oh, Father."

I tried to stop moaning. Jahun, who I thought was asleep, came out slowly and our eyes met, hers strangely shiny and mine filled with tears.

"It's because of you Father," I mumbled, sitting against the sink board.

"I can't take it anymore."

Jahun rushed to me on barefoot. Her emaciated body seemed to float. Lowering herself beside me, she asked me, "What are you so afraid of?"

Under the dim naked bulb, I could see the bluish tinge on her eyelids, a sign of her illness. But her eyes, brighter than ever, looked deep into mine.

"I'm leaving tomorrow," she said.

Dishes and bowls, precariously piled up, crashed down noisily. I picked them up and placed them on the board. A kind of sweet taste in my mouth made me wash out my mouth. There was blood. I had brushed my teeth and gums so hard that my gums were bleeding.

"Why? Why? How can you with that body of yours?"

I slid down beside her. Only silence reigned between us. I grabbed her arms with my trembling hands.

"Forgive me, please." A cold sweat ran down my back. "Where in the world can you go?"

Silence. The kind of silence in which all birds stopped singing and all plants stopped growing. Even the mountains cringed into silence. I swallowed my blood. I couldn't breathe.

How long was it before Jahun began to talk? It was the moment when I could not stand the silence and wanted to scream.

"If you walk east along the shore of Yosu, you get to a small village called Sojei," Jahun began.

"You have never seen it, I'm sure. I happened to get off the bus there because the bus broke down. It was early evening...behind the gentle hills the sun was setting and there were feathery yellow clouds around it. I liked the scenery so much that I began to walk to the village instead of waiting for the next bus. Here and there I saw big round cow dungs. A gray old man herded goats, women covering their heads with white towels were thrashing grains, and young boys helped them.

"I walked on till the rice paddies ended. There, I saw a few round nice-looking graves without any gravestones. It might have gotten dark if I had stayed on, so I turned around. Far down there was a gently curved bay with isles amid the calm ocean that looked like a finely woven blue carpet. I whispered to myself, 'It's beautiful,' and suddenly tears began to flow down my cheeks. On the deserted pier, raggedy tent pieces and broken wooden boards were scattered around while the tides pushed ashore and ebbed. Goats, birds, the wind, and the women...none of these were familiar to me, but I felt deeply that I was finally back in my mother's arms."

Jahun's quiet voice went on.

"I was happy, nervous, uneasy.... I came down to the port and walked and walked. Darkness was nearing at every moment and red and yellow lights came on in Yosu. A few small lights blinked on the isles, too. I couldn't even breathe because I was crying so hard. What.... How...how can you explain this?"

Jahun was sunk in her own emotions, her eyes filled with tears.

"That must have been my hometown. All the places I've been to were strange to me, but I feel everything there very close to me. I was so elated that I wanted to jump into the sea.

I wasn't afraid to die. Death was nothing. It was merely mixing myself with the sky, wind, soil, and water. I wish I could get rid of my body, an annoying burden, so I'd never be lonely again because I would no longer exist.

"I was happy, very very happy, that my poor lonely life was to end in such a gorgeous way. I wanted to shout with joy. I jumped into the mud on the shore and rolled around in mud to injure myself. I wanted my blood to mix with the mud and the mud to flow into my vein...."

Finally Jahun breathed a long sigh, her eyes gazing at some distant spot.

"So, wherever I may go, I'm going there," she said.

As the train passed Yochun, the rain storm was at its wildest. Trees were about to be uprooted, it seemed, while thunder and lighting crashed overhead. After most of the passengers had gotten off at Sunchon and Yochun, the train was only about one third occupied. Empty bottles and vinyl wrappers were strewn in the aisle.

I had to get ready to detrain. I brought down my bag from the overhead rack and took my medicine, a few pills and powder. They slid down my parched throat.

Yosu. Is the dark blue tide still rushing onto the shore? The little inn where I stayed and the tavern on the shore where I lived, are they still there? The darkness in the alley and the wailing-like songs of the barmaids at the tavern, are they there?

The last bit of powder I swallowed and I looked at my hand. It seemed dirty and I wanted to wash it. Nausea assailed me. I didn't want to hold down all the pills and powder. I washed my hands until they were raw.

In a flash I felt the warmth of my sister's palm.

"Big sister, let me go with you. Dad....!" Misun screamed.

I pushed her away and ran. I heard her splash into the water. Turning around, I could see only her small hand and the top of her head sinking amid the foaming water. I screamed and screamed, running and turning, but was caught by my father. I desperately tried to push away his drunken body, his foul breath nearly suffocating me.

I was hoisted up. Father had already thrown Misun into the sea and I was next. I was in the water. The salt water rushed into my eyes, nose and mouth.

When I came to, I was lying on the pavement. The first thing that came into my sight was white clouds in the sky. I heard people standing around me shout, "She's alive! She's alive!" I had thrown up everything on my jacket. My head began to pound.

A woman in flower-patterned work-pants was rubbing her tear-filled eyes.

"Why didn't he die alone? Did he have to take the poor young ones?" she muttered.

Another woman responded. "If her mother were alive, how would she feel?"

"I wonder if it's good for her to be alive alone," a middle-aged man said curtly.

A voice from the speaker announced.

"This train is about to arrive in Yosu. We're about five minutes late. Please be understanding."

The announcement with an accent was the first sign that I was back in Yosu.

Yesterday afternoon, I walked from the clinic to the subway station, where Jahun had lost her purse, and got on the Number One to Seoul Station. Though it was a weekday, there was quite a crowd.

"A ticket to Yosu. 10:30 tomorrow morning. The Tongil Train, please."

Apparently the ticket agent didn't catch my destination. He looked up annoyed, and asked, "To where?" I shouted, "Yosu."

I picked up the change and hurried out of the station. There was a row of public phone booths at the edge of the station plaza. I went into one, pushed two coins into the slot and dialed the number of a friend who came to my mind first. She was a part-time teacher at a high school. A middle-aged woman answered that my friend had left the school hours before. I called her home and her mother said she hadn't come home yet. I called another friend, only to hear her answering machine.

"Please leave your message after the beep."

I dialed two more numbers. No one answered at one, and another said my friend was out on business. Everyone was either busy or unreachable.

It was getting dark. People from the station were hurrying here and there to catch a taxi or a bus.

There was nothing I could do. I walked to the subway station to go home where no one was waiting for me.

As soon as I got on the platform, one car departed noisily. It was near the rush hour and many people were converging. Everyone of them seemed to be made from the same machine—they looked, one and all, lonely and tired. Finally our car arrived, giving each of us a flash of hope.

"Please don't leave me," I pleaded to Jahun the night before she left. I was holding her thin arm as we sat on the cold tile floor of the wash-room.

"I must," she said coldly at first.

"Please don't. Please," I begged.

Jahun drew me to her and stroked me as she would a sick child.

"All right. I won't go," she said.

Her bosom was warm as my mother's might have been and as the Yosu sea on a spring day. My mother who died at twenty five....

Jahun left at early dawn the next day while I was deep in sleep. Wearing the only pair of shoes she owned, she left. The shoes with hardly any soles. Two worn travel bags and one bundle of old clothes were all she ever owned.

When I opened my eyes, it was light. The clothes and things Jahun had scattered around the room were gone. The room looked strange, as if shrouded in a fog.

"She is gone," I mumbled to myself.

I looked down on the floor, patches of it dull with its wax sheen worn away. I stood in front of the notebook-size mirror on the equally dull door. Eyes like those of a long-suffering animal were looking back at me.

I hurriedly looked away as if I had been reprimanded for staring at someone. Slowly and cautiously I returned to my image in the mirror. My lips were parched purple.

"...Father." I whispered.

For three days after Jahun had left, I did not dust the bookshelf or the window sills. I did not feel compelled to mop or to wash the rags. When I lay down on the floor after work, peace wrapped me gently as never before. When I woke up in the morning, the sunlight danced on the window. Jahun's calm face hung in the warm quiet air. A deep sorrow knifed its way into my heart, the pain of it so unbearable that I closed my eyes.

However, I could not stop my habitual nausea yet. "Why are you doing this?" Jahun used to say, but no one was stopping me now. Whenever I felt acutely the absence of Jahun or looked at my unclean hands, I threw up. Jahun's warm hands I had pushed away, her ten fingers hanging helplessly at my rejection began to invade my consciousness, my skin and veins, and even my bone marrow.

The train stopped. Passengers carried their huge bags, some as big as themselves on their heads. Waiting in line for my turn, I stood in the aisle. Out on the platform, the wind blew mercilessly at people whose hair and clothes seemed about to be torn off. Rubbing the rain water off their faces, they hurried toward the station house.

Yosu.

When I stepped onto the platform, the wind whipped me as if it had been waiting for me. The heavily downcast sky threw its icy cold rain drops to my face. From above the pointed roof of the station house, Jahun's giggling floated down in the pouring rain.

A Brief Survey of Modern Korean Fiction

Modern Korean Literature began during the last decades of the 19th century. Before then, literature was a pastime among the aristocrats who regarded literature as a base form of entertainment.

With the opening of the country, however, the situation changed suddenly. Instead of the Chinese ideograms, Korean alphabet was widely used to express a newly awakened nationalistic fervor in face of the influx of foreign culture. Lee Injik, Lee Haecho, and Shin Chaeho were representative writers who produced what were called the "Enlightenment Novels" or "New Novels."

In 1910 Korea was forcibly annexed to Japan and the Enlightenment Novels began to decline, as many of the writers went abroad or attempted works appealing to popular taste. This was the time of Lee Kwangsu and Choi Namsun, Lee with his radical novels and Choi with his new-style poems. Lee's novel *Love* dealt with free love and family life centered around children rather than adults, themes that aroused a great deal of interest and curiosity. Lee can be said to have initiated Korea's modern literature.

After the failure of the Samil Independence Uprising in 1919, the age of Lee Kwangsu and Choi Namsun gradually changed to an age of new self-awareness. Yom Sangsop's "The Frog in The Lab" was an example of the new trend.

From the middle of the 1920s, another new literary trend began to appear in novels. It was the class-conscious proletarian literature represented by Choi Suhhae's "The Escape." The 1920s and 1930s saw a flowering of what was called the KAPF literature based on leftist ideology. Lee Keeyoung's "Wonbo" (1928), Han Sulya's "Transition" (1929) and "Wrestling" (1929), and Hong Myunghee's *Im Kokjung* (1928-1940), were all in the vein of realism and naturalism.

On the other hand, clear signs of modernism were contained in such works as Lee Sang's "Wings" and Park Taewon's "One Day in the Life of Novelist Koo Bo." Koo Inhoe and Lee Taejoon were two prominent theoreticians of modernism.

Following the Japanese victory in the Sino-Japanese War in 1937 till 1945, Korean literature lay dormant under the severe oppression of the Japanese rule. Even after the liberation from Japan in 1945, ideological division and political turmoil made it all but impossible for writers to produce. The polarity of the ideological struggle continued till the Korean War (1950-53).

During the 1950s, the dominant literary theory was existentialism. Kim Sunghan, Sun Woowhee, and Chang Yonghak emerged under the name of "The New Age" literature, and existentialism spread like wild fire. Toward the end of the 1950s, the confrontation between "pure literature" and "engagement (social involvement) literature" intensified and continued till the 1970s.

The 1960s were the age of the young, due to the influence of the April 19 Student Revolution of 1960. The voice of youthful rebels called for reform and against the corrupt Establishment. Choi Inhoon's *The Plaza* was the cry of the young generation.

In the 1970s such young writers as Hwang Sukyoung, Cho Sehee, Lee Chungjoon, Lee Munkoo, Park Sangyong, Choi Inho, and Yoon Hunggil were the flag bearers of the new era. Hwang and Cho concentrated on the social issues of the unjust Korean society; Lee, Park, and Yoon on Korea's traditional views while Lee Chungjoon dealt mostly with the tension between individual and society. Choi Inho, on the other hand, drew the life hidden beneath the superficial modernization of the society. Hwang's

10-volume *The Story of Chang Kilsan* and Cho Sehee's *The Ball That a Dwarf Tossed Up* represented this era.

The 1980s were an age of resistance. The Kwangju Revolt on May 18, 1980 caused a profound sense of defeat and guilt among the intelligentsia. The author of *Toward Tomorrow* was a student-turned-laborer named Bang Hyunsuk. Cho Jungrae's *The Taeback Mountains* was an extremely critical portrayal of the chaos in Korea during the 1940s and 1950s.

The rebellious spirit of the 1980s began to ebb with the coming of the 1990s. Writers tended to create either a kind of "looking backward" memoiristic works or works probing into the inner workings of individual mind. Kong Jeeyoung, Shin Kyungsook, Un Heekyong belong to the latter category with a strong feministic tendency. In contrast to them, Park Kyongni's *The Land* and Choi Myonghee's *The Spirit of Fire* are definitely masterpieces that transcend the limitations of a particular age.

Author Profiles

1. "The Rooster" by Choi Junghee (1906-1990)

Choi Junghee was born in 1906 in Hamkyung Province and began her writing career in the 1930s. One of the early modern women, Choi became a reporter for *Samchulli*, a literary journal, while producing nearly 40 short stories, most of which were rarely above the level of amateurism.

Choi's transformation came during her imprisonment in the aftermath of the 1934 Chonju incident involving the leftist literary movement.

Her first serious work "The Haunted House" published in 1937 in *Chokwang*, another literary journal, and her subsequent works centered on women's life. From 1945 till before the Korean War is the period when her works mainly dealt with Korean rural life and its despair. Choi tried to remain neutral in the raging ideological struggle of the time. After the Korean War, Choi's works concentrated on the everyday life with its mundane but revealing truths about human conditions.

"The Rooster" (1948), a comical folk tale of a story, contrasts Yoon Hansung and his cock. Yoon, an old man in his 60s married to a young woman, finds himself waning in virility which is directly reflected in the weak cowardly behavior of his rooster that loses his hen to a neighbor's rooster. Finally, Yoon accepts the truth that Man and Nature revolve around the immutable natural cycle of life.

2. "The Fragment" by Han Musook (1918-1993)

Born in 1918, Han originally wanted to be a painter but changed her course after marrying into an austere aristocratic family. She debuted in 1942 with her first novel *The Woman Who Held a Lantern*. This book and another of her early work

History Flows On depict the life of early 20th century in Korea, but her later works in the 1950's such as "The Moonlight" and "The Abyss of Emotion" tend to probe into the inner psychology of the characters. In the 1960s, Han moved toward portraying Korean women in such works as "The Screwdriver" and *The Infected Finger*.

"The Fragment," published in 1951, is a searing picture of refugees who had fled to Pusan at the outbreak of the Korean War. The suffering man who had witnessed deliberate drowning of people by the crew of an overloaded ship, a former rich lady with an overpowering animal instinct for survival, a mysterious young man in American Army fatigue, the laborer who brought a fish for the sick wife of a fellow refugee and children scavenging and begging in the railway yard. Despite the unspeakable squalor and despair in the warehouse, there is yet a spark of hope among these people who hang on with the skin of their teeth to the possibility that they would go back home some day.

3. "The Young Elm Tree" by Kang Shinjae (1924-)

A recurrent theme in Kang's novels, as critic Choi Heishil said, is a special quality of beauty that exists in stark contrast to the mundane daily life. Kang has focused on the delicate and sensory beauty in human relationships, away from the tiresome reality. As in her other novels, *Waves and Dandelions of the Imgin River*, Kang depicts women whose absolute sense of beauty or a unique outlook on life fascinates men. Despite adverse criticism on her "tenuous grasp of real life," her works have a mysterious holding power.

"The Young Elm Tree" (1960) revolves around the sentence, "there is always a fresh smell of soap about him," abstract and refreshing, but inconcrete, just as the love between the two young people. A high school girl who falls in love with her stepbrother, the college-student son of the man whom her widowed mother married.

4. "Youngju and the Cat" by Park Kyongni (1927-)

When Park Kyongni's vast serial of a novel, *The Land*, came out in 1994 when she was 68, the entire nation celebrated the occasion. Consisting of 5 parts, 16 volumes, the novel was rightfully lauded to have expanded the sphere of Korean fiction. In Kangwon Province, a literary center for *The Land* was founded and a thesaurus for the book was published.

Born in 1927 in Kyong Sang Nam Province, Park began her career by fictionalizing her life in such works as "Calculation" and "Black Black, White White" and continued to do so till 1960, the year the April 19 student revolt that resulted in a drastic political change. Park's awakened social consciousness was expressed in "The Age of Disbelief," "The Old Woman on Sarang Island," and *The Drift* in which the first person narrator, obviously the author herself, was gradually withdrawn.

Her social criticism and active confrontation became more acute in her long novels like *The Field at the Sunset* and *My Heart is a Pond*. But her magna opus, *The Land* is the novel that crystallizes the uniquely Korean emotion of "Han," a long repressed frustration, expressed in what the critics call "a treasure chest of the Korean language." Her sense of history, culture, social consciousness are all fused in it. *The Daughters of Pharmacist Kim* deals with the life and social conditions Korean women have had to face to live and to love as human beings. Park's *The Market and the Battlefield* was translated into French in 1994 and *The Daughters of Pharmacist Kim* into German in 1996 and into Spanish in 1999.

"Youngju and the Cat," published in 1957 in *Modern Literature*, is steeped in Park's early fatalism. Minhei, the only daughter of her parents, is left alone with Youngju, her own only daughter, because she lost her son in the previous summer. Minhei's father died during the Korean War and her son due to illness. Both she and Youngju try not to show their grief in their daily routine, but their sad acceptance of their fate is the undercurrent flowing through the story. The cat, Adele, is an ironic, symbolic object of their quiet resignation.

5. "The Jade Ring" by Lee Sukbong (1928-)

Lee Sukbong is known for her superb description of human psychology, which is based on her meticulous examination of her characters' inner workings by a careful selection of details.

The critic Lee Kwanghoon said, "Henry James wrote fiction that was like psychological study while his brother William wrote psychology that was like fiction, but Lee's psychological novel is a novel that doesn't sound like a psychological study."

Lee's first published work *The Bay Full of Sunlight* (1964) was followed by *Endless Stairs* (1966), *On the Hill of Fantasia* (1967), *The Dark Field* (1969), *The Forest Filled with Love* (1971), *The Third Man* (1983), and several others.

"The Jade Ring" (1969), published in *The Literature Monthly*, portrays the pathological mentality of a widow who raised two daughters all by herself. When she found out that her daughter Yonju's husband was unfaithful, she gloatingly told Yonju of this news. But Yonju had been estranged from her husband for years and was involved with a married man. Scolding Yonju for her scandalous behavior, the mother left home when Yonju's jade ring disappeared. The mother told Yonju's married lover, Yonju's sister, and the manager of Yonju's tearoom that Yonju suspected them of the theft. After they all left Yonju in anger and hurt, Yonju went to confront her mother. To her consternation, she found the ring on her mother's finger.

6. "The Woman in Search of an Illusion" by Lee Jungho (1930-)

A boy monk in a quiet mountain temple has often been used in literary works. He is a being standing between Nature and the human world, between the world beyond and the world here. He is the ethereal link.

At the beginning and the end of the story is the boy. In between them, fateful human relations are formed and undone. The background of "The Woman in Search of an Illusion" (1969) is the Korean War. The mother and her daughter were separated from other refugees and managed to hide themselves in a temple. Every time soldiers came, the mother desperately hid her daughter.

One night, the mother told a ghost story to her daughter. It was about a girl named Yongnyo, the only daughter of a wealthy family, who became pregnant. No one knew of the baby's father. Yongnyo was imprisoned by her mother in a shed and cut off from any human contact until she bore a boy. The baby boy was sent away. Since then, Yongnyo has been haunting the neighborhood like a ghost.

The most impressive parts in the story are the tantalizingly indirect expressions that hint at the intimate human relations being formed. This is a story of the fate of women, mothers and daughters, who have lived that way for centuries. It is also a story of unchanging human karma.

Published in 1969 in *Yosang*, a literary magazine, the story was followed by such novels as *The Remaining Light* (1969), *The Fog* (1977), and *The Moving Wall* (1988).

7. "Division" by Song Wonhee (1930-)

Born in 1930, Song Wonhee has published seven collections of stories beginning with *Flower Snake* (1971), *The Middle*

(1977), *The Lonely Door* (1978), *The Pipes of Goddesses* (1980), *The Thirsty Land* (1987) and several others.

"Division" (1967), carried in *Modern Literature*, proceeds on two tragic stories in the form of Jinee's mother's monologue. Jinee's mother's brother, the beloved son of the family, had been drafted to the ROK Army during the Korean War and was supposed to be in North Korea, which was tantamount to death.

The husband of Jinee's mother had been married before with three children he had left in North Korea when he came down south to do his job as a war correspondent. The husband, deeply guilt-ridden, refused to remarry for many years till he met Jinee's mother, an old maid school teacher.

Jinee's mother was upset when her husband began working as a researcher at the Unification Research Institute. She was also suspicious of him when he showed fatherly interest in the daughter of his old friend who had been forced to remain in North Korea.

The story ends when Jinee's mother realizes how precious life is when one realizes what little happiness one has and one should treasure it. War destroys men and families, but those who survive it must go on, hiding grief and sorrow behind a teary smile.

8. "The Dreaming Incubator" by Park Wansuh (1931-)

One of the most renowned and beloved writers of contemporary Korea, Park's literary achievement has been proven by the numerous top awards she has received since the early 1980s.

Born in 1931 near Kaesung, Kyonggi Province, she began her writing career rather late in her life. Her first novel *The Naked Tree* was first published when she was forty.

There are three main subjects in Park's novels. First, as in *The Naked Tree* and *Mama's Stake*, the story revolves around a family's excruciating struggle to restore a normal life in the aftermath of the Korean War; second, a searing expose of the mammonism and hypocrisy of the smug middle-class people in the booming economy, such as *The Urban Famine* and *The Teetering Afternoon*; third, the female experience in the patriarchal society that probes deeply and delicately into the issues of family, work, and sex.

"The Dreaming Incubator" (1991) belongs to the third category. It deals with the anger, guilt, and humiliation of a woman who was forced by her in-laws to abort a female fetus with her husband's acquiescence and who eventually succeeded in producing a male child. In 1993 Park received the Hyundai Literary Award for this work and in 1996 it was translated into German.

9. "At Sundown" by Yoon Jungsun (1948-)

In 1986, Yoon debuted on the Korean literary scene with a one-act play "Hodong." In 1991 and 1992, she received honorable mention in some literary contests for her works "The Train and the Star" and "At Sundown" respectively. After a brief stay in Paris, she produced such works as *For You, My Sister's Room*, both novels, and *Dancing Shiva*, a collection of plays.

Yoon's characteristic literary device is her identification with the character, which results in making her work somewhat like a monologue or a diary. There are also bits and pieces of knowledge from everyday life, books, and movies, that might be a jumble of undigested information as in "At Sundown" (1991) that include mentions of Sartre, Beauvoir, Voltaire, and Baudelaire.

Two old people, former lovers now widowed, talk about life, love, and death, which in themselves may not constitute a moving story, but the form, a long dialogue, is well maintained and the general tone is elegiac and beautiful like a watercolor painting of a sunset.

10. "My Wife's Boxes" by Un Heekyong (1959-)

The basic pattern of Un's novels is a pendulum-like movement. At one end, there is the world of reality and at the other, the world of uncontrolled and uncontrollable desire. A single unmarried woman lusting for a married man or a married woman still deeply in love with her first love are two of such examples. But Un's forte lies in her light and lively style and air-tight form that exercise a magic power on her readers.

She began to get a critical and public acclaim in 1995, but in the few years since then she has published *The Gift from a Bird* and *Was It Just a Dream?*, both long novels, and three collections of short stories, *Accosting a Stranger*, *Won't You Have the Last Dance With Me*, and *Happy People Don't Watch the Clock*.

A recipient of the 1998 Yi Sang Award, "My Wife's Boxes" (1997) displays the best qualities of Un's literature. On the surface, it is the story of a barren psychopathic personality, but the story is intimately intertwined with several excellent symbols, resulting in a profound portrayal of the barrenness of human life and modern society.

Prof. Lee Jaesun, one of the Yi Sang Award committee members, commented: "a portrayal of a psychopathic character, the work was an insightful look into the pain and frustration that exists deep in the human relationships. Loss and pain are concretized through a deft and fresh use of symbols such as boxes and dried, horribly scented flowers. "My Wife's Boxes" shows the relationship between body and soul through pain and subsequent awakening.

11. "The Unbearable Sadness of Being" by Kong Jeeyoung (1963-)

There are two distinctly different sides to Kong's fiction: the private emotions hidden behind the loud reform movement of the 1980's and the militant feminism. Beginning with Kong's first short story "Daybreak" (1988), her works fall into these two categories. *The More Beautiful Wandering, And Their Beautiful Beginning, The Mackerel, Courtesy to Humanity* belong to the first category while *Dash Alone Like a Rhinoceros Horn* and *A Good Woman* are distinctly feministic works, which made her a literary lioness of the 1990s.

In the early 1990s, the ardor for social and political reform was waning and writers began to pay more attention to the covert private emotions of characters. Some critics found in Kong's works sentimentalization of life in Korea, while others lauded them for a rediscovery of fundamental human values.

"The Unbearable Sadness of Being," published in 1997, centers on one day in the life of a divorced woman designer, who has just been fired. The psychological distance between her and her lover, who dies in Peru, is symbolized by the geographical one in her reminiscence and fantasy. Reality—her existence as a failed designer responsible for the livelihood of her mother and daughter—and her lover's trip to Machu Pichu and his disappearance, strongly hinted at being caused by her rejection, are delicately and symbolically handled in the story.

12. "Nostalgic Journey" by Han Kang (1970-)

Despite her younger age, Han's works are permeated with the shadow of death, the misty area between life and death, and human obsession with and fear of death.

Like a criminal who cannot stay away from the scene of his crime, Han returns to the theme of death again and again as in her "Nostalgic Journey" (1994), her novel *The Black Deer*, and short stories "The Crimson Sail" and "The Evening Light."

To the character who hovers over the gray area of life and death, there is an alter ego, whom the character has to embrace in love. Han uses the clothes as a symbol. The main character tries to take off or bear up the clothes of his alter ego, replacing them with clean white ones. But the alter ego can either accept or reject the gesture. Life is messy and cannot always be altered by human will.

In "Nostalgic Journey" one sees Han's recurring themes—death, alter ego, childhood trauma and return to the place, Yosu, where everything began. "Yosu" in Chinese ideogram can mean a woman prisoner, nostalgia, or the name of her home town, depending on the selection of homonymous characters.

The main character is leaving for Yosu, her place of origin as well as of her parents' and sister's death. Her journey is a quest for the meaning of human existence and a return to the place of her origin.

Han is regarded as one of the most promising young Korean writers today.

Modern Fiction from Korea

Father and Son: A Novel by Han Sung-won
Translated by Yu Young-nan & Julie Pickering
ISBN: 1-931907-04-8, Paperback, $17.95

An age-old struggle between the generations of modern industrialization and the battle for democratic freedoms in Korea. The author explores the role of the intellectual in modern Korean society and the changing face of the Korean family.

Reflections on a Mask: Two Novellas by Ch'oe In-hun
Translated by Stephen Moore & Shi C. P. Moore
ISBN: 1-931907-05-6, Paperback, $16.95

Reflections on a Mask explores the disillusionment and search for identity of a young man in the post-Korean War era. *Christmas Carol* uses the themes of hope and salvation to examine relationships within a patriarchal Korean family.

Unspoken Voices: Selected Short Stories by Korean Women Writers
Compiled and Translated by Jin-Young Choi, Ph.D.
ISBN: 1-931907-06-4, Paperback, $16.95

Stories by twelve Korean women writers whose writings penetrate into the lives of Korean women from the early part of the 20th century to the present. Writers included are: Choi Junghee, Han Musook, Kang Shinjae, Park Kyongni, Lee Sukbong, Lee Jungho, Song Wonhee, Park Wansuh, Yoon Jungsun, Un Heekyong, Kong Jeeyoung and Han Kang.

The General's Beard: Two Novellas by Lee Oyoung
Translated by Brother Anthony
ISBN: 1-931907-07-2, Paperback, $14.95

In *The General's Beard*, a journalist tries to solve the mystery of a young photographer's death. In *Phantom Legs*, a young girl studying French literature meets a student wounded during demonstrations and begins an ambiguous relationship with him.

Farmers: A Novel by Lee Mu-young
Translated by Yu Young-nan
ISBN: 1-931907-08-0, Paperback, $15.95

The novel is about Korea's Tonghak Uprising the 1894. A farmer-turned Tonghak leader who left the village several years ago in the wake of a severe flogging returns to his village to take revenge of his exploiters.

More titles from Homa & Sekey Books

Flower Terror: Suffocating Stories of China by Pu Ning
ISBN 0-9665421-0-X, Fiction, Paperback, $13.95

"The stories in this work are well written." – Library Journal

Acclaimed Chinese writer eloquently describes the oppression of intellectuals in his country between 1950s and 1970s in these twelve autobiographical novellas and short stories. Many of the stories are so shocking and heart-wrenching that one cannot but feel suffocated.

The Peony Pavilion: A Novel by Xiaoping Yen, Ph.D.
ISBN 0-9665421-2-6, Fiction, Paperback, $16.95

"A window into the Chinese literary imagination." – Publishers Weekly

A sixteen-year-old girl visits a forbidden garden and falls in love with a young man she meets in a dream. She has an affair with her dream-lover and dies longing for him. After her death, her unflagging spirit continues to wait for her dream-lover. Does her lover really exist? Can a youthful love born of a garden dream ever blossom? The novel is based on a sixteenth-century Chinese opera written by Tang Xianzu, "the Shakespeare of China."

Butterfly Lovers: A Tale of the Chinese Romeo and Juliet
by Fan Dai, Ph.D., ISBN 0-9665421-4-2, Fiction, Paperback, $16.95

"An engaging, compelling, deeply moving, highly recommended and rewarding novel." – Midwest Books Review

A beautiful girl disguises herself as a man and lives under one roof with a young male scholar for three years without revealing her true identity. They become sworn brothers, soul mates and lovers. In a world in which marriage is determined by social status and arranged by parents, what is their inescapable fate?

The Dream of the Red Chamber: An Allegory of Love
By Jeannie Jinsheng Yi, Ph.D., ISBN: 0-9665421-7-7, Hardcover
Asian Studies/Literary Criticism, $49.95

Although dreams have been studied in great depth about this most influential classic Chinese fiction, the study of all the dreams as a sequence and in relation to their structural functions in the allegory is undertaken here for the first time.

More titles from Homa & Sekey Books

Always Bright: Paintings by American Chinese Artists 1970-1999
Edited by Xue Jian Xin et al.
ISBN 0-9665421-3-4, Art, Hardcover, $49.95

"An important, groundbreaking, seminal work." – Midwest Book Review

A selection of paintings by eighty acclaimed American Chinese artists in the late 20th century, *Always Bright* is the first of its kind in English publication. The album falls into three categories: oil painting, Chinese painting and other media painting. It also offers profiles of the artists and information on their professional accomplishment.

Always Bright, Vol. II: Paintings by Chinese American Artists
Edited by Eugene Wang, Ph.D., et al.
ISBN: 0-9665421-6-9, Art, Hardcover, $50.00

A sequel to the above, the book includes artworks of ninety-two artists in oil painting, Chinese painting, watercolor painting, and other media such as mixed media, acrylic, pastel, pen and pencil, etc. The book also provides information on the artists and their professional accomplishment. Artists included come from different backgrounds, use different media and belong to different schools. Some of them enjoy international fame while others are enterprising young men and women who are more impressionable to novelty and singularity.

Dai Yunhui's Sketches by Dai Yunhui
ISBN: 1-931907-00-5, Art, Paperback, $14.95

Over 50 sketches from an artist of attainment who is especially good at sketching stage and dynamic figures. His drawings not only accurately capture the dynamic movements of the performers, but also acutely catch the spirit of the stage artists.

Musical Qigong: Ancient Chinese Healing Art from a Modern Master
By Shen Wu, ISBN: 0-9665421-5-0, Health, Paperback, $14.95

Musical Qigong is a special healing energy therapy that combines two ancient Chinese traditions-healing music and Qigong. This guide contains two complete sets of exercises with photo illustrations and discusses how musical Qigong is related to the five elements in the ancient Chinese concept of the universe - metal, wood, water, fire, and earth.

More titles from Homa & Sekey Books

Ink Paintings by Gao Xingjian, Nobel Prize Winner
ISBN: 0-931907-03-X, Hardcover, Art, $34.95

An extraordinary art book by the Nobel Prize Winner for Literature in 2000, this volume brings together over sixty ink paintings by Gao Xingjian that are characteristic of his philosophy and painting style. Gao believes that the world cannot be explained, and the images in his paintings reveal the black-and-white inner world that underlies the complexity of human existence. People admire his meditative images and evocative atmosphere by which Gao intends his viewers to visualize the human conditions in extremity.

Splendor of Tibet: The Potala Palace, Jewel of the Himalayas
By Phuntsok Namgyal
ISBN: 1-931907-02-1, Hardcover, Art/Architecture, $39.95

A magnificent and spectacular photographic book about the Potala Palace, the palace of the Dalai Lamas and the world's highest and largest castle palace. Over 150 rare and extraordinary color photographs of the Potala Palace are showcased in the book, including murals, thang-ka paintings, stupa-tombs of the Dalai Lamas, Buddhist statues and scriptures, porcelain vessels, enamel work, jade ware, brocade, Dalai Lamas' seals, and palace exteriors.

The Haier Way: The Making of a Chinese Business Leader and a Global Brand by Jeannie J. Yi, Ph.D., & Shawn X. Ye, MBA
ISBN: 1-931907-01-3, Hardcover, Business, $24.95

Haier is the largest consumer appliance maker in China. The book traces the appliance giant's path to success, from its early bleak years to its glamorous achievement when Haier was placed the 6th on Forbes Global's worldwide household appliance manufacturer list in 2001. The book explains how Haier excelled in quality, service, technology innovation, a global vision and a management style that is a blend of Jack Welch of "GE" and Confucius of ancient China.

www.homabooks.com

Order Information: U.S.: $4.00 for the first item, $1.50 for each additional item. **Outside U.S.:** $10.00 for the first item, $5.00 for each additional item. Please send a check or money order in U.S. fund (payable to Homa & Sekey Books) to: Orders Department, Homa & Sekey Books, P.O. Box 103, Dumont, NJ 07628 U.S.A. Tel: 201-384-6692; Fax: 201-384-6055; Email: info@homabooks.com

9 781931 907064